I0674984

The Goddess Returns

Book 2 of 2

William A. Jackson, Jr.

The Goddess Returns

Copyright © 2022 William A. Jackson, Jr.
All rights reserved.
ISBN-978-1-7347258-1-0
Cover design by: Nienke Adamse

The Goddess Returns

Dedications

To Nienke, Sebastian, Andreja, Megan, Julian,
Stephan, and Ian

Table of Contents

The Goddess Returns

Acknowledgements

As I do not have a 'Works Cited' section, as such, in my novel, and I am obliged to mention the very gracious individuals and institutions that have granted me permission to use their material in my novel, this Acknowledgements section will also serve that purpose.

I would first like to thank my wife, Nienke, and our eldest child, Sebastian, for reading various sections of the manuscript and critiquing it when the novel was in its earlier stages. They caught all kinds of mistakes that I had made. Nienke even went further in supporting me by permitting me to commandeer one of her paintings, from which I also managed to convince her to design the cover of this book.

I would also be remiss if I did not thank a few of my former colleagues at Country Garden High School in Foshan, China. Catherine McLoughlin was my supervisor in A-Level English. She not only read a bit of the manuscript, but she also introduced me to the world of Irish curses, one of which I incorporated into the novel in the scene in the men's restroom between Mrs. McFarley, the family services specialist, and Alex's lawyer, Stephan Clark. This scene will continue in Book 2 of 2, which will be called *The Goddess Returns*.

Selma Coban, a brilliant philosopher, also read some of the manuscript, and she was very candid with me when she said that there were no surprises. I understood from her comments that I had to dig deeper within myself. She also gave me a few tidbits of her private life that I incorporated into the novel.

The Fosters, a Canadian married couple, were very keen on reading some of the manuscript. The wife, who was the teacher, was so detailed in describing all the preparations that she and her husband made to ready themselves for the reading of the manuscript, that I could not help but think that it had become part and parcel of their foreplay.

Johnny, an English teacher at MCI in Pittsfield, Maine, read the first fifty, or so, pages, and he gave ne invaluable support and confidence when I was at a very low ebb. Thank you, Johnny!

Mrs. Karen Lone Hill, a professor at Oglala Lakota College in Kyle, Pine Ridge Reservation, SD was absolutely wonderful. She translated English words and phrases for me into Lakota, according to the dialect that is spoken on Pine Ridge Reservation, and she did it all gratis. I am in her debt!

Although, it appears in Book 2 of 2, I will thank Dr. Mathias Guenther here for granting me permission to take a quote regarding /Caggen from his excellent book, *Tricksters and Trancers: Bushman Religion and Society,* ©2000. The quote establishes /Caggen as the "first shaman" and not merely a trickster.

With regard to Ervin Laszlo's *Science and the Akashic Field*, I would like to thank Dr. Laszlo and Inner Traditions

International and Bear & Company for granting me permission to paraphrase a bit of Ervin Laszlo's work. As the publisher has specific guidelines regarding citations, it will appear here as follows:

Science and the Akashic Field by Ervin Laszlo published by Inner Traditions International and Bear & Company, ©2007. All rights reserved.

Dr. Chris Low wrote a highly informative article regarding Bushman shamanistic practices and beliefs. It's called *KhoeSan Shamanistic Relationships with Snakes and Rain*. That's where I got most of the material regarding the various ways in which an individual could become a shaman in Bushman culture. I was briefly in correspondence with Dr. Low, and he was very kind when he granted me permission to borrow from his article.

In order to request permission to paraphrase Carl G. Jung, I had to approach. W. W. Norton, the publishing company. However, it was very difficult to reach their point person for 'Rights' because that was around the time when Covid-19 had just started to hit the U.S.A. However, after leaving my name and contact information, several times, and begging, Mr. Bernstein did reach-out to me, and he was kind enough to grant me, on W. W. Norton's behalf, permission to paraphrase some of C.G. Jung's work.

I would also like to thank the *Idler*, whose mission is to make the world a far more relaxing place to live, enjoy culture and play much *more,* for granting me permission to reference them in my novel. That was extremely gracious of them!

I would like to thank the John G. Neihardt Trust for granting me permission to make references to John G. Neihardt's book, *Black Elk Speaks*. And as the John G. Neihardt Trust has specific guidelines regarding the attributing of John G. Neihardt's books, I will attribute *Black Elk Speaks* according to those guidelines:

Black Elk Speaks ©1932, courtesy of the John G. Neihardt Trust.

Finally, I would like to thank Dr. Joseph Cambray for allowing me to use his concept of the *asymmetrical synchronicity*, which I found in his book, *Synchronicity: Nature & Psyche in an Interconnected Universe, ,* ©2009.

Of course, the above-mentioned litany by no means exhausts all of the individuals and institutions that I am indebted to. For the genesis of *A Girl Called Thunder* came to me approximately forty years ago, when I was living in Frohnau, West Berlin, West Germany. While I was washing dishes, I was listening to the World Service of the BBC; I was listening to a report on 'child soldiers in Uganda.' After the report had concluded, I asked myself a question: How can I make a story about child soldiers in Uganda that involves an African-American boy?

During the course of these forty years, a plethora of people, institutions, and countries have nurtured me, influenced me, inspired me, and loved me. I thank all of you!

The Goddess Returns

The Goddess Returns

A Gentle Reminder:

In the previous book, "A Girl Called Thunder," my Kaka, grandfather in Lakota, made me reach out to my father, Alex, because the Department of Social Services (DSS) decided to take my little cousin Misun away from us because we were poor. My Kaka was desperate to get Misun back, and he believed that Alex, my father, was the only one who could help us do it. I was against the idea because my father had never come for me, and I was afraid that he didn't want me. But Kaka wasn't hearing any of that, so off I went, to Bozeman, Maine, with my best friend Esther.

Things were somewhat bumpy at first, but after a while, things started to click between us.

Alex did come to the Rez., Pine Tree Reservation in South Dakota, and we did manage to get Misun back, with the help of Alex's lawyer friend, whom I didn't very much care for because he always called me Lightening Girl.

Oh, yeah, I forgot to tell you that I am a shaman, and I am trying to become the Calf of the White Buffalo, which, among other things, means that I hope to be on the Council of the White Buffalo when White Buffalo Calf Woman, San Te Winn, returns. Besides being able to communicate with the spirits and our ancestors, there was only one of Alex's ancestors that I could communicate with. He referred to himself as being the 'collateral ancestor.' Spoiler alert!

The Goddess Returns

He lied. He isn't our ancestor at all, but an ancient Bushman trickster god. He kept hassling me to get Alex to get in contact with him, and /Caggen—that's his name with the backslash representing a clicking sound—was so annoying that although Alex was afraid of meeting /Caggen because of a previous encounter with him when Alex was a child, Alex had to because I gave him an ultimatum: "Meet with him or I will break off all contact with you." Alex couldn't afford to lose me because his wife Roya and their four children appeared at his front door the day after I had arrived. This was significant for Alex because he hadn't seen his other children in over a year, and he hadn't seen his estranged wife Roya for over three years. He saw it as being more than just chance or a coincidence.

/Caggen, besides being the one who started patriarchy in the world, is also the Great Mother's husband and son. His mischief making is not limited to that, either, oh, no! He is also responsible for scattering all the other gods and goddesses "throughout the cosmos," Alex told me. This included The Goddess Mother, but she knew what would happen, which is why she went along with it.

At this point, things got interesting because The Great Mother didn't like the idea that Alex had come into my life, because as he was my father, and my mother had died several years earlier, Alex was next in line to help me prepare for my role as Calf of the White Buffalo. However, She doubted his worthiness, which means that he has to undergo the 'Ordeals' (This made me think that there had to be some kind of connection between The Great Mother and Pte San Winn).

Besides having to contend with the "Ordeals," which are still ongoing, Alex has a few serious issues that stem from his past with his parents, my grandparents, which is why he went to Charleston, South Carolina, which is where the first chapter resumes.

1
Meeting the Gatekeeper

The next morning, after Alex washed himself, dressed himself, and descended the stairs to a vacant house, the telephone rang. Although Alex had no intention of answering it, he heard his landlady's voice on the answering machine, threatening to kick his butt—she, of course, used another word instead of butt—if he did not answer her call, considering that he was unemployed and all. After Alex picked up the phone, she informed Alex that she had spoken to Jerry's social studies teacher, Mrs. Sullivan, and that she would expect to see him "today at 3:30, sharp. After having given Alex the directions to get to the school, she underscored the significance of the appointment.

"An' yo' sorry, unemployed ass betta be dere, an' on time!"

Needless to say, Alex arrived at the school thirty minutes early. He read a book on his e-book reader while he waited. It was a book that he had started reading a few days previously. At 3:21, a tall, black, voluptuously-shaped woman with frosted colored, short-cropped, curly hair entered the office. However, because the bench that Alex was sitting on was hidden by the door that she passed by, she did not initially see him. After entering the room, she turned left, took a few steps toward two waist-high swinging doors, passed through them, and proceeded to the six partitioned desks, where she tossed some books and papers inside of one of the cubicles. She then turned around to see Alex with eBook reader in hand at the bench, which was in front of a partial counter.

"You must be Mr. Alex Madden, Jerry's tutor," she stated.

"Yes, and you must be Mrs. Sullivan, Jerry's social studies teacher," Alex responded.

"It's good to see someone reading for a change," Mrs. Sullivan stated. "Is it any good?"

"Yes, it is. It's entitled, *The Evolution of Beauty*," Alex replied.

"Hum, what's it about?" Mrs. Sullivan enquired.

"I'm reading it because the author makes a strong case supporting the notion that in bird species, at least, the females choose their mates," Alex replied.

"Didn't Charles Darwin write about that in one of his books?" Mrs. Sullivan enquired.

"Very good!" Alex exclaimed. "Yes, the author mentioned that Darwin wrote about it in *The Descent of Man*."

"I remember, now," Mrs. Sullivan stated. "We had to read excerpts from it in a radical feminist class. Are you a feminist?"

"I'm trying to be, yes," Alex replied.

"My husband needs to have a one-on-one with you!" Mrs. Sullivan exclaimed.

"I'm reading it because it makes a strong case against patriarchy, especially in chapter 12," Alex stated.

"Just for the sake of playing devil's advocate, why would a man be interested in reading books against patriarchy?" Mrs. Sullivan enquired. "I mean, why would you, as a man, be interested in reading something that could potentially lead to you losing your advantage?"

"Whoa! That is the kind of question that goes right for the jugular!" Alex exclaimed. But to answer you, patriarchy is not only the source of sexism, misogyny, and generally suppressing females and everything related to being a woman, but it is also the source of racism, homophobia, xenophobia, white supremacy, it is anti-nature, and a whole host of other things."

"It's the source of racism and xenophobia?" Mrs. Sullivan enquired somewhat skeptically.

"Oh, yes!" Alex exclaimed.

"How?" Mrs. Sullivan enquired. "I see how sexism is connected with patriarchy, but not the others."

"In a nutshell," Alex started, "patriarchy is the propagation of the conviction that men and everything that men are, do, and make, is better than everything women, are, do, and make, which requires multiple layers of violence to buffer that conviction. So far so good?"

"Yes, it's clear cut so far," Mrs. Sullivan stated.

"Good," Alex stated, somewhat relieved. "Now, other concepts are built into the notion of patriarchy as well, such as alterity, which, as you know, is about otherness. Another thing that's part and parcel of patriarchy is that it's dichotomous—it tends to compare things in opposites..."

"Like man-woman and white-black," Mrs. Sullivan interjected.

"There you go, you got it," Alex concurred. "And it's hierarchical."

"Are you saying that patriarchy started with comparing men to women, and afterwards, men, white men to other men because of their otherness, their differences?" Mrs. Sullivan enquired.

"Yes, something like that," Alex replied.

"Okay, I understand that, but how did it start?" Mrs. Sullivan enquired. "How did patriarchy start?"

"Are men generally bigger and stronger than women?" Alex enquired.

"Is that all it's based on!" Mrs. Sullivan exclaimed amazed.

"It seems that somewhere along the line, because men were bigger and stronger than women, it was assumed that men were 'better' than women," Alex concurred.

"You can't make that kind of an assumption on strength and size alone!" Mrs. Sullivan declared in outrage.

"No, you can't," Alex concurred. "But to answer your original question, let me use a real-life situation. Do you still have time?"

Mrs. Sullivan looked at her watch and nodded her head.

"An African-American male, for example, who hates racism and is active in the Civil-Rights Movement simultaneously subscribes to sexism—he is convinced that men are better than women--and he hates homosexual men..."

"Then, he is a hypocrite, because he actually subscribes to the same thing that he is vehemently against?" Mrs. Sullivan interjected.

"Yes, racism, sexism, homophobia, xenophobia, and hating nature all have the same origin, patriarchy. You can't embrace one expression of that and revile other expressions of it, which is one reason why I, at least, choose to reject all of its expressions."

"Wow! Not just my father and husband, many black men are in that predicament," Mrs. Sullivan added while walking to her mail box and taking out a folder. "Thank you for sharing that with me, but I guess you are really here to talk about Jerry's project."

She handed the folder to Alex, explaining that Jerry had to do his project on a prominent figure that was local. By local, Alex asked if the figure had to be from Charleston. Mrs. Sullivan widened the scope area to include North Carolina, South Carolina, and Georgia. She then informed Alex that there were five rubrics: one for social studies, one for English, one for math, one for science, and one for art. In order for Jerry to get an overall passing grade, which he would have to achieve to pass to tenth grade, he would have to meet the lion's share of the criteria of each subject rubric. Alex was a bit shocked when she announced to him the due date, which was in three and a half weeks.

"How much time did Jerry have in total?" Alex enquired.

"We gave Jerry's cohort the assignment two and a half weeks ago," Mrs. Sullivan replied.

Examining the rubrics, Alex enquired as to whether Jerry could have a bit more time. However, Mrs. Sullivan informed him that Jerry and the others knew about the project at least two weeks prior to having received it. She decided to contact the students' parents to cover herself for when the due date transpired and no projects were done. Before Alex left, she stressed the fact that the project culminates in a presentation, which has to have "all the stops and whistles," such as a well-designed poster and a power point presentation. When Alex informed Mrs. Sullivan that Jerry did not have a computer, she asked if Alex had one.

"Of course, but I don't like the idea of letting other people, especially careless kids, use my computer," Alex replied.

"Mr. Madden, I don't know what your relationship with Jerry and his mother is," Mrs. Sullivan stated, "and I don't need to know, but I do know one thing. Unlike many of our parents, Ms. Mary cares. She cares more about that boy's success than he does, and in order for her to keep him out of the gangs and away from the drugs, she's going to need all the help she can get. You seem to be well-educated and stable."

"Are there any school laptops that he can borrow?" Alex enquired.

"We only have desktops in our labs, and most of them are broken," Mrs. Sullivan replied. "May I be frank? We know that most of our students will not take us up on this project, and before I met you, I thought that Jerry would be one of them. You can make the difference in that boy's life, if you choose to."

Before leaving the office, Alex quickly looked over all the rubrics for a second time, and then he enquired regarding Jerry, whether he was still in school. It just so happened that Jerry was in detention for skipping his English class.

"Do you want to talk to him?" Mrs. Sullivan enquired.

"If it's not too much trouble," Alex replied.

After signing Alex in and attaching the sticker with his name on his chest, Mrs. Sullivan escorted Alex to the detention room, which was on the third floor in room 302. When they arrived, she asked the detention monitor if she could speak with Jerry. The detention monitor first looked on her digital roster, and then called Jerry's name while pointing to the door, where Jerry could only see Mrs. Sullivan. When Jerry arrived at the door, he saw Alex and was a bit taken aback.

"I'll be back in five minutes to take you back out," Mrs. Sullivan stated.

"Is you gonna tell Momma that I'm in detention?" Jerry enquired with some cheekiness.

"No, but I will tell her that you've been sitting on this project for two and a half weeks without lifting a finger, if you don't check the attitude," Alex replied. "And now, you only have three and a half weeks."

"Don't tell Momma," Jerry pleaded.

"Okay," Alex replied, but you need to come home right after detention, so you can start."

"I get out in twenty minutes," Jerry stated.

"Then, I'll be expecting you no later than 4:30," Alex stated.

At 4:33, Alex glanced at his cell phone for the time. He took it out again, five minutes later. At 4:42, he took it out again. However, this time, he left it out. Jerry did not return home until 6:15. When Jerry saw Alex at the dining-room table, he simply stated that he had things to do and walked to the kitchen. A minute later, Jerry returned to the dining-room with a glass of milk and a peanut butter and jelly sandwich.

"Take a seat," Alex stated.

"How long this gonna take?" Jerry enquired impatiently.

"Fuck it!" Alex exclaimed, thoroughly vexed by this point.

He then stood up and ascended the stairs to go to his bedroom.

A couple minutes later, there was a knock at Alex's bedroom door.

"Jerry, I'm tired of your bullshit," Alex stated, "so just tell your mother that you don't really care if you fail. Just leave me alone."

"Mr. Alex, Mr. Alex," Jerry repeated, "come on, Mr. Alex. I already know who I wanna do my projec' on."

There were sounds of movement in the room behind the closed door. Then, Alex opened the door.

"So, you have been thinking about it," Alex stated, somewhat relieved. "Who is it?"

"Dr. E. E. Just," Jerry replied.

"Why do you want to learn about him?" Alex enquired, to test Jerry's motivation and to ensure that Jerry would actually learn something new.

"He was a black spy that the Nazis caught in…" Jerry replied. "I wanna know if he made it or not"."

"He was not a spy," Alex stated, attempting not to laugh. "He was a pretty outstanding biologist, though."

"I remember my six' grade teacher tellin' us that he was caught by the Nazis and was in their prison," Jerry responded.

"Yes," Alex continued, "E. E. Just was in France when the Germans invaded France during WWII. He was working there because he was a famous scientist in Europe, and several countries invited him to come and work."

"Why didn't he stay here and work?" Jerry enquired.

"What do you think!" Alex exclaimed/

"He was famous all over the world, right?" Jerry enquired.

"Jerry, I should let you discover this for yourself, but I'm going to tell you. Ernest Everett Just was at the very top of his field. I even think that he was the absolute top of his field, and he still couldn't work in his field here. Why not?"

"Was it racism?" Jerry enquired.

"Damned straight it was because of racism!" Alex shouted.

"But he was famous. He was the best!" Jerry exclaimed.

"Jerry, at the time, white America couldn't give a shit!" Alex exclaimed.

"Shit!" They must really hate us!" Jerry exclaimed

"No! It's not about hate, but fear," Alex said. "Do you still want to do your project on E. E. Just?"

"Yeah, I wanna know what happened to him when he was a prisoner." Jerry replied.

"Jerry, it's good that you have someone in mind, E. E. Just," Alex stated. "It doesn't look like you know that much about him, so you should learn a lot. But if you start on him and decide in a few days that you don't like him, you won't have time to change to someone else."

"I wanna do it on him!" Jerry insisted.

"Then, let's get started," Alex stated while taking his laptop out of his backpack, which was on the floor.

"Why you takin' that computer out?" Jerry enquired.

"I want you to read something about E. E. Just," Alex replied.

While looking at the laptop, Jerry asked if Alex already had the article on Just. Alex informed him that he was getting it from the Internet.

"But we don' got no Internet," Jerry stated.

"I always have Internet access," Alex responded, while pointing to his hotspot. "This hotspot gives me Internet access. Okay, read this short article on E. E. Just, and then we will talk about it."

Alex was quite relieved to hear that Jerry could at least read, but what about Jerry's comprehension?

"What does valedictorian mean?" Jerry enquired.

"Write it down in the vocabulary section of your notebook," Alex insisted. "It means the best in the whole graduating class. Write it down!"

"How do you say this word?" Jerry enquired as he pointed to it.

"Magna cum Laude," Alex replied.

"What does it mean?" Jerry enquired.

"Write it down!" Alex shouted.

"Okay, I'm writing it down," Jerry replied. "What does it mean?"

"It means that he got 'A+' for each one of his classes," Alex stated. "Write that down, too, and it means he was the best in university."

"Wait, wait," Jerry repeated. "New Hampshire is in the north, right?"

"That's right," Alex replied, "it's in New England, where I live."

"Was he the only black student in his class in New Hampshire?" Jerry enquired.

"I'm not sure if he was the only black student, but the far majority of his classmates were white," Alex replied. "You should look that up."

"And he was better than all them white people?" Jerry enquired.

"I wouldn't use the word 'better,'" Alex replied. "I would say that Just achieved a higher academic level than anyone else in his class."

"And in college, too," Jerry added, visibly quite thoroughly impressed.

"Okay, E. E. Just it is," Alex stated as he handed Jerry two sheets of typed paper, hot off his printer.

"What is this?" Jerry enquired.

"That there is your product descriptor. It's a list of questions that you can start with as you are gathering information on E. E. Just. You don't have time to generate, make, your own questions."

"Do I haf' t' fin' the books on my own?" Jerry enquired anxiously.

"No, we will do that together," Alex replied. "But you first need to go to E. E. Just's museum tomorrow and answer as many of those questions as you can. And based on what you learn there…"

Alex ceased speaking mid-sentence because of the ostensible pessimism on Jerry's visage.

"What?" Alex enquired.

"We ain't got no E. E. Just Museum heia in Charleston," Jerry replied.

"What the fuck!" Alex screeched in disbelief. "You must be mistaken, Jerry."

For the next fifteen minutes, Alex scoured the Internet in search of a museum in Charleston, SC, named in E. E. Just's honor, and although there were various schools, non-profits, and even a digital museum, Alex could not find, in Charleston, a brick-and-mortar museum with Ernest Everette Just's name on it.

"Damn! You're right!" Alex exclaimed. "Looks like we'll have to look online.

After Alex managed to recover a moderate portion of his composure, he informed Jerry that the latter needed to generate at least five new questions pertaining to E. E. Just all on his own. Once the questions were approved by Alex, then, Jerry was also expected to have to look for and find the answers himself. On that note, Alex handed Jerry a notebook for documenting his answers.

After handing Jerry the notebook, Alex handed him a smaller book.

"What's this for?" Jerry enquired.

"It's a journal," Alex replied. "It's kind of like a diary, but instead of writing down the events and thoughts of your life, you are going to write down everything you do, think, and feel that's related to your project."

"Why should I do that?" Jerry enquired. "It jus' sounds like extra work that I don't really need t' do."

"Do you want that 'A+' or not?" Alex enquired.

"Can you picture Momma's face when I tell her that I got a 'A+'?" Jerry enquired.

"No, you won't tell her. You will show her!" Alex insisted. "Jerry, you have to keep an accurate journal because it is not enough to just do the project, but you have to think about it constantly. You not only have to record everything that you do, but you also have to give your project direction. In other words, you have to plan it out, and you have to make changes if something is not working. And to know that, you will have to be able to reflect on everything you do. Keeping an accurate journal will come in handy."

"Is you sayin' I can't get the 'A+' without doin' that?" Jerry enquired.

"No!" Alex stated categorically. "Everybody makes silly mistakes. Even the brilliant ones like Einstein and Stephen Hawking made mistakes, but they always went over their work to catch those silly mistakes."

After Alex showed Jerry how to make daily entries into his journal, Alex also informed Jerry that he would give Jerry two more articles and the wiki on E. E. Just. Jerry protested strongly against using the wiki because three of his teachers are of the opinion that wikis are unreliable. Alex did concede that anybody, "and their grandmother," can make a wiki. However, in many instances, the people who make wikis are professionals, "experts." As Jerry continued to protest the use of wikis, Alex brought it to his attention that he, Jerry, could check to ensure that the information in the wiki on E. E. Just was reliable. When Jerry enquired as to how he could do that, Alex turned his computer screen toward Jerry.

"You can start confirming it with the information in this book, if you think you can trust it," Alex stated.

Jerry read the title of the book out loud, "'Black Apollo of Science: The Life of Ernest Everett Just,' by Kenneth R. Manning."

"Does it seem reliable?" Alex asked.

"Yeah, yeah," Jerry admitted, "but how many pages does it have?"

"It doesn't matter for the people who want an 'A$_+$,'" Alex replied.

While Alex was searching for something in his backpack, Jerry enquired of Alex what he should do if he can't get the book from his school or the public library. Alex took out his e-reader and turned it on.

"Is that a e-book reader?" Jerry enquired.

"Yes," Alex replied.

"Mrs. Sullivan has one, too, but a different kin'." Jerry added.

"Is she your homeroom teacher?" Alex asked.

"Yeah, she fine! ain't she!" Jerry exclaimed.

"Jerry, neither you nor I will ever have a physically intimate relationship with Mrs. Sullivan, so let's not think about it or talk about it," Alex recommended.

. "You mean we won't git to hit it with 'er," Jerry said.

"That's right!" Alex exclaimed. "But there's so much more to her than just her body. She has a warm personality. She's highly intelligent, and most importantly, she has compassion."

"What is that?" Jerry enquired.

"What? Compassion?" Alex enquired.

"Yeah, that," Jerry replied.

"This is how you spell it," Alex said. "Write it down in your notebook, and tomorrow I will get you a dictionary, so you can look it up and we can discuss its meaning."

Since the e-book reader had booted up, Alex downloaded the book he had just bought. Then, he showed Jerry how to use it. Afterward, Alex handed it to Jerry, telling him that he was loaning it to Jerry and to keep it away from all liquids. As Alex was explaining these things to Jerry, the landlady entered into the kitchen.

"Good, you took Momma's mea'loaf out o' de freeze', like I to'd you," the landlady stated. "How's Jerry's projec' goin'?"

"I'm gonna do it on Ernest Everette Just," Jerry announced.

"I've heard o' dat name befo'," the landlady interjected. "Wha' did 'e do?"

"He dead now, but he was a famous black scientist that was born in Charleston," Jerry replied.

"In Cha'leston or North Cha'leston?" the landlady enquired.

"Charleston, Charleston," Jerry repeated. "Oh, yeah, Momma, Alex jus' bought a book f' my projec'. You have t' pay 'im the money back."

"How di' you jus' buy a book an' dere ain't no damned bookstores anywhe'e t' be seen?" the landlady enquired.

"He bought it with his computer," Jerry replied while pointing at it.

"Le' me see," the landlady stated. "I'll be goddamned! How cin you do dat wit'out de Inte'net?"

"He can git on the Internet with this," Jerry replied while indicating the hotspot by means of his index finger.

"So, you not a bum afte' all!" the landlady exclaimed. "How much is de book?"

"It doesn't cost anything," Alex replied.

"Dis de U. S. of A., an' heia, ev'ry damn thing cos' money, ev'rything!" the landlady stressed.

"You don't need to pay because I am also reading the book," Alex added. "Jerry, read the two articles by this time tomorrow, and answer the first ten questions."

As Alex was collecting his things to go upstairs to his room, the landlady asked him if he wanted to have some meatloaf, string beans, and mashed potatoes for dinner. Before he accepted her offer, he asked whether he could eat it in his room because he wanted to start reading the book.

"I don' give a damn wheia you eat it," she replied. "Shouldn' Jerry start readin' de book, too?"

"No, I want him to read those two articles first," Alex replied. "Afterward, he will read the wiki, and then, he can read the book."

"Alex, what do cells do?" Jerry enquired.

"Does the library in your school have encyclopedias?" Alex enquired.

"Yeah," Jerry replied.

"Tomorrow, go to the library and look it up, copy the pages, and take some notes in your notebook," Alex stated. "In your notes, answer what, where, when, why, and how. Also, be sure to write down in your journal what we did today, what you will do tomorrow, and your question about what cells do."

"Jerry, go git my babies from Momma's," the landlady stated. "And when you git back, hi' dem art'cles."

While Alex was in his room writing in his own journal, the landlady called upstairs for him, but he didn't hear her initially.

"Negro, don' make me come up these damned steps 'cause you gittin' pretty damned close to gittin' yo' ass whupped on a em'ty stomach." The landlady shouted.

"Yes, Ma'am," Alex replied.

"'bout damned time!" the landlady exclaimed. "Is Jerry goin' t' make it?"

"If he keeps working, thinking, and caring like he has done, I think so," Alex replied.

"Da's goo' to heia'," the landlady stated. "I'm only callin' yo' ass once when de food ready."

"I'll be on the lookout," Alex replied.

Later that night, while Alex was undressing for bed, besides learning how to make it rain, he recalled that he had to visit the domain of his ancestors as well. He recalled my deliberate act of misinforming him, that he had to turn left. As he fell asleep, he also wondered whether the Great Mother would summon him for his second 'Ordeals' this night. However, as it turned out, what he had anticipated, with regard to the Goddess Mother, did not come to pass.

Having transported himself to the great Drakensburg Mountains immediately after he had fallen asleep, and passing through the blue-light emitting, craggy crevices, Alex soon found himself walking, almost wandering, as if he were in a dream, in what seemed to be an eternity through an empty, open expanse. Alex could barely make out many scattered structures in the far distance. Having walked a long time still, he could finally identify those structures, and they were huge. They were huts. Hoping that there would be at least one such hut that would be open to him, Alex realized that these thatched huts were as expansive as some of the mega apartment complexes that he had seen in several communities in China. He attempted to go to a couple of them. However, it wasn't possible for him to even approach them, let alone enter them. So, the only thing he could do was continue walking in the hope that there would be at least one that he could enter. After a while longer, Alex had become thoroughly impatient, and he began to imagine that I was laughing my "head off" for putting Alex on such 'a wild goose chase.' At this point, Alex genuinely wanted to turn back, and he did stop a few times to do so. However, one simple thought kept nagging at him when he stopped—what if there is something there that can help me get through the next two 'Ordeals?' As a result, Alex was obliged, as they say, to press on. Then, all this walking caused a past image to resurface in his mind, one in which he was walking in a desert, crossing all those lines in the sand that continuously marked "Freedom." And every time that Alex saw the term "Freedom," there were a myriad of dead black and brown bodies piled up high all around the demarcation. Alex recalled the biliousness he experienced because of the degree of death associated with the recurring moniker. He too recalled the utter meaningless of it all, except, that is, for a dying black girl who held up a rather voluptuous Venus figurine in the air with her left hand. Then, as the girl lowered her hand as she died, the Venus figurine, however, remained suspended in the air. And in his mind presently, it floated higher and higher, and it became bigger and bigger, to the extent where it occupied all of heaven and the Earth, which caused Alex to make a connection.

Suddenly, Alex experienced the sensation of a very sharp object poking him in his stomach. Then, he saw the one who was poking him.

"Hey! hey you!" the man shouted with a fierce grimace on his visage. "You are not dead. Go away! You don't belong here. Go away! Bugger off!"

Amazed that he could understand the man's language, Alex grabbed the stick and yanked it out of the man's hand. Then, Alex broke it and dropped it. The man became visibly alarmed as Alex stepped closer toward him.

"I am looking for my forefathers and mothers," Alex stated.

"They are not here!" the man exclaimed. "So, go fuck off!"

Alex, thinking that this was all some kind of sick prank on my part, decided to leave. As he did, two women, one middle-aged and the other quite old, walked up to the old man and enquired regarding the visitor.

"He say he was looking for his forefathers," the old man stated.

The two women looked at each other a little alarmed.

"Why did you not invite him to rest with us?" the older woman enquired.

"We cannot afford to take any chances with these riff-raff beggars," the old man replied. "And it has been left to me to protect our kinfolk."

"Could he speak our language?" the younger woman enquired.

"Yes, he did, somewhat," the old man replied.

"Then, he must have been ours," the older woman interjected.

"No!" the old man responded. "The first fathers tell us that our children, if they come, will come to us in a very special way. And he did not come that way."

"But still, he is the first to come here in over seven-hundred years," the younger woman declared. "If you would have let him in, he could have brought us tidings."

The old man grunted, rolled his eyes at them both, and stepped away, in search of a bigger and stronger poking stick.

2

How Screwed Is Screwed?

Of course, Mr. Reynolds, the director of the Department of Social Services, was not going to let well-enough alone. On several occasions he taunted Thunder openly when she was on her way home from school. Fortunately, she was always with her friends, Esther and Olivia. Both Esther and Olivia urged Thunder to inform Alex as well as her grandfather. Thunder was clearly shaken by Mr. Reynolds's crass antics. However, she feigned laughing it off, as they say, informing the girls that there was "no need to worry Kaka or Alex. I can take care of myself." Needless to say, neither Esther nor Olivia was buying it, as they say. It was Olivia who informed Daniel and Jonathan, soliciting their protection and that of their friends. Daniel informed his father and Uncle Joe, who praised him for "watching over our sister." They then told Daniel to inform his Uncle Dana, who would bring this to Alex's attention. When Daniel enquired as to whether he ought to inform Thunder's grandfather with regard to Reynolds's actions, Uncle Joe thought it was better for them to wait for Alex. However, they did encourage Daniel to continue watching over Thunder.

It wound up being a godsend that Alex no longer needed to be gainfully employed, for now he had the time to make the occasion to do the things that he really wanted to do, such as check-in with Roya and the kiddos, and to check-in with Thunder and her family in South Dakota. It is not as though they had not been in contact at all since he had left South Dakota. They would text each other a few times each week to let the other know that they each were still alive and okay. However, they had not had any long, thorough conversations, yet. So, he texted Thunder to suggest that they have an enhanced phone call, so they could see each other, and Alex wanted to say "hello" to Thunder's grandfather and all her cousins. When they saw him, the first thing Thunder noticed was that Alex looked a little plump in his face.

"You must really be enjoying the food down there in South Carolina," Thunder stated.

Alex chuckled and admitted that he was and commented that it must show. When he started talking about going on a diet, Lucy protested.

"No! Don' do that, you look much jollier when you are fat," Lucy said.

On hearing that, Alex laughed again, in that deep, hearty, reassuring laugh, which made Thunder feel very proud to have him as her father.

Thunder knew that he would want to know Misun was getting along and how they were managing with their finances, so she started those conversations. Alex became somewhat alarmed when she told him that, initially, Misun had a hard time of it, because he would often have nightmares in which the police would come to our trailer, banging hard on the door and walls until the door and walls came crashing down to the ground. And then, the police took on the appearance and shape of big, blue bears that not only grabbed him with their large, bright, shiny teeth, but they grabbed everyone, including their grandfather. Then, these bears would all run away with them in different directions. However, they never informed Alex that Misun had urinated nearly every night in his bed for the first few weeks, due to his nightmares. However, he has now stopped the nightly urinating, and Thunder could honestly report to Alex that Misun has become a much happier boy, almost his old self. About two weeks after Alex had left them, Thunder's grandfather came to get her while she was helping her cousins with their homework, just before he started cooking. He brought her some rather disturbing news. One of her grandfather's drinking buddies, Bull Man, was recently diagnosed with liver cancer, which was in a late stage. Thunder didn't feel at all comfortable hearing him speak of such matters, and her grandfather acknowledged that fact. However, he told Thunder that the only one that he trusted with taking care of his grandchildren was her.

"Wakinyan, you will do a fine job in raising your cousins, and your father will help you," he stated quite confidently.

Thunder really didn't want to hear this, but all she could do in protest was imagine herself running away from his voice. When she started hearing his voice again, he was telling Thunder that he wanted her to take care of the budgeting of the household finances, so that when his time came, she would be ready.

She relayed this to Alex, and she could hear the dread in his sighs. Then, she had to present Alex with more abysmal news. However, Alex interrupted her, for there was something on his mind, something that Dana had brought to his attention. After Alex had informed Thunder's cousins that they had to discuss some private matters, Alex jumped right into it, as they say.

"Thunder, why didn't you tell me, or your grandfather, about that fuck, Reynolds?" Alex enquired.

"I didn't want to bother you, either of you," Thunder replied.

"Yet, here I am, quite bothered because I heard it from Dana and not you, which makes me doubt our relationship, at least your commitment to it."

After a few seconds of silence, Thunder began to speak.

"I'm sorry, Alex," Thunder stated. "Even when Daniel told me that he told Dana, and I knew that Dana would tell you, I was just too afraid to say anything."

"Thunder, you gave me your red-ribbon dress, and it seems as though it holds three of us bound together, your mother, you, and myself. A Lakota woman named Gina, whom I spoke with on the phone after I read an article on the significance of the various colors for the Lakota, told me that red was your most spiritual color and that when you wore your red-ribbon dress when you first called the house for me, you were asking me to be your father and protect you. And she said that when you gave me your red-ribbon dress, that you then accepted me as your protective father. But I can't protect you if you don't let me in, if you don't tell me what's happening in your life."

"I'm sorry, Alex, but you don't have to worry because Daniel, Jonathan and the other boys pick-up me, Esther, and Olivia in the mornings to take us to school, and they take us home every day after school. And it looks like Esther and Daniel are getting close."

"Will Daniel and his friends be able to do this beyond the short term?" Alex enquired.

"They like doing it, Alex," Thunder replied, "and although I do see Reynolds's ugly head from time to time, he keeps his distance."

After Alex made a mental note to speak to his lawyer regarding the possibility of requesting a restraining order for Reynolds, Alex then enquired of Thunder if she had anything else to report to him.

"That's right, Esther, Olivia, Joy, and me met with our tutors today. They are Lakota, but they live off the Rez. They live in Rapid."

"Did you all feel comfortable with them?" Alex enquired.

"I think it will work," Thunder stated.

"Good," Alex replied. "Is there anything else?"

A few days ago, when Thunder called Sana'a, Sana'a sounded as if she were heartbroken. It took a while before she could calm-down enough for Thunder to understand what was amiss. Not only was Sana'a distressed because of what she wanted to tell Thunder, but she was also torn because Roya made her and her siblings promise her that they would not, under any circumstances, say a word to Alex regarding a recent decision that she, Roya, had made.

"Alex. Sana'a knew that Roya would not have wanted her to tell me either, but Sana'a felt as though she'd be betraying you if she didn't somehow try to get the news to you."

"What is this big news?" Alex enquired.

"Alex, Roya and her mother decided that the family would return to Iran, for good," Thunder stated.

"So, that's why she hasn't returned my calls!" Alex exclaimed, after Thunder divulged the news to him.

Alex went on to tell her that Roya was the only person that he had ever met that who was constantly and consistently busy maintaining her integrity. She could not lie, or deceive, or omit.

"Roya is the only person that I have ever met who reminded me of Diogenes," Alex admitted.

"Who is this Diogenes?" I asked.

"Diogenes was an ancient Greek philosopher," Alex said. "Many people consider him to be a nut case."

"But you don't," Thunder stated.

"No, not at all," Alex replied. "For example, he lived in caves, and one time,

Alexander the Great, a great general and emperor, went to Diogenes's cave and told Diogenes who he was and that he had heard many good things about Diogenes. Alexander the Great then told Diogenes that he would give Diogenes whatever he wanted."

"Why would a powerful emperor be interested in a homeless thinker?" Thunder enquired.

"Well, one of Alexander's teachers just happened to be none other than Aristotle, one of the early great western philosophers," Alex replied. "But to continue with Diogenes, Alexander the Great was blocking the sun from shining on Diogenes. So, Diogenes said something to the effect of, "please move. You are blocking my light."

"What!" Thunder exclaimed, utterly flabbergasted. "He could have asked for anything. He could have asked for a house, a big house, with servants."

"But he didn't," Alex replied. "He wasn't preoccupied with having. He was far more interested in being and becoming."

"Is that why you respect him, for his integrity?" Thunder enquired.

"Yes, but there was something else he did that I think about quite often," Alex added.

"What's that?" Thunder enquired.

"He would walk around during the day with either a lit candle or lantern," Alex started. "And when people asked what he was looking for, he said, 'a genuine human being.'"

"Oh, I get it!" Thunder exclaimed. "For you, Roya is one of those 'genuine human beings.'"

"Yes, you understand what I mean," Alex responded.

"I don't know about other people, but I've known a few Lakota and Kiowa who I consider to be 'genuine human beings,'" Thunder remarked.

"Yes," Alex stated, "like your grandfather."

"And my mother, and my grandmother, too," Thunder added.

"At least I now know why Roya hasn't returned my calls and emails," Alex sighed.

"What do you mean?" Thunder enquired.

"Roya cannot lie or hide something or deceive," Alex continued. "If she spoke with me on the phone, she would tell me everything that's happening in her life, including the kiddos and her mother."

"But isn't she hiding the trip to Iran from you?" Thunder enquired.

"Yes, you're right, Thunder," Alex concurred. "What I'm trying to say is that you have people who can lie to you to your face and not bat an eyelash. Roya can't do that. And she is concealing this from me in silence because she is afraid that I will talk her out of it."

"Alex, aren't most of the countries over in that part of the world not very friendly to girls or women?" Thunder enquired.

"Oh, yeah, big time!" Alex exclaimed.

"Alex, I'm sorry for saying this, but Roya doesn't take no shit from you, and you're her husband," Thunder stated. "So, why would she go to a country where she would have to take tons of shit from all kinds of men?"

"Thunder, honey, that is the sixty-four-thousand-dollar question," Alex replied. "Thunder, did Sana'a happen to say when they would be leaving?"

"No, Alex, she didn't, and I didn't think about asking her," Thunder replied. "I'm sorry."

"Thunder, listen!" Alex exclaimed. "You have absolutely no reason to feel sorry. Without you, I would have been left in the dark. So, thank you for telling me!"

Needless to say, as soon as they ended their enhanced call, Alex booked his flight for Quebec City, which took a tad over nine hours with a two-hour layover in Chicago's Airport. Initially, Alex was annoyed during the first leg of his trip, for there were no direct flights between Charleston and Quebec City. But once Alex arrived in Chicago, other thoughts began to take center stage. The first thought to take the stage was his student Shorty, the one whom Alex had pummeled quite severely. And closely following the shame and guilt,

Alex relived Mrs. Rawlins, his high school principal at the time, who disparaged Alex, "a teacher," for, "unleashing such a violent hate on a poor, confused, and troubled boy." The vehemence with which she spoke those words was so utterly chilling to the quick, that deep down, it convinced Alex in believing that he himself went too far, that he himself, and not Shorty, was, and is, the monster. It cinched it for him that night when he went to visit Shorty in the hospital. Alex only wanted to express his deep compunction for hurting Shorty so terribly. At least that's what Alex thought he wished to do. However, when Alex slipped into Shorty's room, there was an elderly gentleman who was watching television. Shorty's bed was on the other side of his, but Shorty was sleeping. As Alex moved toward Shorty's bed, the elderly gentleman noticed Alex and began to speak.

"Bo', yous go'n' be in a worl' o' trouble, when dat bitch of a nu'se fin's you heia dis time o' night."

His voice woke Shorty, who first looked startled and confused. However, when his eyes could focus and found Alex standing over him, sheer fright caught hold of his face and would not let go. With an elevated cast arm and a leg, Shorty screamed at the top of his lungs. Although something was ostensibly amiss with his voice, he was nevertheless quite able to produce a loud, shrill, piercing scream, which reminded Alex of the scream one of his female students had unleashed when he was on the floor after Shorty had pistoled him. Reliving that night and that day was too painful for Alex. So, he tried to shift his thoughts to Roya and the kiddos. However, no matter how hard he endeavored, he could envision neither Roya nor the kiddos. The only thing that came to Alex were words, viciously cruel words that he had uttered to Roya when she was at a low ebb, "There is no forgiveness."

Then, Alex recalled his first 'Ordeals' with the Great Mother and wondered how in the world he could have passed it, for he has always known in his heart of hearts that he was, and is, "a stone, cold patriarch," Alex's words, not mine. Finally, he recalled the spirit and the medium and Reverend Montague, and made a mental note that he be present in church this coming Sunday morning, because the trip to visit the spirit and the medium was fast approaching.

When Alex arrived in Quebec City, he went directly to one of the car-rental establishments. Alex was in such haste that he did not so much as hear when the woman behind the counter informed him that they only carried E-vehicles, so Alex would have to pay close attention to the charge. Alex followed her outdoors, and when she stopped, she bid him to elect one of four E-vehicles.

Although Alex did not particularly care about the fabricant of the E-vehicle, as long as it ran well, he was surprised when the sales woman stated, "Wise decision." At that point, Alex looked and saw that he would be driving the most popular EV.

Driving through Quebec City was challenging for Alex, though, for the direction of the flow of traffic had altered. Before Alex could properly park the EV, Roya's maid had come to inform Alex, in French, that their offspring were not at home and that Roya was playing her piano in her parlor, which meant that Roya ought not be disturbed. However, as Alex understood none of what the maid had stated, except, "Madame," to the maid's chagrin, she was obliged to bring him to Roya.

As Alex entered the house, he heard the final notes of Schumann's '*Kreisleriana, Op.16.*' Not wanting to disturb his estranged wife, he took a seat on the divan. However, after a minute, Alex found himself running to Roya's parlor, for a cacophony of noises had arisen from Roya's piano. When Alex forced Roya's parlor door open, he found Roya there, at the piano, weeping. On seeing Alex, Roya made a gesture to wipe away her tears, but it was only a gesture, for Roya's tears continued to stream. As a result, Roya turned her visage away from Alex and wiped her tears away, but this time with her kerchief. Convinced that she had her tears under control, Roya's visage returned once again within Alex's gaze, where she smiled at him. Alex then walked towards her, and she scooted over for him to join her on her stool. Then, she began playing Chopin's Ballade Number 4. After a minute, Roya's weeping resumed. After another minute, Roya's hands abandoned the keyboard abruptly and found rest on her lap. Alex recalled the last time that he had heard her play. It was in Bozeman, in her studio. Roya was playing Grieg's sonatas. Roya then turned toward Alex and began to speak.

"Alex, I am losing, and Ahriman is winning," Roya stated.

Alex was at a loss for words, wondering, doubting, whether I could genuinely hold up my end of our deal.

"Yes, Sana'a told me that she asked Thunder to tell you about the new plans," Roya stated without looking at Alex.

"Why, Roya?" Alex enquired as he took Roya's right hand in his.

Still, she wouldn't look at him, although she did allow him to keep her hand, which caused Alex to recall something he had read from Jean Paul Sartre.

"You don't have to go all the way to Iran to get away from me," Alex stated. "All you have to do is tell me to get out of your life, and I would do it."

"No, you wouldn't!" exclaimed Roya, now looking at Alex and laughing. "Anyway, you are not the reason why we move back to Teheran."

"Then, please help me understand how an ultra-liberated woman like yourself would voluntarily elect to go to one of the most repressive regimes today for women?" Alex enquired.

"My mother is getting on in years, and most of her friends and acquaintances are dead," Roya stated. "One Indian couple have moved back to India, which leaves three widowed, childhood girlfriends, who are in Teheran and Shiraz. Besides, when it's her time, she wants to die in Iran and be buried next to my brother and father."

"Then, give her a big send off, and send her on her merry way," Alex stated.

"Alex," Roya stated somewhat disappointedly, "you know she won't go anywhere without me and the kiddos."

"Yes, yes, I know," Alex admitted, disappointed in himself for having thought such a thing. "But still, I never thought that there would be a day when you would be sporting a chador and a hijab, like your mother does when she's out in public."

"I wore them when I was in Bozeman," Roya stated.

"Yes, I noticed," Alex acknowledged.

"Besides," Roya continued, "I can wear a hijab and still be 'liberated.'"

"And what about the girls?" Alex enquired. "You are raising them to be ultra-radical feminists. That is definitely not going to fly in a country like Iran."

"The girls will be fine," Roya stated. "Besides, regardless of the regime in Iran, our kiddos are of Persian heritage. So, they should be fluent in Farsi. They all speak good French and English, but their Farsi is suffering."

"That can't be the main reason why you are picking-up and moving to Iran," Alex stated.

"There is no one main reason, Alex," Roya stated. "it's all the reasons I mentioned in aggregate."

"Since I can't stop you, I guess this will be the last time that I see you and the kiddos," Alex stated as he returned her hand.

"That is not true!" Roya exclaimed. "We can have holidays together in Dubai, or on the Corniche in Abu Dhabi, or Muscat, or Manama, or Doha. And you don't need to get a visa to go to any of them."

"Seeing you guys only on holidays won't be enough, not for me at least," Alex replied.

When their offspring arrived home, on seeing Alex, they just ran to him, collided into his stomach and sides, and wept. Roya and her mother left them alone. After a while, Alex's children began talking, initially, one at a time, and then, they talked over each other, sometimes in English, sometimes in French, and there were a few times when Alex thought he heard Farsi. He did not understand most of what they were saying. However, he did not have to, for he knew very well how they all felt.

After dinner, which Roya and her mother had prepared, Roya and her mother retired to their chambers, giving Alex and the kiddos the final hours together. When Roya said, "Good night," Alex enquired as to where he should slumber.

"I will keep our bed warm for you," Roya stated."

Then, she climbed the stairs. After about an hour of eating ice cream and watching cartoons, Darioush and Shotvah began to yawn. So, Alex carried them both to their bedroom, where they undressed and put on their pajamas. After the nightly ablutions, Alex carried them again to their bedroom and threw each one on his bed, something that they loved. However, on this occasion, it fell flat, which disappointed Alex. After reading them their bedtime story, Alex tucked them in, kissed their foreheads, turned off the light, and stated, "*Dorm bien, mes enfants*," which he learned from Roya.

When Alex returned to the living room, there was only Sana'a.

"Where is your sister?" Alex enquired.

"We decided that she should go to bed, so we can talk," Sana'a replied.

"Is Marjan afraid of me or something?" Alex enquired. "Why can't the three of us talk together?"

"Marjan is afraid of *Ma'man*," Sana'a replied.

"And you're not?" Alex enquired.

"Nope," Sana'a replied.

"Well, I guess that makes you unique," Alex stated. "Okay, what do you want to talk about?"

"What will happen if we never come back here again?" Sana'a enquired.

"Of course, you will come back," Alex stated. "In a year or two, you all will speak good Farsi, and your grandmother will be settled-in. Then, *Ma'man* will bring you back."

"Baba, *Ma'man* is not going to leave *Ma'mi* alone, and *Ma'mi* will die in Iran!" Sana'a declared. "So, Marjan and me want to know what will you do if we never come back here?"

"*Ma'man* told me just today that we could spend our holidays together in either the U.A.E., Oman, Bahrain, or Qatar," Alex stated in desperation, attempting to convince his daughter of something that he himself found difficult to believe.

"Baba, will you come to Iran to see us, or not?" Sana'a enquired bluntly.

After a few seconds, "Yes," Alex replied. "If *Ma'man* doesn't bring you all to one of those countries, so we can be together, I will apply for a visa and come to you in Iran."

On hearing those words, Sana'a stood up, walked to where Alex was seated, took his hand, shook it once, kissed him on both of his cheeks, and wished him a good night as she climbed the stairs.

Shortly afterward, Alex went to bed himself, and although he did embrace Roya for most of the night, which was his custom whenever they slept together, on this occasion, nothing erotic transpired.

For the remaining two days, although the general mood was quite somber, Alex tried tirelessly to cheer his children up. However, nothing proved successful. Nothing special had transpired.

After Alex had seen his family off from the airport in Quebec City, he flew back to Charleston. While waiting for his flight, Alex could not help but reflect on the conversations he had had with Roya and Sana'a repeatedly. At one point, he was overcome with remorse for not having done enough to stop Roya from going through with the trip. Then, he asked himself what could he have done to stop her. 'You could have gone to the police and complained that Roya was violating your right of custody of the kiddos,' he thought to himself. Although he signed full custody over to Roya after that time when he loaned his car to Pieter to visit the widow of Wells, by the time the Quebec Canadian police would get to the bottom of the case, they would at least have missed their flight. When Alex came to his senses, however, he knew that if he had pulled something like that, he would most definitely never see them again.

During the flight, Alex felt as though he needed to think about something else or he would lose it for sure. However, it was initially quite difficult for him to stop thinking about losing his wife and kiddos. Only when he recalled what I had told him, "I will give you back your entire family, your entire family," was Alex able to relax, somewhat. To prevent his mind from wondering back to his family, Alex made a to-do list for the things he would have to attend to once he arrives in North Charleston. The item that topped the bill was 'go to church this Sunday and try and convince Rev. Montague to let me go on the trip to Chicago, which will take place in a week.' The second item was 'check up on Jerry's progress and evaluate his writing skills.' Based on Alex's fourteen years of teaching secondary school-aged children, Alex considered it to be a given that Jerry will have done next to nothing because when the cat's away, the mice, as they say, will play. Third on Alex's list was calling his driver during the stopover in Chicago, so Alex would have a ride to get to the house. However, by the time that Alex had endeavored to enter a fourth item, his thoughts had returned to his family, whom he would call to ensure their safe arrival in Teheran.

Once his plane had landed, Alex turned-on his phone to find a message from his driver that he was waiting for Alex just outside of arrivals. When Alex stepped out of arrivals, he saw his driver who was waving at him. Alex also noticed that his driver had a lady friend on his arm who had to be at least thirty years his driver's junior. 'How the hell can a geezer like Mr. Micky get such a young woman?' Alex enquired of himself.

"Hey, Mr. Mickey," Alex said as Mr. Mickey reached for Alex's bag.

"An' i's goo' t' see you, too," Mr. Mickey stated. "Mr. Alex, dis hia' is Lucille. Lucille, dis is Mr. Alex. He one o' my steady custome's."

"Nice t; mee' tyou," Lucille announced.

"Likewise," Alex replied. "Are you his daughter?"

They both laughed at each other and laughed heartily.

"He ain't my daddy, but he is my sugar-daddy," Lucille added.

They were laughing and pawing each other to such a degree that Alex made the comment that they had to be the happiest couple that he had ever seen or heard about.

When Alex arrived at the house, everyone was sleeping, so he went to the kitchen to drink a cup of water. While he was drinking his second cup of water the kitchen door opened. First, there was the baseball bat, and then the landlady followed.

"Alex, are you playin' stupid or what! Didn't I tell you 'bout that tiptoein' through the tulips bull shit!" the landlady exclaimed. "When you do that, you makes me think you somebody that don' belong heia."

"Hey, Ms. Mary. I'm sorry. I forgot," Alex confessed.

"'Bout time yo' ass got back heia," the landlady stated.

"Why? What's wrong?" Alex enquired, somewhat concerned.

"Don' tyou know?" the landlady said. "That boy done made hisse'f a got-damned nuisance askin' me, Eugene, and Mama if the questions you to'd 'im t' write up was good, or stupid, or unde'stand'ble, or importan', or related, or shit, I don' even 'member ev'rythin' he asked us 'bout dem damned questions."

Alex just smiled at her.

"What the fuck you smilin' f'?" the landlady enquired. "Ain't nothin' I'm sayin' is funny!"

"I'm not smiling at you, Ms. Mary," Alex stated. "I was just worried that it would be like pulling teeth to get Jerry to work. But fortunately, it doesn't look that way at all!"

"Oh, hell yeah!" the landlady exclaimed. "You bette' believe his ass motivated!"

Alex detected something ominous in those cryptic words, so much so that Alex pressed her to explain what she meant. Yet, she would not divulge a sound. After a few moments, Alex concluded that she threatened Jerry with a pummeling if he did not do his best. However, Alex found out a couple of days later that the source of Jerry's motivation was not the looming threat of violence, after all. Indeed, it was the promise of largesse, money, as they say.

A couple of days after Alex had returned from Quebec City, Jerry's grandmother enquired after her grandson's progress when Alex entered the kitchen to make himself a salmon salad sandwich. Of course, she only did so after she informed Alex, again, that he would not be getting any of her fried chicken, mashed potatoes, and collard greens.

"To be honest with you, I think Jerry is going to make it," Alex replied.

"I knew it would work!" Jerry's grandmother exclaimed.

"What do you mean?" Alex enquired, recalling the conversation he had had with his landlady two days previously.

"I tol' Mary that she would have t' offer that boy some money, so he would work hard t' git a good grade f' this assignment," the land lady's mother said.

"How much money are we talking about?" Alex enquired somewhat perturbed.

"If he gits a 'C', she'll give him fi'ty dollars," the landlady's mother started. "If he gits a 'B', she'll give him one hund'erd dollars. If he git a 'A', she'll give him a hund'erd and fi'ty dollars. But if he git a 'A+', she go'n give him two-hund'erd and fi'ty dollars."

"So much for intrinsic motivation," Alex stated under his breath.

There was a knock on Alex's bedroom door early in the morning, the day after he returned from Quebec City. It was Jerry, who informed Alex that he had his questions and that he had read the first two chapters of the book. After commending Jerry on his work, Alex asked Jerry if he had anything important to do after school. Jerry's reply was, "Yeah, I gotta work on my projec'." Alex was pleased with that response, and they agreed to start working on the project at the house at 3:00.

Because he had read only the first chapter of "Black Apollo," Alex was going to read the second and third chapters right after breakfast. However, the Great Mother had other plans for him. She summarily summoned him to her to succumb to the second 'Ordeals'. After Alex bowed, and then toward the other goddesses, he raised his hand, as if he were a school boy in class.

Although the other goddesses were visibly taken aback, turning toward each other in mild shock, the Goddess Mother went on unperturbed.

"Yes, Alexander, what will it be today?" the Goddess Mother enquired.

"Your Grand Worshipfulness," Alex started, "/Caggen, your husband…"

"Estranged husband," the Great Mother interjected.

"Of course, Your estranged husband," Alex quickly correcting himself, "recently told me that he was a god who has worn many masks throughout the ages. For example, he told me that he was Shiva, Dionysus, Yahweh, Satan, and Eshu-Legba. And I was wondering if your Grand Worshipfulness has been many other goddesses as well?"

"Surely, /Caggen must have told you that he was Marduk as well," the Great Mother added.

"Yes, your Grand Worshipfulness. He did," Alex responded. But Alex didn't feel comfortable talking about the Babylonian high god Marduk, for Babylonian mythology has it that Marduk smoot the Canaanite goddess, and Alex had a premonition of sorts that the Goddess Mother was Tiamat. And he didn't want to get any more on her bad side than he already was. So, Alex remained silent, for a moment, divulging nothing, and neither did the Great Mother. After what seemed half of eternity, the silence between them became excruciatingly unbearable for Alex. Knowing that he would have to pose the enquiry that he dreaded posing, to soften the effect, Alex apologized profusely in the more-than-likely event that the Great Mother becomes offended by his enquiry. She smiled faintly at Alex and gestured that he should get on with it.

"Were You not Tiamat?" Alex enquired

"Do you not feel better, now, that it is all out in the open?" the Great Mother enquired.

"Your grand worshipfulness, may I be candid with you?" Alex enquired.

"Alexander, although I do not like you one little bit, We do feel generous," the Great Mother candidly replied. "So, I shall explain a few of the finer minutiae of how these 'Ordeals' function. In order to prevent filibustering, procrastination, or any other form of time squandering, you are brought before Us. We put the 'Ordeals' to you. And you respond as best you can, as EXPEDITIOUSLY as you can. For time, and yours is about up, is nonrenewable. Once it is dispensed with ... well, there you have it. Notwithstanding that, to answer your question, yes, We are Tiamat. Who else do you think We might be?"

"Are You also Inanna, the ancient Sumerian Goddess of Heaven and Earth?" Alex asked.

"Of course!" the Great Mother replied. "Shall We commence with your second 'Ordeals' now?"

Alex nodded, and waited for Her to initiate his 'Ordeals'. She began to say something, but nothing came out of Her mouth. After a few seconds, She attempted to speak again. However, again no utterances came forth out of Her mouth. With a visage full of determination, She struggled a third time to speak and failed. Finally, with the mien of being somehow wounded, with one fel stroke of Her left hand, Alex found himself awake, staring at the book "Black Apollo," which was opened to chapter two. Alex continued staring at the book for some time, wondering about what had just transpired during his second 'Ordeals', which seemed to have backfired. He could not help thinking that he was in some seriously deep trouble--of course, he would not use the term 'trouble.'

Shortly thereafter, Alex heard the familiar sound of a myriad tiny insect feet shuffling and scurrying on the floor. He thought it was under his bed, so he looked. However, there was no activity there. Then, he realized that the sounds were coming from his closet. After a few failed attempts to open the closet door from the inside, there was a knock at the closet door. When Alex opened the door, he found himself looking at the back of my head.

"Oh, so that was the correct door," I stated.

"That's the only door," Alex replied while shaking my hand.

"Alright, now that the pleasantries have all been dispensed with, what the hell happened?" I enquired.

"How did you find it out so quickly?" Alex enquired.

"I have my spies, of course. However, Coti sees everything," I replied. "Alex, as Coti's realm is in a rip and roar, as they say, it would behoove us all if you divulge what transpired during your second 'Ordeals' before Coti causes the universe to implode prematurely!"

Alex went on and divulged to myself of how he had been curious as to whether Coti, the Goddess Mother, too, had donned multiple deific guises, not unlike what I had revealed regarding myself. As Alex proceeded with his spiel, seeing where this was headed, I quickly became uneasy, and at one point, I simply gestured to Alex with my hands to cease speaking. Then, I enquired as to whether Alex enquired as to whether Coti is, among other Goddesses, Tiamat. Alex explained how, after hinting in "that general vicinity," he wanted to avoid talking about Marduk and Tiamat. However, the Great Mother brought up Marduk and She "practically forced" Alex to enquire whether She is Tiamat. Despite everything, Alex was quick to point out that the Great Mother didn't seem angry or distraught in the least.

And although I did manage to retrieve a portion of my erstwhile composure, Alex could still sense that my mind was frantically racing to account for what transpired during Alex's second 'Ordeals'. When Alex finally arrived at the part where he enquired as to whether the Great Mother is Inanna, the Sumerian Goddess of Heaven and Earth, my face fell into my cupped hands, followed by general cringing and several moans.

"You know, I don't mind fucking up, as such, because we all do," Alex started. "But the thing that really gets on my tits the most is when I fuck up and I don't have a clue as to how I fucked up, like with Roya. Do you know what I mean?"

"Actually, no," I replied, "because I always know exactly how I fuck up, but until recently, I was always indifferent to it."

"Okay, how did I fuck up?" Alex enquired. "The suspense is killing the fuck out of me!"

"Ereshkigal," I replied.

"What the fuck are you talking about now?" Alex enquired.

"Ereshkigal," I repeated, "she is the Sumerian goddess of the underworld and Inanna's older sister."

Although Alex had read *The Epic of Gilgamesh* many years previously, he didn't immediately recall much of it. So, after some cajoling on my part, I managed to tease it out of him.

Alex did recall that Gilgamesh and Enkidu killed the Bull of Heaven, who was Ereshkigal's husband. It was Inanna who had the Bull of Heaven go after Gilgamesh and Enkidu, because Gilgamesh refused her entreaties to wed. As a result, Ereshkigal blames her sister for her husband's death. When Alex enquired as to whether the Great Mother is Inanna, She undoubtedly recalled the great pain that she had brought to her sister.

"But that's just not real," Alex stated. "There was never a Goddess of the Underworld, and there was never a Bull of Heaven."

"Alex," I started, "what is real? Are archetypes real? Are the most primary building blocks of thought real?"

"I believe they are," Alex replied after a few seconds of considering the enquiry.

"They are, indeed!" I exclaimed. "There are thousands of millions of you who, every single day of their miserable existences, wake up and create and recreate for themselves a myth, a story, in which they are the hero or heroine. Are these myths real? Without them, many thousands of millions of people would have given up the ghost a long, long time ago, Alex. When you take out your bill fold to purchase something, say a cup of coffee, is the note that you surrender over to the one who is vending you that coffee really real?"

"Is this story about Inanna and her sister, the Goddess of the Underworld in The Epic of Gilgamesh?" Alex asked.

"Of course, Inanna is mentioned in the epic," I continued. "However, Inanna's decent into the underworld is in a book by Wolkenstein and Kramer. The book is called *Inanna: Queen of Heaven and Earth*."

Alex started writing the title of the book to remember to buy it. However, I instructed him not to bother. When Alex asked why not, my reply was, "Because you already own this book."

"When I started my ascension to be the Supreme Patriarch, it was not at all subtle. It sent shock waves throughout heaven as well as the rest of the cosmos. It reeked sheer pandemonium. Indeed, I was myself initially terrified by the scope of my success. Coti, the Great Mother, even she was taken aback, not knowing how to respond. And because I was her son, her first creation, she initially went along with it. Of course, you should not regard the story of Inanna and Ereshkigal literally. Try to regard what happened during your second 'Ordeals' in the manner that I do. When you enquired as to whether Coti is Inanna, you recalled in her the time when she started allowing females, her daughters, to suffer unjustly and relentlessly at the hands of men, causing some women to adopt the tactics of men for their own survival, often at the expense of their sisters, daughters, friends, and mothers."

"So, how screwed is screwed?" Alex enquired.

"Well, if what you tell me is correct, then you should be safe, for the time being," I replied. "For Coti did allow you to pose your enquiry. However, Alex, you should be wary now. Coti will take this personally. From Her perspective, you snubbed Her, and She will most definitely return the favor, ten-thousand-fold, at least. And when She does, Alex, She will come at you when you will be least aware and most vulnerable."

3
Eugene Returns to Richmond

When I left Alex, Alex still had ample time to read the second and third chapters of *Black Apollo*. After organizing his notes, Alex generated a list of questions that he would have Jerry gravitate toward in the event that he didn't include them in his list.

At 3:30, Jerry called up to see if Alex was home and to let Alex know that he was there. As Jerry was finishing up the peanut butter and jelly sandwich and glass of milk that he had made for himself, Alex had come downstairs and sat down at the dining-room table. As Alex was asking Jerry about how his day at school had gone, Jerry opened his notebook and handed Alex his list of questions. Although it was clear that Jerry had worked hard, he had asked several of the questions multiple times, using different words. So, Alex crossed the redundant ones out.

"Wha' tyou doin'!" Jerry snapped.

Alex explained to Jerry that he was simply crossing out the questions that Jerry had asked more than once. For example, Jerry had read in chapter three that black people who strove to succeed in a white professional arena had to be better than their white colleagues. Jerry posed the enquiry as to in what way was E. E. Just was the best in no fewer than five different occasions.

Alex also told Jerry that the two most important question words, why and how, were missing from his list. Alex explained how the question words why and how can unlock much more and deeper information than the other question words, so he should focus on them. Moreover, Alex introduced Jerry to Bloom's Taxonomy with regard to thinking and learning. Alex wrote the word knowing, and above it, he wrote understanding. Then, he drew a line over it. After he drew the line, Alex wrote Analysis. Beside it, he wrote compare and contrast in parenthesis. Above analysis, Alex wrote evaluation, and above that, he wrote synthesis. Beside synthesis, Alex wrote creating in parenthesis. After explaining what each term meant with examples, Alex informed Jerry that thinking and working below the line means only a 'C', maybe a 'B-', But working above the line means 'A' and 'A+'.

As Jerry started answering his questions, Alex saw only simple sentences, so he had to teach Jerry about the importance of having a variety of sentence types. Therefore, after teaching Jerry the difference between coordinating and subordinating conjunctions, he taught Jerry how to make complex and compound-complex sentences. And Jerry's writing did improve. He even took care to make sure all the words were spelled correctly.

As soon as Jerry had come home from school on Friday, he did put a few enquiries to Alex.

"Hey, Al, where's New Hampsha," Jerry enquired.

"Look it up," Alex replied.

"I'm tryin' t' find it on this map, but it's no' clear," Jerry stated.

Alex then came over to look at the map, and saw that it was a pretty poor one with no color distinctions between the states, and the names of the towns and cities were barely legible. Alex opened his laptop and found a good road map of the United States.

"Okay, this is a better map of the United States," Alex stated. "I seriously hope that you know where New England is."

"Why?" Jerry enquired. "Wha's in New Englan'?"

Shaking his head in disbelief, Alex bade Jerry to Find New York, which Jerry was able to do.

"We gots peoples in New York City, I think," Jerry stated. "Naw, naw, i's New Jersey."

"Have you been there?" Alex enquired.

"Naw, I only been t' Raleigh to visit my gran'mothe' on my fathe's side," Jerry replied.

Turning back to the map, Alex informed Jerry that all the states directly north of New York including Connecticut make-up New England. Then, Jerry found New Hampshire.

"Damn!" Jerry exclaimed. Why the hell did he have t' go all the way up there t' go to a white-boy school? Couln't he fin' one in New York or New Jersey? They in the north, right?"

"Yes, they are in the north," Alex replied. "The Mason-Dixie line is between Pennsylvania and Maryland."

"So, Pennsa'vania is in the north and Mer'lan' is in the south?" Jerry enquired while looking at the map.

"That is correct," Alex replied. "But to answer your question about why they went so far away from Charleston to go to school, what do you know about life in America for black people back in the day?"

"Black people and white people had to stay away from each other," Jerry replied.

"What was that called?" Alex enquired.

"Segregation," Jerry replied.

"Jerry, do you happen to know the Supreme Court case that cemented segregation in America?"

"No, I don' know that," Jerry replied.

Okay, no problem," Alex stated. "Look up Plessy versus Ferguson."

"Can I go to Wiki?" Jerry asked.

"Sure, Wiki can be a good place to start your research," Alex replied, "but it shouldn't be the only source you use. And make sure that the information you find in Wiki is corroborated in the other sources you find."

"Oh, shit! Oh, shit!" Jerry repeated. "He bustin' out with them big-ass words."

"To corroborate just means that the information you find in one source is also in other sources," Alex explained. "And if it isn't, then you can't use that information because it's probably not reliable."

As Jerry was making steady progress regarding his project, Alex made a point of only being cautiously optimistic that Jerry would follow through without any major hiccups, for Alex had been burned so many times by students who initially seem to be all gung-ho to jump into a project only to run out of steam at the first sign of challenge. Although Jerry did eventually disappoint Alex, it wouldn't be in the academic arena.

That Saturday morning, Alex woke up at 5:30 am because he was going to visit the Carolina Islands to listen to some Gullah and eat some authentic black sea food. This time, as he moved around the house, he made a point of being loud, and to his surprise, the land lady didn't wake up. However, he later found out that that she had worked a double shift. So, she wasn't home. However, Eugene was up, and when Alex found him, Eugene was sitting on the sofa, crying.

"Damn, Eugene!" Alex exclaimed. "What the hell happened?"

Initially, Alex thought that he and the land lady had broken up and that she kicked him out, for Alex had heard them arguing a few times behind their bedroom door lately. But that wasn't the reason why Eugene was crying.

"Alicia, my little girl, always asks me when I'll be comin' home," Eugene started. "The las' time I spoke with her, she even told me that she got her grandmothe' to promise that she would be nice to me when I come back. She such a sweetheart."

"Shit!" Alex exclaimed. "I was thinking that Ms. Mary kicked you out."

"No, it's jus' the opposite," Eugene stated. "I been thinkin' about goin' back to my family. I been thinkin' hard about what you said about kids growing up and not having a lot of memories of the absent parent."

"Yeah, man, out of sight, out of heart," Alex stated.

Eugene continued to inform Alex that he found out from his wife that Alicia had broken her collar bone while playing on the monkey bars at school. The whole time during the journey to the hospital as well as while Alicia was at the hospital, she only asked for her father, which was why Eugene was weeping.

"Eugene, man, I once heard a famous rock star say that you don't stay because of the children," Alex said. "if I were to ever meet him, I would tell him that he is so incredibly fucking wrong. Will your wife take you back?"

"Yeah, every time we talk, she asks me to come back, every time," Eugene stressed.

"Eugene, aren't you afraid of that day when you talk to her and the conversation ends without your wife asking you to come back?" Alex asked,

"Every fuckin' time, man," Eugene admitted. "Will it happen because I'm fucking other women or because she's fuckin' some dude, or because the kids start hating me, or because she doesn't love me anymore?"

"Then what's keeping you here?" Alex enquired.

"Alex, have you ever been with a woman that loves to give you head?" Eugene enquired. "I mean really loves it. It's almost like she is worshipping your private parts. Most of the women I been with would do it but only if I asked them to. Mary just does it, and sometimes that's all that happens. I don't know about you, but it's hard for me to tear myself away from that."

"I hear you, Eugene," Alex responded, "I really am, but no matter how particularly well Ms. Mary may be doing you right now, but when you are an old, lonely man and your kids resent you or worse, they don't want to have a mother-fucking thing to do with you, I bet that you will come to hate those sucks that seem to be so mind-blowingly sweet right now."

"So, I should go back home?" Eugene said.

"While the going is still good, bro" Alex concurred.

"Mary's gonna be pissed," Eugene acknowledged.

"She's a big girl," Alex stated. "She'll get over it."

4

Anarchism and Beer in Kreuzberg

Although Alex had planned on spending Friday
and Saturday visiting a couple Carolina Islands
and getting stuffed on the seafood, he decided to
stay around the house. He didn't understand why
he had changed his mind so abruptly. However,
when he thought about it, the only conclusion he
could come to was that it must have something to
do with the conversation he had with Eugene.

On that Sunday, his driver, Mr. Micky, came
and fetched Alex, as usual, to transport him to
church. Mr. Micky enquired as to whether Alex
had secured a ticket for the coach to Chicago.
Alex responded by informing Mr. Mickey that he
was "still working on it." And after Mr. Micky
enquired as to what "the holdup' was, Alex
divulged the particulars. Mr. Micky became a tad
bit distraught and stated that he would talk to
Reverend Montague himself. However, Alex
assured him that he would be on that coach "one
way or another." Then, Mr. Micky reiterated to
Alex that there were only a few days remaining.

"I know, I know," Alex replied.

As soon as Alex had staked out his seat by
placing his jacket over the back, he sought out
Rev. Montague. However, the good reverend was
actively engaging various members of his
congregation. When it was time for the service to
commence, which was signaled by the music,
and everyone had got settled, something quite

unusual transpired. Up till now, all announcements would only be made near the end of the service. On this occasion, however, Rev. Montague himself approached the dais and began with the announcements, even before the prayer.

"Good morning brothers and sisters," Rev. Montague started. "I know that this is highly irregular, but we have an emergency. And when you hear what I have to say, you will understand."

The first thing that the reverend spoke of was that the journey to Chicago would have to be postponed because although there were five members of their church who desperately needed to go, they didn't yet have the necessary funds to pay for the coach and the hotel accommodation. Then, Rev. Montague pleaded to his congregation, entreating them to pray for those sisters and brothers "to ask the Lord to see fit, in his infinite wisdom," to find a way to get those brothers and sisters on that coach to Chicago. In addition, the reverend pleaded for the members of his church to put in a little extra in the plate, whatever they could, "because every little bit counts."

Alex saw this as his chance. At the end of the service, he would talk to Rev. Montague and offer to pay for all five church members' passage to Chicago and their accommodation. Alex saw this as his lucky break. He suddenly became quite confident that he would be on that coach.

And at the end of the service, one of the deacons made an additional announcement. Reading it from a sheet of paper, the deacon informed the congregation that, Roger, the pianist, will take part in a competition next Thursday at the local high school auditorium. The winner will be able to compose a score and play it in a feature film. The deacon then suggested that the members of his church come out in support of the pianist. Alex made a mental note to be there to support him. Nevertheless, his primary focus was on meeting with Rev. Montague.

After the service had concluded, Alex patiently waited for Rev. Montague to return to his office, alone, where he would make his offer.

Forty-five minutes later, Rev. Montague descended the stairs along with two other brothers, who were both deacons. Rev. Montague waved at Alex and shouted that he would be there shortly. The three men stopped walking and continued their conversation where they stood. Although the three brothers believed they were engaged in susurration, Alex could hear them quite easily. The older brother was the deacon who made the concluding announcement. Alex heard him say that the money that came in today was barely enough for two of the five people who didn't have the money for the journey. The younger brother talked about hearing a few brothers and sisters disliking the fact that they had to wait because they had to make arrangements in order to travel to Chicago. After the younger brother enquired as to when the journey would transpire, Rev. Montague declared that both brothers inform everyone that, "We will all be going only a week later than originally planned."

When Rev. Montague had almost reached the bench where Alex was seated outside of his office, he extended his hand to Alex and enquired, "How can I help you today, Brother Madden?"

Alex stood up and they shook hands. After Alex had exhausted the civilities, which he acquired through my tutelage, enquiring after Rev. Montague's health and that of his family, he struck while the iron was hot, as they say. He made his offer. Alex could see from Rev. Montague's body language that the reverend was very much tempted to agree, and Alex was quite convinced that he would. However, after a few seconds of what looked like internal conflict, Rev. Montague thanked Alex for his very gracious offer and reiterated to Alex that his hands were tied, that Alex would have had to have been a member of their church for at least three months before he could allow Alex to go on the trip. After Rev. Montague retired into his office, Alex, again, found himself slumped over the bench. Shortly afterward, Roger, the pianist, descended the stairs and was walking towards the reverend's office.

"Man, you must be the biggest sinner in the world," the pianist stated. "It looks like every time I come down here, I see you on this bench. I'm startin' to think you live here."

"Hey, Roger," Alex managed to utter.

"I don't mean t' be too nosey or anything, but what's up between you an' the Rev.?" Roger enquired.

"No, it's no secret," Alex replied. "I need to go on the trip to Chicago, but Reverend Montague won't let me?"

"Did he say why?" the pianist enquired.

"I haven't been going to the church long enough." Alex replied,

"Yeah, they got that stupid-ass rule," the pianist replied. "Alex, you say you need t' go, why?"

"When I was little," Alex started, "I think I was about seven, my mother left my father and we came to Charleston to get away from him. But somehow, he was able to find us. We went to that church that burned down, the one that housed the spirit, I mean angel. Something happened at that church between my mother and my father, but for some reason, I can't for the life of me remember. I was hoping that the angel and the prophet could help me remember."

"What do you think happened?" the pianist enquired.

"Some seriously heavy shit," Alex replied. "That's the only thing I know for certain."

"Well, if you happen t' have some extra paper lying around somewhere, maybe if you offer to cover for them five brothers and sisters, the Rev. will let you go," the pianist added.

"Been there, done that," Alex replied. "And I was convinced that that would work."

"Ah, damn!" the pianist interrupted, "man, I'm sorry f' cuttin' you off, but I gotta hurry up and ask the Rev something. Then, I gotta go practice with the guys at the bar."

"That's okay. Thanks for listening," Alex stated as the pianist knocked on the door.

"Oh, yeah, you coming to the try-out, right?" the pianist enquired as he was opening the door.

"You know it, baby!" Alex exclaimed.

When Alex left the church, he wasn't yet prepared to go home, so he caught a taxi that took him to downtown Charleston. While walking around, he ventured up a back street and found this small, cozy Italian restaurant that for some reason cause him to reminisce the time when he lived in West Berlin, and as soon as he entered the restaurant, he was transported back to that time. A short, stocky, elderly woman wobbled before him, leading him to his table. At first, Alex was confused. Shortly, the elderly woman returned to his table bringing a glass of water, a few slices of bread, and a small container of olive oil all on a tray. While placing the items in front of him, she enquired vis-à-vis his abstinence. Thinking that the woman was enquiring as to whether Alex engaged in sexuality or not, on reading the confusion of his body language, she clarified herself by enquiring as to whether he was "abstaining from the alcohol." Alex thought that was a strange way to pose the enquiry. However, "No," was his reply.

After pouring some olive oil on a saucer, she left and returned with a half-liter container of red wine. The vessel actually marked one-half liter. After she poured his wine, she pointed to the menu, which was already on the table. Then, she wobbled away. After about five minutes, a much, much younger woman rushed to Alex's table and apologized for his wait. However, Alex didn't really notice that he had been waiting at all because he was trying to figure out why the place caused him to recall West Berlin.

Alex ordered a Greek salad, spaghetti Genovese, and some calamari in garlic white sauce. While Alex was eating the pasta, it came to him. As he smiled, he placed his fork on his plate and reminisced.

The place was West Berlin, the district of Kreuzberg, and his time there started in January 1981 and ended in July 1983. Although Alex was staying in Schoeneberg, which was contiguous to Kreuzberg, he spent virtually all of his waking hours in Kreuzberg, because that was where all the action was. When Alex arrived on the scene, as they say, it was the time of the *Hausbesetzers*, squatters, as in unlawful tenants. For the most part, these squatters were young adults in their late teens and early to late twenties, laborers as well as university students, who had a hard time finding appropriate housing. Although the government blamed supply and demand for the acute housing shortage, the squatters noticed early on that very many apartment buildings were totally vacant. These young people demanded that the government force the landlords of these vacant apartments to make them available. However, the government was not inclined to do so. So, these young people decided to take matters into their own hands and they squatted these vacant apartments. As this was illegal, the police were quick to move in, especially when the owners complained to the authorities. However, to avoid being forcibly removed, the squatters had a strategy. They would try to fill their entire apartment building with people, so the police would have a hard time removing them.

In the beginning, the squatters would just invite people to come to their apartment building to help them stay there. However, that wasn't always effective, so others got the bright idea of throwing parties. This is how Alex got involved with the squatter scene in Kreuzberg. As Alex was walking down a street in Kreuzberg, a man with a guitar walked up to him and enquired as to Alex's origins. After Alex informed him that he was American, the man invited Alex to a party and stating, "We have the beer. You can bring anything else you want." The man's name was Johannes Klein, or Hansi. He was in his early twenties. While he was giving Alex directions to his apartment building, two women joined them. After interrogating Hansi, in German, of course, whether Alex was coming to the party, Hansi insisted that they speak English, and then he confirmed that Alex would come. Then, the shorter woman, Brigitte, or Biggie, introduced herself, and she introduced the taller woman, whose name was Katherine, or Kati. Kati didn't utter a sound, and she looked upon Alex suspiciously. All three of them were punk rockers.

A couple hours later, Alex arrived at Bergmann Strasse 103. In Germany, the number comes after the name of the street. He was met warmly at the door by Tuan, who turned out to be of Chinese heritage, fluent in English, German, Mandarin, French, and Catalan. He was also fluent in Spanish. However, as his girlfriend, Raquel, a Catalan activist for a liberated Catalan from Spain, he stopped speaking Spanish

"Thanks for bringing the potato chips and pretzels," Tuan said. "Most of the other people didn't bring anything. Take it to the first floor. Hansi will be there."

Despite the punk music, which was blaring, no one was dancing. Biggie came up to Alex and led him to the table where he could put the potato chips and pretzels.

"What do you prefer?" Biggie asked while holding up the bag of potato chips and the bag of pretzels.

Alex pointed to the chips. After putting the bag of pretzels down, she opened the bag of potato chips and told Alex to take what he wanted now because there wouldn't be anything left over later.

Within an hour, the first floor at least had become full, and the dancers had finally arrived. The dance of choice was the pogo. That, however, doesn't mean that they did it all the time. Generally, the punks Alex saw would move somehow, either from side to side or back and forth. But when the music became faster and more intense and louder, that's when everyone on the dance floor pogoed, which entailed jumping up and down and deliberately intending to collide into the other dancers. Yes, dancing the pogo was an extremely hazardous business, and Alex did see people get hurt. Despite that, Alex had to try it. He loved it. Initially, Alex wasn't going to drink because he didn't know anyone, and from his days in Bristol, England, he knew that some punks were racists. But he so thoroughly enjoyed the dancing that he felt comfortable enough to drink a couple beers. There was even a kind of comradery associated with doing the pogo. At the end of a song, people would pat him on the back, admiring how he moved. When Alex went to the hallway to get a beer, he finally found Hanzi, who made sure that no one would steal the crates of beer. Alex was surprised that there was still so much beer.

"Hansi, when you told me that you had beer, I thought I would have to share it with three or four other people," Alex shouted.

Laughing, Hansi shouted back that "you can't call a party a party if people have to share ze beers."

"But how can you afford to buy so much beer?" Alex enquired.

"We can afford ze beer because we don't pay for it," Hansi replied.

Alex recalled the old adage that 'Ignorance is bliss' and decided that it would be best to embrace its counsel, so he didn't pose any additional enquiries regarding the beer. Hansi, however, well aware of all the elephants in the chamber, laughed and added.

"Zey steal everyzing from us, Alex. We just steal a little bit of it back."

While pondering on Hansi's statement and sipping his beer, someone slapped Alex's behind quite hard, which caused Alex to spit out the beer he had in his mouth, and it almost caused him to drop his half-full bottle of beer. When he turned around and found Kati smiling at him, his anger subsided almost as quickly as it was provoked. Kati uttered something in German while still smiling, and Hansi translated it.

"She said you should know how your face looked," Hansi stated.

As Alex gazed upon Kati, he was picturing her as some kind of twisted Dr. Jekyll and Miss Hyde, totally reserved by sobriety and an out-of-control bitch from hell when intoxicated. Kati continued to speak, and Hansi continued with the translation.

"Kati said zat she nefer was zo near to a black man before," Hansi translated.

Kati stated more, much more, while Hansi blushed all over his face and ears. Then, he he shook his head and said, "Nein, nein," which Alex understood as 'No.' After waiting a few seconds for the translation, Alex enquired as to what was stated.

At this point, both Alex and Kati were pleading with Hansi to relay Kati's enquiry to Alex. While gazing upon both Alex and Kati and contemplating the daunting task before him, Hansi reiterated to Alex that these were not his words, "but Kati's." Then, Hansi took a huge gulp of beer, ostensibly to muster up the courage, and proceeded to relay Kati's enquiry to Alex.

To make a long, drawn-out, translated conversation short, Alex did end up sleeping in Kati's bed that night and many nights thereafter. At about 4:00 am, Alex was startled from a nightmare he had had and woke up frazzled. In his nightmare, Kati woke up, frantic, screaming at the top of her lungs, "Rape! Rape!" And striking Alex with a rather imposing staff. After about twenty minutes of deliberating what the best course of action would be, he decided that it would be best if he left. However, when he started to slowly get out of the bed, he accidently stroked her left nipple. Before he could place his other foot on the floor, she was awake and spoke to him. All Alex could say in German was, "I don't understand." Then, Kati grabbed Alex by the genitalia and pulled him back into the bed.

After about forty minutes, Kati said something quickly about Hansi, and then, she jumped up out of bed, put some pants on, and ran out of the room. Not knowing what to expect, Alex decided to get up and dress himself. A few minutes later, Kati returned to the room with a very sleepy Hansi, who could not stop yawning or rubbing his eyes. While still rubbing his eyes and yawning profusely, Hansi began again with a precursor.

"Alex, remember, zese are Kati's words."

Fortunately, on this occasion, there were only three things that Kati wanted to know. The first was the most embarrassing for both Hansi and Alex. She made it known to Alex, via Hansi, that she did enjoy their copulation. However, she felt that her orgasms would be more "*explosiv,*" if she were on top. After Hansi excruciatingly and painfully got through relaying this to Alex, Kati insisted that Hansi put it to Alex as to whether he could agree to this. After that was settled, Kati went on to inform Alex, via Hansi, that although she was a punk, she did not particularly like punk music, that she preferred artists such as Barbara Streisand, Shirley Bassy, Diana Ross, Aretha Franklin, Dionne Warwick, Gladys Knight, and Roberta Flack. Then, she enquired, via Hansi, as to whether Alex could agree to listen to these artists, which Alex did. After that was settled, Hansi was obliged to inform Alex not to be too late tonight and left.

"Not too late for what?" Alex enquired.

"A date, I zink,"Hansi replied.

After about a minute, Kati returned to add one more 'important' item. She made it known to Alex, while addressing Alex directly, via Hansi, that when she gets bored, she will move on. When Hansi relayed this to Alex, Hansi had to repeat it several times because Alex could not believe what he was hearing. However, every time Hansi repeated it, he interchanged 'when' and 'if.' When Alex asked if Kati had said "when" or "if," Hansi replied that he was not certain, because, to him, they are the same.

Although Hansi was the one who first started talking to Alex about anarchism, between his strumming and singing, that is, it was Tuan who was on a mission to proselytize. When Hansi first mentioned anarchism to Alex, Alex rejected it outright because he understood it to be chaotic and disorganized and degenerate. But Tuan was quick to correct that generally held misconception of anarchism.

"Alex, we want there to be order, too," Tuan stated. "But the question is whose order? If it's the order of the few, this order of the so-called representative democracies, then, no, we don't want it."

Alex agreed that representative democracy, especially as it was in America, left a lot to be desired, especially since over fifty percent of the voting population doesn't even participate in the process, and nobody seems to care enough to try and change that state of affairs.

"I admit that American democracy is a sham; it only serves the rich, and the rest are too stupid to see that," Alex admitted. "But how would your anarchism be any better?"

"Alex, when America kicked the English's ass, America was heavily involved in the slave trade," Tuan stated. "Several of your presidents even had slaves. And even after slavery was supposedly abolished, there was the one-hundred years after slavery. From what I learned in school, your ancestors were not much better off than their slave parents."

"Okay, okay," Alex interrupted, "but how is anarchism better?"

"Alex, anarchism is better because it is about freedom," Tuan replied. "The issue is power, Alex. In both the West and the East, power is meant to be abused, managers over workers, teachers over pupils, men over women. But it is not like that in anarchism,"

"In theory, maybe," Alex stated, "but you don't know that because there has never been an anarchistic…what would you call it? State, community, country?"

"My friend, you need to read George Orwell's *Homage to Catalonia*, Tuan stated.

While Alex and Tuan were in heated discussion, Hansi was strumming his guitar, playing with a few punk riffs. But when Tuan mentioned George Orwell and *Homage to Catalonia*, Hansi just had to jump into the discussion.

"It *war so tol, eh*! I mean cool," Hansi partially corrected himself, "to read how the generals didn't order the soldiers around, but they patiently explained what they had to do and why, *dass war so tol*!"

Before Tuan left Hansi and Alex, to go to work, Tuan handed Alex a copy of *Homage to Catalonia*, which Alex started reading right away, while Hansi returned to his strumming.

"Hansi, what kind of work does Tuan do?" Alex enquired.

Hansi smiled and responded, "He works in a *Brauerei*. I don't know that word in English."

"I think you mean brewery," Alex stated. "The place where they make beer, right?"

Smiling, Hansi nodded his head. Then, it dawned on Alex how they were able to get all that beer for their parties.

By the time Alex had finished his meal in that Italian restaurant, he was still perplexed as to why it reminded him of *Kreuzberg* and the squatters of Bergmann Strasse 103. Although he was enjoying his stroll down memory lane, as they say, he had to know how the Italian restaurant triggered it. Alex was going to stay at the restaurant until he got to the bottom of how this restaurant triggered these recollections. However, when he discovered, from the woman who served him, that they did not serve cappuccinos, he paid and left. While he was walking, he developed a bit of a sweet tooth. So, when he passed a cafe, he went in and ordered a cappuccino and a slice of hot apple pie.

In the beginning, it was difficult for him to get back to Hansi, Kati, and Tuan. Then, it finally came to him. Alex remembered how tantalizingly provocative Kati appeared in her hand-made black dress and her dyed blond hair.

The occasion was their one-month anniversary. By now, Tuan had gotten Alex to read Jean-Jacque Rousseau, whose quote, "Men are born free and everywhere in chains," resonated with Alex, partly because of his dream when he and other persons of color were walking in the desert, continuously passing under those placards that bore the word 'Freedom.' Kati invited Alex out to dinner for this evening. Alex had also read some Mikael Bakunin, Emma Goldman, Rosa Luxembourg, and even Anton Pannekoek as a critique of Marxist Leninism, which, ironically, is perceived as being right-wing. It was also around this time when Tuan was 'let go' from his job at the brewery. During those days, Alex did not see him much because Tuan was busy looking for a job, again, in a brewery, only, in a brewery.

"Man is born free, and everywhere he is in chains."

When Kati woke up, she woke Alex up by trying to smother him with her breasts. When

Alex woke up, he was in the process of being asphyxiated. Alex woke up trying to catch his breath with Kati laughing the whole time. When she finally stopped laughing, she kissed a very angry Alex all over his face and head and chest until all of his anger had dissolved. By now, Alex had learned a bit of German, so between some basic words accompanied by hand signals, they were able to communicate in a very rudimentary manner. When she informed Alex that it was their one-month anniversary, she suggested that they had to celebrate.

"Wir mussen es fueren."

When Alex repeated Kati's words, Kati laughed again but harder because Alex exchanged the term 'fire' for 'celebrate.'

When she stopped laughing this time, she invited him out to dinner, and told him that he had to dress nicely. That meant that Alex would have to go back to Cheruska Strasse in Schoeneberg, where he stayed. Alex stayed with Helga and Diethem, a couple of graduate students he met through SERVAS. Although most people think SERVAS is some kind of religious organization, it isn't, not in the least. SERVAS is an organization for peace. Basically, SERVAS believes that if everyone in the world knew everyone else, in the world, there would not be any more war, which, of course, is debatable. Nevertheless, working toward that goal, SERVAS has SERVAS host and SERVAS travelers. The hosts open their homes up to travelers, who generally stay with the host for about two days and nights, and during that time, they eat and drink and get to know each other's interests, tastes, and views. In Alex's case, Helga and Diethem felt sorry for him because he arrived in West Berlin with only 3.00 D-mark, which wasn't even enough to cover the 5.00 D-mark transit visa through the German Democratic Republic. The only reason why Helga and Diethem found this out about Alex is because the gentleman who was kind enough to offer Alex a ride from Hannover in West Germany to West Berlin, wanted his money back in full. So, he took Alex all the way to Cheruska Strasse to get his 5.00 D-mark from Helga and Diethem, which they gladly paid.

To get Alex on his feet, they found him work, under the table, as they say, , of course, and lots of it. His first job involved sitting at a covered bus stop and pushing three separate counters, one for if a lorry or van drove by, one for when an automobile drove by, and the third one was for motorcycles and bicycles. It was so incredibly monotonous that Alex fell asleep, and he was chided for falling asleep. Alex didn't expect to get paid, but they did pay him the agreed amount. However, they never asked for him again. Alex's second job was something that Alex never could have imagined. Helga had a cousin in West Germany, in Lubeck, who was a contractor. He had recently won a bid on a job for the German navy, on a naval base. Alex was looking forward to hitch-hiking his way to Lubeck, but Helga insisted that he take the train. Alex had to change trains several times, and it amazed him how everything was like clockwork. When Alex arrived in Lubeck, he stepped out of the train, looked for the nearest clock and saw that his train had arrived in Lubeck to the minute of its estimated arrival time. Heinz Peter, Helga's cousin met Alex as Alex was walking along the perrone of his train and took his backpack. Being with Heinz Peter was awkward because he didn't speak to Alex at all, not while they were walking to his vehicle and not while they were riding to God only knew where.

As Heinz Peter was parking his vehicle, he blew the horn, and a couple of long-haired, full-bearded Bohemians came to the car and welcomed Alex warmly in fluent English. Before Alex got out of the car, he said, *"Danke schoen,"* thank you, to Heinz Peter, who shook Alex's hand without looking at him. Heinz Peter said something in German to the two men and then sped off. These two men were Markus and Dieter who were vehemently against atomic energy, *Atomkraft, Nein Danke."* They lived in a very lively house with four bedrooms. They both had sometimes-live-in partners. Markus's was named Elke, and Dieter's was called Marion. Elke was an elementary-school teacher, and Marion was a bartender. Both women kept their own apartments, though, just in case "we need to escape our men," Elke once stated. However,

Elke tended to be at the apartment from Friday evening to Monday morning. Then, she wouldn't be seen until the following Friday. When Alex enquired as to whether Markus sometimes sees her or speaks to her on the phone during the week, Markus smiled, wryly.

"No, she wants to keep her two lives apart. Here, she can be loose. Here, she smoke hash, drink, fuck, and stay up all night. But in the week days, she play the perfect school teacher."

On the other hand, Alex did occasionally see Marion during the week. But the real character of the bunch was Markus and Dieter's dealer, Bernhardt. If you were to see him walking down the street, you would think that he were a lawyer or some kind of business executive, because he always dressed to the nines, always wearing a suit and tie, and he carried a black leather briefcase that actually contained bonified-looking documents.

The day after Alex's arrival, their dealer, Bernhardt, showed up at about 5:00 pm. After being introduced to Alex, Bernhardt shook Alex's hand and hugged him. Then, he went to the large, round, wooden table, where he put his wares on display. The sight of this impeccably dressed hash dealer, and that's all that he dealt in, going about his business to make a sale, or two, was such a motley occurrence that an uncontrollable laugh protruded deep from Alex's abdomen and erupted out of his mouth into an unsuspecting living room. All three men looked at him for only a second, ostensibly, to ensure that Alex was alright and went back to their business.

Three days later, Bernhardt returned, this time, at 6:30 pm, and again, he made his way to the big, round, wooden table to spread out his wares. A few minutes later, there was a knock on the door, and with the speed of a cat, Bernhardt tossed a red table cloth over the table and placed a deck of playing cards on it. When he saw that it was Marion, he removed the cards and the table cloth and resumed his business. That whole episode made Alex wonder why Bernhardt trusted him, so Alex put it to him.

"Alex, you are just like us. You don't vant to spend your whole life slaving for some stupid *Arschloch*."

After enquiring as to whether Alex knew what *Arschloch* meant, which Alex did, Bernhardt, despite Alex's nodding, had to scream it out loud.

"It fucking means 'asshole'. If you did, you would not be here *reisen durch Europa*. You would be *zu hause,* worried about not being able to pay your *Rechnungen. Was bedeuten Rechnungen auf Englisch?*"

"It means bills," Alex replied.

As Alex was drinking his cappuccino in the cafe in Charleston, he thought about how that big, oaken table was the center of life during his time in Lubeck. It was where they ate, drank, talked, smoked, played poker, listened to sixties and seventies music, and although Alex had never thought of it before, he realized that that table must have carried some hot lovers engaged in some rigorous copulation, which it had.

Three days after Alex had arrived in Lubeck, he started working at the naval shipyard. With a limited amount of English, Heinz Peter explained and taught Alex how to quickly spray paint large metal pipes. This was Alex's job for the next four days. Heinz Peter was generally pleased with Alex's work, and after a few days, he started opening up to Alex. The breaks were too short to be spent together. However, they did all eat lunch together. There were four other men working for Heinz Peter as well. One time during lunch, Diego, a migrant worker from Barranquilla, Colombia, spoke to Alex, "The German Polizei will neber catch us here."

It was also during lunch when Alex was informed regarding Heinz Peter's relationship with Markus and Dieter. About eight years previously, Heinz Peter lived with them in Flensburg. He was working at the German-Danish border. He inspected the hogs that were being brought into Germany. At that time, he was seeing Elke, who was still a student. After a particularly tough day at work, Heinz Peter's boss was on his case, as they say, because Heinz Peter took too much time processing the hogs. That was because he had to inspect nearly twice as many hogs as he would normally do. At one point, Heinz Peter informed his employer that he, the employer, had his, Heinz Peter's, permission to kiss his ass and resigned. A day later, Heinz Peter and the others threw a party. Elke could not come because she had to study. However, she felt so guilty for not being there for Heinz Peter, that she went to visit him before her classes would begin. She had the key, so she let herself in and found Heinz Peter naked and in bed with a likewise naked woman laying on him. And the musky, pungent scents of coitus, alcohol, and hash were clearly in the air. Elke slapped him awake, screamed at him at the top of her lungs, and left.

Heinz Peter attempted, on multiple occasions, to speak with Elke. However, she was, as they say, 'deaf to him'. After a few months, she started coming around the house, again. However, by that time, he had moved out and was starting up his contracting business. He figured that she came back to the house on account of the big oaken table.

"*Es hast etwas bestimmtes*,"—It has a certain something.

In all, Alex worked with Heinz Peter for three weeks. Heinz Peter had a lot more work to do at the naval base – however, Helga called him back to West Berlin because she, Diethem, and a group of their closest friends had applied to buy an old dilapidated apartment building for one D-Mark to restore it and live in it themselves. However, most of them were either graduate students or professionals. So, they only had time on the weekends to do the work, which is why they needed people like Alex, who had time during the week to work. Alex was flabbergasted when he found out that the local government gave them D-Mark 1,200,000.00 to restore the building.

"That is a deal and a half," Alex stated, "one D-Mark and some paperwork for D-Mark 1,200,000.00."

It was about one week after Alex had returned to West Berlin when he was due to go out again with Kati.

Fortunately, Alex had a passable jacket, which was given to him by an elderly SERVAS host in Frankfurt. Alex called her Frau Anhalt. As soon as she saw Alex, she went through the chest where all of her late husband's clothes were. When she found it, she made Alex wear it. Indeed, she forced him to stay an additional two days just so she could reminisce a bit longer about the good old days when her husband was alive. Yet, Alex still had to find a half-way decent pair of black slackss, which he did manage to find in the third second-hand clothing store he visited.

When Alex arrived at Bergmann Strasse 103, Biggie was at the door and yelled.

Kati, dein Liebchen ist endlich da."

Then, to Alex, Biggie stated, *"Du bist spaet,"* which means 'You are late.'

Alex was convinced that Kati would be furious with him for his tardiness. Ironically, perhaps not all that ironically, she was all giggles and smiles and even somewhat shy, as if she were ashamed of some dastardly thought she was harboring.

"*Du siehst gut aus*," Kati stated.

Biggie translated for Kati, informing Alex that he looks good. Yet, when Alex finally got to see Kati in all her full splendor, he felt dismally underdressed. Kati was wearing a sleeveless black sequin tunic dress that stopped just above her knees. Although there was nothing special in the back half of the dress, the front half, from the waist down, had various layers of frills and ruffles that all extended outward as they approached the knees. From below the waist on the front half, the dress sported various values of black and gray. And in contrast, Kati had dyed her now blonde hair with pink streaks here and there. She looked absolutely divine.

After having walked to the Sued Stern U-bahn station, descending the stairs to the subway platform, Kati walk passed the ticket turn stiles, pulling Alex along with her, walking straight to the opposite exit. While ascending those stairs to leave the U-bahn station, she spoke to Alex.

"*Es gab zu viele Buellen.*"

Realizing that she was not being understood, Kati repeated what she had stated, replacing '*Buellen*' with '*Polizei*,' which Alex understood, which means police. So, Alex figured that she wanted to 'ride black,' ride without paying, something that he had done many times. So, they walked for approximately twenty-five minutes.

Then, they entered into an Italian restaurant, one which closely resemble the one with the short, old woman who wobbled. As they were being seated, Kati commanded Alex to order whatever he wanted.

Both Kati and Alex ended up eating a five-course meal with soup, salad, pizza, the entree, and dessert. For the entrée, Alex had pork that was roasted in a white wine sauce. Because Kati didn't eat red meat, she ate pasta with pieces of filleted fish, shrimp, and mussels in a light, creamy tomato sauce. When they finished off their first bottle of wine, Alex raised the empty bottle, signaling to the waiter to bring another one. However, before the waiter could see Alex, Kati grabbed Alex's arm, pulled it down, and spoke to him.

"Nein, nicht besoffen worden."

Recalling how Hansi had once deliberately translated something that Kati had said incorrectly, Alex instantly knew what she meant. Kati was commanding Alex not to get drunk.

When Kati was about halfway through her dessert, she started to snicker. Alex assumed that she was quite happy and looking forward to when they close the door of her bedroom at Bergmann Strasse 103. But in actuality, she was giggling for a whole other reason. Then, her giggling ceased abruptly, and her entire body language took on a grave aspect. Alex noticed this change, and, at first, he thought that he had done something wrong to cause it. But she wasn't looking at

Alex, nor was she deliberately avoiding his gaze. Kati's eyes were fixed on the waiter, watching his every move. The waiter also noticed how intently she was watching him, which made him come to their table immediately.

"*Moechten Sie etwas anderes, gnaedige Frau?*" the waiter enquired.

Alex understood that the waiter was enquiring as to whether Kati desired anything else. Kati ordered two cappuccinos. But as soon as the waiter had disappeared into the kitchen, Kati pulled firmly on Alex's arm and spoke to him.

"*Komm schnell mit!*"

Not yet registering what she meant, Alex didn't budge. After taking a quick glance at the kitchen door, while practically dislocating Alex's left arm, she exclaimed, "*Geh schon!*" Finally understanding what she wanted to do and why she was giggling, Alex raced after her out of the front door and down the street.

After a block, they turned into a side street but kept running. While still running, his entire experience with Kati flashed before his eyes— How she looked at him as if he were the personification of the plague when they first met, when she made Hansi to enquire of Alex whether he were too intoxicated to copulate, and the coitus that followed; all their walks, the wrestling in her bedroom that always ended in coitus, when she instigated heated arguments between Alex and Tuan, for Tuan was a staunch follower of Mikhail Bakunin. Besides being a bit of an anti-

Semite, Bakunin believed that it was necessary to violently destroy Bourgeois society in order to create an anarchist society. Although Alex had taken to anarchism, he could never come to terms with the blatant contradiction. For anarchism, at least in the manner that Alex regarded it, anarchism was meant to promote freedom and peace by keeping institutional authority, along with private property, to an absolutely bare minimum, if at all. He had a problem with the notion of anarchism's first act being coercive and violent. Kati made a point of regularly getting Tuan's goat by mentioning Alex's view of anarchism. Finally, Alex thought of Hansi's songs and how he would miss them once his relationship with Kati ended. And it would end, sooner rather than later, not so much because he couldn't keep up with her caliber of 'interesting,' but because he was not willing to go as far as she would demand of him.

Don't get Alex wrong, he was no goody two shoes, not by any means. Alex rode the major subway systems of Europe—West Berlin, Paris, London, Stockholm, Stuttgart—black, not unlike the best. However, what Kati had done left a rather bitter taste in his mouth. There was the possibility of being apprehended for something that he didn't want to do, something that he knew would have fallen on deaf ears at the police station, as well as on the docket. However, not tonight. Their relationship wouldn't end tonight, but 'tomorrow, tomorrow, tomorrow.' For tonight, Kati was full of giggles, which, for her, meant that the foreplay had already begun. Coitus was imminent and inevitable!

5
Alex Goes to Chi-Town

Jerry was making consistent progress with the research for his project. Alex figured that he liked seeing those dollar signs in his eyes. After they had finished reading E. E. Just's biography, there wasn't enough time for Jerry to understand the main points of Just's cellular research. So, Alex suggested that Jerry focus on the two types of cells—prokaryotes and eukaryotes--and mitochondria. While Jerry was working on getting his presentation together, he was consistently anticipating questions that some of his classmates and teachers would pose.

"Hey, Alex, in my class, we got two Vietnamese girls, a boy from Nepal, wherever that is, white whites, blacks, and some Guatemalans," Jerry stated.

"What's your point?" Alex enquired.

"Of course, Plessy v. Ferguson ended, 'Separate but equal' ended, but how did it end?" Jerry enquired.

"Good thinking!" Alex replied. "Look up Brown v. the Board of Education."

"Damn! What don't you know!" Jerry exclaimed.

"Jerry, every half-way decently educated American knows about the landmark decision of Brown v. the Board of Education," Alex replied.

The Goddess Returns

As the day of Jerry's presentation drew nearer, Alex underscored the necessity for Jerry to become so thoroughly familiar with his material, and the order in which he would present it, that he ought to be able to present it "blindfolded."

That Thursday evening, Alex went to the school auditorium to see Roger compete in what was familiarly dubbed 'The Battle of the Pianists.' There were eight pianists in total. Each of them was obliged to play three pre-arranged pieces of music--a classical piece, a jazz piece, and an R&B piece. The classical piece was Chopin's Scherzo number 2 in B-flat minor, Opus 31. The jazz piece was from the Yellow Jackets' "Green House" album. And the R&B piece was from Earth, Wind, and Fire's "Fantasy." Afterward, they all were again obliged to play a self-composed piece.

Of the eight pianists, there was only one woman, Yvette Summers, a twenty-four-year-old graduate in Business Administration. Early on, starting from the first round, Yvette was in the lead. Although, in Alex's mind, she was not the best pianist, she was by no means the worst either. However, her performance paled in comparison to Roger's. Indeed, she even omitted several of Chopin's chords and notes throughout her performance of the scherzo. Alex only started to realize what was transpiring when it was made known to the audience who the judge was, one judge. He was the same man who had organized the competition, Mr. George Archibald Moore

III. He was a retired music teacher with alleged connections in the music industry.

The winner of the competition would sign a recording contract with a major record label, yet to be named, and compose a song that would be incorporated into a feature film. By the end of the second round, half of the male performers had become visibly distraught. Alex did not know whether it was because they realized that the entire event was a farce, one that cost each of them $250.00 to enter, or because they, too, knew that the best among them was ostensibly not upset that he was not in the lead, nor was he going to win, which suggested that Roger, as they say, was on the take.

Ostensibly, no one in the house, except for Alex, enjoyed listening to Chopin's scherzo. However, when the performers started playing the piece from "Green House," things began to liven-up. And when Roger played it, several people rose-up from their seats and began to dance. However, when he played "Fantasy" from Earth, Wind, and Fire, everyone danced, not only the spectators, but all the other pianists as well. Indeed, even the 72-year-old George Moore showed the younger crowd a step or two. Nevertheless, at the end of the round, Yvette remained well in the lead.

By the final round, three of the pianists had departed the public house, and another three withdrew their names from the competition, stating that they just wanted to hear Roger play.

Yvette was called up first to play her self-composed piece. There was something strangely nebulous and other worldly about it, and Alex felt as though many chords were being omitted from this piece as well. He even found himself adding the missing chords as he was listening.

In stark contrast, when Roger began playing, it seemed as though his piece would even be more disjointed and solemn than Yvette's. However, it picked up rather quickly, and once again, the whole house, as they say, was "jumping."

After the competition had concluded, and Yvette received her trophy, which already had her name etched on it, along with the promise of a recording contract, she and George departed the school auditorium, together. Although the night was still young, only 9:37 pm, Alex felt disgusted and wanted to talk to Roger regarding the sham they had all participated in. Roger, on the other hand, was preoccupied at the piano, playing his fans' requests. So, Alex ordered a taxi, and departed.

Early that next morning, Rev. Montague phoned Alex to offer him a place on the coach to Chicago, provided that Alex was prepared to pay for "the transportation and accommodation expenses of three of our brothers." This was a very pleasant surprise for Alex, for he had resigned himself to the thought that he would not be having a spot on that coach. As Rev. Montague was obligated to make the payments by 4:00 pm later that day, they agreed that Alex would come to the church at 1:30 to make the payment to Rev. Montague.

While Alex and Rev. Montague were completing the transaction in Rev. Montague's office downstairs, there was a knock on the door. It was Roger, who started smiling profusely after seeing that Alex was paying the reverend money. Roger apologized for disturbing them and stated that he could come back later.

Still incredulous to the fact that he would be going to Chicago after all, Alex sat down on the bench after he departed the reverend's office. On exiting Rev. Montague's office, Roger signaled to Alex that he was obliged to relieve himself. After departing the WC, still drying his hands with the paper towel, Roger walked over to him.

"I guess that means you'll be goin' to Chi-Town after all!" Roger exclaimed.

"Don't it!" Alex replied.

However, the bad taste of the sham of the previous night was still with Alex.

"Roger," Alex began as he handed Roger a piece of gum, "you were way better than Yvette, last night."

Roger stated nothing in response.

"Aren't you pissed that you lost?" Alex almost shouted.

"Nope," Roger declared.

"What about the $250.00 entry fee?" Alex enquired.

"What about it?" Roger retorted.

Alex found out to, his dismay, that Roger had a leading role in the sham. George Moore begged him to take part in the competition, offering Roger $350.00. After he had divulged this to Alex, he continued.

"That might be," Roger replied, "that I was better than Yvette. But one thang is fo' sho'. An' do you know wha' dat is?"

"No," Alex responded.

"Is you lis'nin'? Is you ready for this truth?" Roger enquired.

Alex gestured that he wanted to know.

"Okay, I'll tell you. First, that woman is fffffffine! I mean GOD DAMN SHE IS FINE! Secon', DID YOU SEE Dim LEGS! OH, MY GOD, DID YOU SEE 'EM...you betta tell me you saw 'em! Tell me! Tell me, damnit!"

"Yes, yes, I saw her legs," Alex finally admitted.

"Evert single time I saw dat woman's legs, an' I mean, EVERY, SINGLE FUICKIN' TIME, I couldn' help but wonder 'bout just how fuckin' amazin' being caught up in dem lips mus' be."

After looking at Alex for a sign that he understood, Roger shook his head in frustration.

"You really ain't gittin' what I'm drivin' at, is you? Roger enquired "Well, it's like this, remember the judge?"

"Yes, of course, the balding geezer," Alex replied.

"Well, the only reason he set up this little contest was so he could git him some young, wet, tight pussy. And I be' tyou he is hittin' dat ass right now like thay's no t'mar! Can you feel me now?"

Gesturing that he did, Alex changed the subject back to the fact that he was now going to Chicago. However, he felt as though something was not quite right.

"Don't get me wrong," Alex stated, "I am as happy as pie that I'm on that bus. But that man was not going to let me go. He's a stickler for following the rules if ever I'd seen one!"

"Damn, man!" Roger exclaimed. "You even bitchin' when you in. You know, it could be that Rev. Monty changed his min' 'cuz he had to gi' 'em other brothers on the bus, too."

"I don't think so, because when five brothers and sisters needed help to pay for the trip, he refused my offer," Alex replied.

"Maybe, the Holy Ghost go' to 'im," Roger suggested.

"Maybe," Alex concurred. "And I guess the Holy Ghost gave him my phone number, too."

"De lawd does work in mysterious ways, you know!" Roger exclaimed.

Looking upon Roger, Alex enquired as to whether there was anything that Roger wanted to tell him.

"Naw, man. I ain't got nothin' t' say 'bout it," Roger replied as he looked around, avoiding looking upon Alex. "Tha's between you an' the Rev."

After a pause, Alex looked at Roger and brought it to his attention that he knew that Roger had got him on that coach to Chicago, and Alex thanked him. However, Roger simply listened as if he had no idea as to what Alex was referring to.

After briefly recalling just how dogged and recalcitrant Rev. Montague had been, Alex went on about how he hoped that Roger didn't have to do anything too unsavory or against his principles to get Alex on that coach. On hearing that, Roger's eyes fell toward the floor directly under him and shook his head. And after a short silence between them, Roger spoke.

"Man, you too much!" Roger exclaimed.

"How am I 'too much?'" Alex enquired.

Man, you was frettin' yo' ass off about how you was goin' t' get on that bus," Roger replied. "And now, when yo' ass is finally on that Goddamned bus, I thought yo' ass would be as happy as a mother fucker who has never had any lucky breaks in his sorry-ass life but hits the number. Bu' tyou ain't! Here you is askin' all kinds o' questions—How did I git on that bus? Why did I git on that bus? When did I git on that bus? Shit! The way you carryin' on, I'm afraid you liable to not even show up t' git on that bus."

Regarding things from Roger's perspective, Alex smiled and assured him that he would "definitely be on that bus."

"It's just that I believed that nothing short of an act of God would permit me to see the angel and the prophet," Alex clarified.

"I feel you," Roger stated as, vis-a-vis his body language, he was visibly considering something.

Thinking that Roger was regarding him as being ungrateful, Alex quickly stressed his joy, relief, and gratitude.

"Don' worry, Al. You still okay in my book! Roger exclaimed. "The reason why I got you on the bus is because you remind me of something my grandfather taught me. My grandfather used to teach me a little philosophy because even though we ain't officially slaves, he never believed that we was free, and we ain't, not really. He would always tell me that the beginning of freedom was knowing what the people in power know. I never forget one of those philosophers he told me 'bout. His name was Diojean."

Alex corrected Roger by saying that the philosopher's name was Diogenes in English.

"As I was sayin' befo' I was rudely interrupted," Roger continued, Diojean was so bad ass that he could diss' Alexander de Great and git away wit' it. Diojean was also a little freaky. He often walked around with a lit candle in broad day light. When fo'ks ast him what the hell he was doin', he would say that he was lookin' fo' a human being. F' the longest time, I was tryin' t' break it down because f' me, a human bein' was just another way of saying a person, nothin' special. Then, about four years ago, it hit me. My best friend, somebody who I thought was my best friend, tried to destroy my relationship with my girlfriend at the time, tellin her that I talked behind her back and that I was cheatin on her. He wasn't true-blue, he was bogus."

While taking a pause to see if Alex was listening because Roger knew Alex's propensity to not listen while others are in dialogue with him. However, Alex was clearly listening intently.

"Da's you, man! Da's you. From the firs' time I me' tyou, I thought of Diojean. You one o' dose people Diojean was lookin' fo', you one o' dose people I been lookin' fo', too."

Alex could only look at Roger in amazement, incapable of speaking, for although Alex, too, was looking for Diogenes's true-blue human being, Alex would never have considered himself to be one in ten-thousand years.

"Remember how you told me that I played f' the music and how I reminded you of Beethoven? It was like you was the firs' person, the only person who saw me, who I was. So, when I realized just how bad you needed t' go t' Chi-Town," Roger continued, "I had t' gi' tyou on dat bus."

After thanking Roger and shaking his hand profusely, Roger thanked Alex for teaching Roger something about himself, something that he believed he never would have realized about himself if it weren't for Alex.

As Jerry's presentation was only three days away, on next Monday, Jerry was a tad bit nervous but he did believe that he would get at least a 'B'. However, Alex, because of the Chicago trip knew that Jerry's confidence was tied up with the fact that Alex would be present during the presentation. But now that Alex probably wouldn't be able to attend Jerry's presentation, because of the trip to Chicago, he wondered how his absence would affect Jerry. On the way back to the house, Alex even contemplated not going to Chicago. At one point, Alex thought to himself that it was settled, 'I'll just go to Jerry's presentation.' And for a few minutes, Alex even felt relieved that he wouldn't have to disappoint Jerry. However, all of that self-assurance fell by the wayside as Alex climbed the stairs to the porch, for he remembered what Pieter had said regarding the female architypes, that there were none in Alex's psyche.

As soon as Alex entered the house, he was surprised to find Jerry in the living room with another young man. Alex thought it was Alphonso. However, he was not certain.

"Jerry, why aren't you in school?" Alex enquired.

While Jerry was explaining how there was no water, so school was let out early, Alex could not, for the life of him, keep his eyes off of

Jerry's guest. On hearing that, Alex enquired as
to whether the young man were Alphonso. Then,
Alex brought it to Jerry's recollection how his
mother did not want him to have anything to do
with Alphonso, who just laughed with his eyes.
Alex knew all too well what Alphonso was
thinking. He had seen it often enough in his
career as a teacher. Recalling Shorty and desiring
to avoid further escalation of the predicament,
Alex enquired as to whether he and Jerry could
speak privately.

"I know what Mama said," Jerry stated.

"No, it's about something else," Alex replied.

Standing up from his seat, Alphonso made it
known that he had "to roll." However, prior to
his departure, Alphonso enquired as to whether
Jerry was "sure." After seeing Alphonso to the
door and affirming that he was certain, Jerry
closed the door, turned toward Alex and stated,
"What!"

"What are you so sure of?" Alex enquired.

"None o' yours!" Jerry exclaimed. "Is that all
you have t' say?"

"No, no," Alex repeated, shaking his head,
"there's something I have to tell you."

"Go 'ead," Jerry stated.

"Jerry," Alex started, "you know…"

"No! I don' know!" Jerry exclaimed.

"The church … I go to … is organizing a trip
… to Chicago, and I … I really have to go," Alex
stated with some difficulty.

"So? Why you tellin' me dis?" Jerry enquired.

"We leave tomorrow … and we will probably get back Monday afternoon," Alex stated, again, with difficulty.

After a couple of seconds, it dawned on Jerry what Alex was attempting to get across to him. Alex wanted desperately to explain why he was obligated to go to Chicago. However, Jerry screamed at him, informing Alex, with the aid of not a few expletives, how he was no different from Eugene and all the other men that his mother had brought into his life.

"Y'aw come, get whatever it is that y'aw want, fucks, sucks, a place t' lay low for a while, whatever the fuck it is dat y'aw want. An' after a while, us kids start t' see y'aw as bein' hie' finally fo' good. But y'aw mother fuckers always end up leavin'. An' the stupid thing dat I jus' don' git is dat we always fall fo' it, ev'ry God Damned time, ev'ry fuckin' one! If you know, cin you tell me why we always fallin' fo' dat shit? If you know, please tell me, 'cuz I'm fuckin' tired of always feelin' so damn stupid when y'aw gone!"

6
The Furies Condemn Alex to Death

While Alex was standing around outside of the church, waiting for the coaches to arrive, two of the three men for whom he had paid came up to him and thanked Alex for allowing them to make the trip. But when Alex thanked them, they became confused. Then, he explained that he was only allowed to go on the trip because he paid for them, considering that he was new to the church. The two elderly gentlemen looked at each other, and the younger one laughed.

"Do you mean t' say we done he'ped you out by takin' yo' money?"

Alex smiled and nodded in agreement. As they moved away from Alex, he could hear what the older of the two gentlemen said.

"It look like that boy really need t' gi' t' Chi-town bad!"

Alex also noticed that Rev. Montague kept looking at him disapprovingly. At one point, Alex believed that Rev. Montague was going to change his mind and not allow Alex on the coach, but that never transpired.

Having the habit to go to the restroom before embarking on a long trip, Alex quickly made his way to the restroom in the basement of the church. But before he reached the door, his phone rang.

"Al, is that you?" the caller asked.

"Hey T-Man, yeah, it's me," Alex replied. "Why are we whispering?" Alex asked.

"My wife is still sleeping. We hit it pretty hard and long last night." Alex's lawyer replied.

"You got married and didn't invite me!" Alex exclaimed disappointedly.

"Sorry 'bout dat Al Man, but we didn't invite anyone," the lawyer replied. "We eloped. I always wanted t' do that shit! A little Vietnamese brother who was tryin' t' impersonate somebody white married us."

"Are you both happy?" Alex asked.

"Hell yeah!" the lawyer exclaimed. "You know, Al, you can find happiness and pure pleasure in the strangest places."

"Why do you say that?" Alex asked.

"Remember when we got Lightnin' Girl's cousin back?" the lawyer asked.

"How could I forget that!" Alex replied.

"Remember the case manager we had to deal with?" the lawyer asked. "You know, the Irish one?"

"Oh, FUCK!" Alex exclaimed. "No, T-Man! Don't tell me that you married that ... you did, didn't you?"

"You know it, baby!" the lawyer exclaimed proudly.

"T-Man, I never thought that I'd ever have to ask you this, but are you on crack, or L.S.D., or some other shit like that?" Alex asked.

"Naw, man, jus' love, L-O-V-E.," the lawyer replies. "Let me break it down t' you what happened. Man, that shit was jus' like Romeo and Juliet! Remember how I was makin' fun of her accent?"

"Of, course," Alex answered.

"Well, that shit pissed her the fuck off big time, an' she's one of these women who don' let shit go. So, she had to get me back before I left, because, otherwise, she would have never seen me again..."

"Why did you do that?" Alex asked.

"Al, have you ever read James Joyce's *Ulysses*?" The lawyer enquired.

"Funny that you mention that book," Alex replied, I finished reading it recently."

"Well, you know redheaded women are talked about and described so much as if they were actually painted all across the books pages," the lawyer enquired.

"That wasn't quite my experience while reading *Ulysses*," Alex replied.

"You see, Al," the lawyer continued, "during my junior year of college, I still had to get a few electives out of the way. So, for English, I was planning on doin' one on African-American writers, you know, like Zora Neal, Richard Wright, and James Baldwin. And if they were all full, I figured that I could get into a class on black writers from the Caribbean Islands. But every god-damned thing was full. Then, this short, phat, as in P-H-A-T, white woman with long, shiny-black hair walked up to me and asked me if I was looking for an English class. I told her I was, and then she told me that her name was Shannon Fitzpatrick and that she was a visiting professor from Cork in Ireland. As she was talking, she guided me over to her own personal booth and signed me up for her Irish lit. class. In that class, we read Joyce's "Portrait of an Artist," "Ulysses," of course, Synge's "Playboy of the Western World," which was some seriously whacked-out shit, Beckett's "Waiting for Godot," and Yeats's poems, especially the ones that were inspired by his muse, Maud Gonne, yes, you guessed it, a redhead. And Maud was so deliciously freaky—she has to take the cake for freakiness—that she hooked-up with her ex-husband at their deceased child's burial site, on the child's birthday, mind you, to make a new baby that would have their deceased child's soul and spirit."

"Did they do it right there, at the grave site?" Alex had to ask.

"I kid you not!" the lawyer exclaimed. "Who knew that old-school white folks could show an' glow their freak with the best of us black folks?"

"You gotta a point there, T-Man," Alex said. "I don't know of anything that can top that!"

"Al, man, by the time that class was over, I jus' knew I had to get me a redheaded woman, but I never met any…"

"Not until that day we showed up at the DSS building in Rapid City," Alex interjected.

"What the fuck, man, this is my story!" the lawyer exclaimed rather vexed.

"My bad, T-Man," Alex stated with some contrition, Go ahead, man."

"After I left you and Lightening Girl, I went to put out the fire, and that's when she slipped into the men's facilities and locked the door behind her, calling me a 'patetic little shite.' Al, she did mean to call me a 'turd. She told me, but it's all good and proper."

"But I don't understand how her calling you a piece of shit can end up in you guys getting married and living happily ever after," Alex interjected.

"When she said all that," the lawyer stated, "I turned around to make sure she wasn't about to shenk me in the back, and in so doing, I inadvertently exposed myself to her."

"Ah, T-man," Alex interrupted, yet again, "getting shanked means being stabbed in the stomach, not in the back."

Ignoring Alex, the lawyer continued.

"'Tanks for showing me dat,' she said. 'Now when I tell de autorities about how you forced me in here, locked de door behind us, and treatened dat you'd kill me if I didn't perform fellatio on you, dey will most definitely believe me. And I will be having de last laugh, everyday of my life while your patetic, sorry arse languishes away in prison, because you, a big black man raped a white woman, me.'"

"Al, man, she had me. God damned, she had me!" the lawyer repeated. "She knew it. I knew it, and she knew that I knew she knew it. She had me by the balls like I had never been had by the balls before in my life. And you know what, Al? I loved the fuck out o' dat shit!"

Alex had always known that his lawyer was somewhat of a loose "and freaky' canon. However, Alex was finally captivated by the story, that he remained quiet and keen for the lawyer to continue with the story of his exploits.

"I saw it as a challenge, and I had every intention of getting out of it, and in her life, permanently. So, I started by telling her about that Irish lit. class I took and that I fell in love with redheaded Irish women."

"'Bullocks!'" she shouted. "'You are telling me dat you're foolish enough to believe in dose stupid stereotypes—dat we're armory bitches, yakking gossips, and easy.'"

"I told her that I prefer to focus on what that Mulligan dude in Ulysses said about them, that redheads like to hit it like there's no tomorrow," the lawyer stated.

On hearing this, an expression of confusion initially erupted over her visage. Afterward, however, a smile began to take shape over her countenance.

"But you do think that I'm easy," she stated.

"Since, that Irish lit. class, you have been the only redheaded woman with whom I came into contact, and I guess I didn't want the encounter to just come and go uneventfully," the lawyer confessed.

"I don't know," she stated. "Your words bit deeply into my soul, as if you wanted your words to erase me, to make me disappear, as if you were trying to take away my dignity."

"I am terribly sorry," the lawyer confessed, yet again. "I admit that what I actually said was cruel, but I had to engage you in some kind of meaningful and intense way, so something would stick."

"As I said before, I don't know," she reiterated.

"Then, let me take you out to dinner, so I can wine and dine you," the lawyer replied.

"What if I am married?" she enquired.

"It's too late for me to care about that, now" the lawyer confessed. "We have started a relationship, and I need to get to know you very intimately, even if that doesn't include sex. But don't get me wrong, I'd really prefer if there was some sex, and lots and lots of it, you know, like walt-to-wall. But, hey, I would accept the platonic, celibacy thing, if I have to. But will I?""

"T-Man, you still sound happy and excited about being married, congratulations," Alex stated whole heartily.

"Oh, yeah! Shit! The lawyer exclaimed. "I almost forgot the reason why I wanted to call you."

"What up?" Alex enquired.

"It looks like your boy, you know, that piece o' shit Reynolds at the DSS in Rapid, has some major-league protection in his pocket," the lawyer stated.

"What are you saying?" Alex enquired.

"What I'm sayin' is that the restraining order that we requested won't stick," the lawyer elucidated further.

"Shit!" Alex exclaimed.

"You bette' let Lightening Girl know and keep her surrounded 24/7," the Lawyer added. "It looks like the K.K.K. and Jim Crow are still very much alive and well in America."

"Thanks," Alex stated, "thanks for keeping me in the know."

"You got it, man," the lawyer concluded.

Forty minutes after the designated time, the coaches showed up, three of them, with one already three-quarters full. As Alex boarded a coach, he not only found out that members of two other churches had been picked up, but that they would also make one more pick-up before they got on their way to Chicago.

There was a toilet on the coach, and the elderly gentleman who sat next to Alex insisted on sitting in the aisle seat because he had "a weak bladder." Alex didn't like the idea of being closed in by a big man whose old, black suit reeked of mothballs. However, he acquiesced because he didn't want to give Rev. Montague a reason to kick him off of the coach. Fortunately enough for Alex, though, his neighbor had members of his church sitting all around him, so he had no need to converse with Alex. It was not as if Alex had become a-social, but he was anxious and becoming more so as the coach ploughed its way nearer and nearer to Chicago. At first, he was anxious about what would transpire. Then, when he became tired of being anxious about 'nothing', he attempted to direct his thoughts toward other things, such as Roya and the kiddos, Thunder and Esther, Pieter, Jerry's upcoming presentation, etc. However, no matter how hard he tried, the anxiety kept popping up.

There was quite a bit of talk and laughter throughout the bus, in the front, in the middle, and in the back of the bus. To Alex, most of the conversations that he was in earshot of revolved around establishing connections. Although two of the sisters found out that their mothers had married and divorced the same man, the others were not looking for anything that was nearly as formal. Simply having a mutual acquaintance, or even an acquaintance of an acquaintance, would suffice. By the time the coach had reached the Illinois state line, the only one who had not established the remotest of connections was Alex, although he did have a strong feeling that a few of them, especially some of the older sisters, must have known his mother and even probably pinched his cheeks.

However, all the while, the anxiety had swelled inside him. For, on the one hand, he contemplated the possibility, the strong possibility, that it was all a hoax, the chest, the spirit, the medium, the lot. And, on the other hand, what if it is real, even, perhaps, too real? What if what he finds out is too unbearable, the reason why he probably forgot it in the first place? That was the fear that held him the deepest as well as the longest.

Because the trip was an "express," the brothers and sisters had brought their own food and drinks on board, and it was good. Although Rev. Montague had failed to inform Alex that he had to bring his own sustenance, the brothers and sisters shared what they had very generously. A couple brothers had even brought liquor, it was rumored. However, that was not offered to Alex.

After the meal, some sisters in the front started humming and singing, and in a matter of minutes, the holy spirit made its way through out the entire coach, even Alex couldn't help but sing along, despite the fact that he didn't know most of the lyrics.

As the lion's share of the brothers and sisters were late-middle and elderly, almost everyone was asleep at around 9:00 pm. However, as the coach drew nearer and nearer to Chicago, Alex's anxiety increased. So, sleeping became impossible. On top of that, Alex's seat partner tended to break-wind quite a bit in his sleep, and when he did so, he turned his rear end toward Alex. 'So far away from Maine,' Alex thought, 'and I still can't escape Pieter.' Then, he figured that he must have done some pretty horrific things in a previous life to deserve this.

After several hours, at around 1:00 am, sleep did finally catch hold of him. However, it was a miserable sleep, for he was having a nightmare. In this nightmare, he was cattle prodded into an over-crowded courtroom. When he attempted to sit down with the public, he received two red-hot cattle prods in either butt cheek, which propelled him forward, so far forward that he landed next to the dock on his knees, where he was obliged to stand. After a short while, he was first joined by Stephen Daedalus, and finally, Orestes was ushered in. However, Alex noticed that they were treated much more humanely than he had been. It was obviously influenced by *The Oresteia*, and *Ulysses*, both of which he had recently read.

Although Alex had no idea as to why he was there or of what he was being accused, Stephen and Orestes were both quite absorbed in their thoughts, perhaps wondering what the outcome of their trials would be. After what seemed like a long time after Orestes stepped-up to the dock, the three Furies entered the courtroom. All three defendants knew of their arrival because an immediate, breathless, ominous silence swept through and stifled the bustling noises in the courtroom, which caused the three defendants to lift their heads to see what was transpiring around them. Initially, they could not see who it was. However, the gasps of the spectators were quite palpable. Yet, it still took some time before any of the trio could see who was coming, which obliged Alex to pose the enquiry to himself, 'Who could possibly walk this fucking slowly?'

It was Daedalus' who saw them first.

"Oh! Bugger! Bugger! Bugger!" he exclaimed. "It's the three hell bitches."

Alex, still unable to see them enquired, "Who is it?"

"They are the Three Furies," Orestes stated to Alex.

"Oh! We are so mother fucked!" Alex exclaimed.

And the three men gazed upon each other in despair. However, as the Three Furies passed the dock, they suddenly stopped, contorted their wrinkled, old, withered bodies around to look at the three defendants, taking a particular interest in Alex. When they had unraveled themselves and moved on, Orestes enquired as to what both Alex and Daedalus were being charged with. However, before they could respond, the trial had begun.

In their cracked, squealing, piercing voices, the Three Furies began with a synopsis of their cases against the three defendants. They began with Orestes's crime, matricide, killing his own mother. Daedalus' crime, refusing to pray for his mother's soul while she was on her deathbed, which, to the Three Furies, was synonymous to wishing her to go to hell. However, when they got to Alex's case, their whole tone and demeanor had altered quite considerably, so much so that Alex was left with the strong impression that the their terrifyingly spooky, macabre appearance and behavior was merely a front, a façade. Based on their pronouncement, as well as on how they were not making that pronouncement, Alex could only surmise that they were far more terrified of him than he could ever be of them. When the Three Furies finally got to mentioning what Alex was being charged with, they broke off, abruptly, before they could utter the words, for it appeared as though one of them had fainted, which made the entire courtroom gasp, incredulously.

"What did he do? What did he do?" several voices shouted in the courtroom.

When Alex gazed around, he could not bear the sight of dread in the faces of everyone who attempted looking upon him. Even his dock-mates became visibly wary of Alex.

"What did you do that you terrify pure terror itself?" Daedalus' enquired."

Alex replied by stating that he did not know.

"That's bullshit if ever I heard it!" Orestes exclaimed angrily.

When the one Fury recovered, somewhat, the three of them wobbled slowly to their seats. And they all seemed rather fatigued and downtrodden.

Before Alex could see who would be defending the three of them, he was awoken by a head butt from his farting neighbor. Both men apologized to the other while they were both rubbing their heads, and since his neighbor was awake, Alex took this opportunity to go to the

WC at the rear of the coach. On returning to his seat, approximately ten minutes later, Alex had to wake his neighbor to get to his seat. Not even considering the possibility that his nightmare would resume, Alex sought the rough sleep that his seat had to offer, and he found it quickly.

The nightmare resumed, and there was Athena. At first, Alex could not make out the words she was uttering. However, after a few seconds, he could hear what She was saying. And to his shock and dismay, Alex realized that Athena was only defending Stephen and Orestes. In his sleep, he figured that Athena and the Furies must have made a deal when he was briefly awake. The Three Furies were more than willing to let Stephen and Orestes walk as long as they could have Alex, he thought.

When the trial had adjourned, Stephen and Orestes were crying in each other's arms, for they were acquitted. When they left the dock as free men, they never once looked back at Alex to wish him well.

While still in the dock, alone, Alex was able to see Athena and the Three Furies hugging, kissing, and congratulating each other. Yet, Alex felt no bitterness or animosity toward them. What he continuously thought to himself was, '*Mea culpa, mea maxima culpa*, but for what?'

Before Athena left the courtroom, she went to the dock to take one final look at Alex. shortly before she departed, she grimaced at him and said, "Good riddance, you piece of abominable shit." As she moved away, Alex realized that he was not ever likely to get another opportunity to find out what his crime was if he didn't enquire Athena now.

"Your worshipfulness! Your worshipfulness, Athena", Alex shouted.

She had to have heard him. However, she continued toward the exit.

"Your worshipfulness, Athena, please!" Alex screamed.

"What?" Athena screamed back as She turned toward Alex, thoroughly perturbed. "How dare this abomination address me!"

"Your worshipfulness," Alex started, "I understand why you didn't speak on my behalf like you did for Orestes and Stephen."

"Do you now?" Athena enquired cynically. "To be honest with you, Alex, I find that highly debatable, for if you had, you would have fallen on your own sword by now."

Alex considered his words carefully, for he did not want to upset her more than he had already done.

"Your worshipfulness, I accept that I am guilty," Alex responded carefully. "Indeed, I had already accepted that a long time ago. My problem is that I don't know what I am guilty of. I don't know what I have been charged with."

Looking at Alex incredulously, shaking her head, her entire body almost rebelling, cringing, in disbelief, she turned her back toward him, took a few steps, then quickly turned toward him, pointing her right index finger at him.

"Your charge. Your charge?" she repeated, the second time as an enquiry, a rhetorical enquiry. "Orestes deserved a defense because he was only obeying the law, the custom, and the mores of Sparta as they pertain to the unlawful murder of a father and king. Daedalus deserved a defense because although he declined to bless his mother on her death bed, it was because he was not ready to lose her, hoping that by foregoing he blessing, she would live a bit longer, which, unfortunately was not the case. But you, Alex, you are truly undeserving, for you are, as you correctly surmised, the guiltiest of all. And as such, your crime, your sin, is unpardonable, for you, Alex, have damned us all, mortals and gods alike."

"But what did I do? Tell me, please!" Alex entreated.

Several guards rushed to the dock, but with a slight gesture, waving her hand, they stood down and returned to their posts.

"I will tell you, Alex, and then, I will leave you my sword. You volunteered for the task of reconciling the masculine and the feminine principles, to bring them once again in balance. We told you, we all told you just how insuperable this task would be for you. But nooooo, you refused to listen. 'I got this,' you said. 'It'll be a cinch,' you said. 'It'll be a piece of cake,' you said."

The Goddess Returns

After turning her gaze away from Alex, Athena began to slowly walk in what became a circle. And when she came around, she turned again toward Alex, with both of her palms open as if surrendering herself. In the slightest susurration, Athena spoke.

"Alex, you failed, utterly, and now, we are all damned."

After a few moments, with her head down cast, she moved a few steps away from him, stopped, turned back slightly toward Alex, and raised her chin as if she wanted to speak. However, she didn't and walked off, but not before her scabbard with sword still inside fell to the ground. Alex picked it up with every intention of going after Athena and returning them to her. Despite that, he unsheathed her sword, placed the tip at his navel, and behind him, he heard the Three Furies murmur, "Dooooo iiittt!" Then he woke up.

3
The Goddess Returns

7

The Minister Confesses

Alex woke up from his nightmare to his bus vigorously maneuvering its way through the streets of South-side Chicago. It was still dark, almost dawn, and Alex remembered hearing a deacon saying that because there were so many brothers and sisters on this trip, one of the buses would go directly to the angel and the prophet. Alex wondered if that was his bus, but when it stopped, he saw that the bus had parked right in front of the hotel.

Getting the luggage out of the bus and into the hotel took ages. One reason was because the bellboy was recently fired. He was caught taking pictures of hotel guests while they were having sex. He would upload the footage on a porn website, and he was well paid for it. The only reason he got caught was because one of their guest's mother-in-law, who was a widow, had a new boyfriend who supposedly needed to see porn in order to get in to the mood. That's how the mother-in-law got to see her son-in-law pound away on a woman who was definitely not her daughter.

Another reason why the unloading went so slowly was because almost all of the brothers and sisters were old and suffering from two or more ailments, which meant that the younger brothers, of which there were only four, had to do the lion's share of the unloading. And yes, that included Alex.

It was arranged in advance that each guest would be issued a number when they checked in at the hotel, and they were all told to "guard that number with your life," for they would not be able to have an audience with the angel and prophet without it. But because Alex, as well as the other three men, was busy moving the luggage from the bus to the hotel lobby, and then to the rooms, he was the very last one to register, and he would be dead last to have an audience with the angel and the prophet, at least from his hotel. As a consolation, he was told that things change rapidly, but Alex accepted that he wouldn't have an audience

until late Sunday afternoon, somewhere around 4:00 pm. Unfortunately, Alex failed to consider the fact that he would also have to help with bringing all the luggage from the rooms and loading it back onto the bus.

After bringing all the luggage to their designated rooms and checking in, Alex went to his room, which was on the 7th floor, 717. As he exited the elevator with his one, brown bag, he figured with the way his luck was going, Alex assured himself that his farting neighbor on the bus would end up being his farting roommate. But when Alex entered the room, there was only a slight hint of mildew in the air, no gassiness, none. There was no one else in his room. Rev. Montague, later that Saturday, told Alex that one brother had canceled at the last minute, so he put the gentleman who would be Alex's roommate in the room where the brother who canceled would have been.

Alex went to bed almost immediately, which was about 8:25 am, and he didn't awake until 3:30 pm to go to the bathroom. He went back to bed, but he couldn't sleep, so after about twenty minutes, he got up, took a shower, got dressed, and went down to the lobby to find out if there were any changes in the "pecking order." There were none. Although he wasn't hungry, Alex thought it would be better if he got a bite to eat to keep his strength up. Because, if this thing with the 'angel and prophet' were real, he would more than likely need it. So, after having been directed to an all-day breakfast diner a couple blocks away, he left the hotel to get a very belated brunch. As Alex was walking through the cool Chicago afternoon, he remembered the feeling of when he lived in Chicago. Then, while paying attention to his surroundings, he realized that during those two years when he had lived there, not once had he ventured into the southside of Chicago. Of course, he went to the aquarium several times, and he took in the free, open-air classical music concerts, but he spent much of his spare time in Joliet because his Uncle Charlie move there to be with his college sweetheart, Anne Marie Sullivan. Alex stayed with Uncle Charlie when he lived in Bristol, England.

In the late 60s and early 70s, some ivy league universities opened their doors to black people, even if they weren't ready for the rigor. Uncle Charlie, after returning from the Vietnam War, was admitted to Cornell University. While other black people were more concerned about acquiring concessions, power, from the university, Uncle Charlie wanted an education, but he started to flounder very quickly. In desperation, he approached Anne-Marie, who was a petite, shy, red-headed, Catholic woman, for help. She taught and showed Uncle Charlie how to plan, how to study, and how to be disciplined with his time. As Uncle Charlie's grades improved, he and Anne- Marie became more attached to each other. And although they spent a lot of time together and kissed and hugged, they had not yet had sexual intercourse.

When the final exams rolled around, they often spent all night together studying, mostly at Uncle Charlie's studio apartment. When the grades were posted, Anne-Marie was the one who first knew that Uncle Charlie had passed all of his courses. He even had an '-A' for his history class. To celebrate, they went to the Jukebox, which was a dance club where black and white people could mingle. And truly, that night was about dancing and exerting all the energy that they had pinned up since they had met. But by two in the morning, they both came to the conclusion that all dancing from now till kingdom come wouldn't quench the fire that they felt for each other. So, they went to Uncle Charlie's apartment and made love.

To make a long story short, Anne-Marie was with child that first night. After missing her second cycle, she told Uncle Charlie, While they were discussing what they would do, Uncle Charlie remembered the last thing Uncle Buggs had told him and his brothers just before Uncle Buggs blew his brains out, "Never love a white woman, because they will never let you keep her." But that was in the 40s, Uncle Charlie told himself. And he was seeing plenty of mixed couples everywhere, in college, in the park, at clubs. And he was convinced that between the Women's Movement, the Anti-war Movement, and the Civil-Rights Movement, there was nothing else for America to do but accept them, together, and their biracial baby because "America's bound to become a more open and accepting society." And with that new-found optimism, he convinced himself and Anne-Marie that they should get married and have their baby.

It turned out that Uncle Charlie was a little bit before his time. He suggested to Anne-Marie that he would put his education on hold, so that she could finish hers first. His reasoning for that was simple. Anne-Marie was a straight 'A' student who was hellbent on becoming a lawyer. Figuring that she would make the most money, she should finish first, he thought. Anne-Marie did think that was considerate of Uncle Charlie, but she didn't see him being a happy, stay-at-home dad. But he insisted on it.

As Anne-Marie was allowed, and even encouraged by her mother, to bring Uncle Charlie to Sunday dinners, she thought her parents would not necessarily like hearing that their oldest daughter was going to marry a black man, but she was confident that they would eventually get used to the idea. Needless to say, she was wrong, dead wrong.

During one of those Sunday dinners, the last one, after her father announced that he was opening his third furniture store, Anne-Marie decided right then and there to share some good news as well.

"Mom and Dad, Charlie and I are getting married," Anne-Marie said.

Anne-Marie's mother and two younger sisters rose from the table to kiss and hug Anne-Marie and Uncle Charlie. Her father stayed seated, though, and continued eating.

"Dear," Anne-Marie's mother started, "aren't you going to congratulate your daughter for this wonderful news?"

Putting his knife and fork neatly beside his plate, Anne-Marie's father wiped his lips with his serviette, looked at Anne-Marie, and asked, "Why?"

"What do you mean?" Anne-Marie asked.

"Why get married now?" her father asked. "You are supposed to be this bigshot lawyer who's gonna clean-up New York City, 'all of it, remember?"

"Daddy…," Anne-Marie started, but her father interrupted her.

"No, now's a bad time," Anne-Marie's father continued. "No! You both should finish your studies first. And you still have to go to law school, Anne-Marie."

Still not letting Anne-Marie, or anyone else speak, her father went on.

"If you get married now, you will have a very hard time of it. Being Catholic in this country is already hard enough. But being Black and Catholic together will be impossible. No, not now! If you want, do it after you become a lawyer, but not now," Anne-Marie's father concluded once and for all and recommended that everyone return to their meal.

"Daddy, look at me! I'm pregnant!" Anne-Marie shouted.

Slamming his knife and fork against his plate, chipping it, "I don't give a damn! Pregnant or no pregnant, you are going to be a lawyer!" her father exclaimed. Then, he rose up and left the table.

Anne- Marie's mother excused her husband and herself, following him to bring him back to the table. But after a few minutes, it was clear that they would not be returning to the dinner table any time soon. So, Uncle Charlie gestured to Anne-Marie to leave. While they were putting on their coats, they could distinctly hear Anne-Marie's father shouting.

"No daughter of mine is going to marry a nigger! You can count on that!"

At first, Alex wondered why he was thinking so intently about his uncle and aunt, but the story demanded to play itself out in his mind.

Uncle Charlie and Anne-Marie somehow managed to stay together until shortly after the birth of their daughter, Indigo, who was immediately put up for adoption.

During the last trimester of her pregnancy, my grandparents paid Charlie a visit. They stayed in New York for a week, which is when they met Anne-Marie. My grandmother, Mildred, and Anne-Marie took to each other right off the bat. Besides shopping for baby clothes and more comfortable clothes for Anne-Marie, they did a lot of talking, most of which revolved around life after the baby. As my grandmother was a firm believer in 'having your cake and eating it', she spent most of their time together convincing Anne-Marie that her baby and Charlie were worth fighting for. And by the end of the week, Anne-Marie was sold.

"You're right! There is absolutely no reason why I couldn't be a great mother, wife, and lawyer!" Anne-Marie declared.

However, the conversations between Uncle Charlie and my grandfather were altogether different. First of all, my grandfather ridiculed Uncle Charlie for desiring an education, "A white education" because, from my grandfather's perspective, there was only power, and everything else was being used as an obstacle to prevent those without it from ever getting it. In other words, they were distractions to power. When Uncle Charlie argued that all you need were a good education and money to have a good life in America, my grandfather laughed at him.

"Damn! You still don' git it, little bro!" my grandfather exclaimed. "If I read you right, you sayin' that as long as you got a education an' some money, you in, Right? But what if the economy crashes? What then? Then, your money ain't wort' shit. A' what if your education becomes obsolete because there's some new, more advanced knowledge? What then? Your money's gone, an' yo' education's gone, so you back in the shit, believe it or not, where you've always been, even with your piece o' paper and your chump change."

"If power isn't having an education or money, what is it?" Uncle Charlie asked.

"Having power means that you will always be accepted an' respected, no matter what kind o' threads you wearin', or ride you sportin', or the amount o' big, fancy words you have in yo' rap, or the amount o' money you can pu' down. Everything else is bullshit."

The second argument that my grandfather presented to Uncle Charlie was in the form of a question. Charlie had told his mother, my great-grandmother, what he had overheard Anne-

Marie's father say, "My daughter is not going to marry a nigger!" And she, in turn, told my grandfather, which is why he asked Uncle Charlie why would he marry a woman whose father will detest his biracial grandchildren.

As for the third and final argument, my grandfather hardly needed to say a word because for Uncle Charlie, during the months before his daughter, Indigo, my second cousin, was born, hardly did a day go by when he did not think of Uncle Buggs—my grandfather telling him and Walter not to follow him inside, the gunshot, the one dollar bill that Uncle Buggs sent all three boys to the store with, and those almost prophetic words, "Boys, don't love a white woman because they will never let you have her."

Ironically, the education that Uncle Charlie was enjoying was also battering his resolve to fight for Anne-Marie and their child. There were two courses in particular that stayed with him. He had taken one of them with Anne-Marie. The first course was on Shakespeare's four great tragedies-- "King Lear," "Hamlet," "McBeth," and "Othello." The other was a course on James Baldwin's oeuvre. This was the course they took together.

In Uncle Charlie's mind, while reading *Othello* and Baldwin's *Another Country*, he had found too many similarities between himself, Othello, and Rufus. In the comparison with Othello, both fathers disapproved of the marriage, an interracial couple, the man was constantly under scrutiny, always having to prove himself, to name a few. Initially, both in Othello's case and in his own, Uncle Charlie could justify blaming those on the outside for attacking and, potentially, destroying their relationships. But the more he thought about it, he had to accept that there was something fundamentally, perhaps even inherently, flawed about Othello as well as himself. Although he could not yet see it in himself, he could easily see the fatal flaws of Othello. For Iago to have been able to so thoroughly play Othello, there must have been something there, lurking in the depths of Othello's unconscious. After reflecting on this for a while, Uncle Charlie came to the conclusion that Othello was incapable of actually, deeply believing that such a wonderfully beautiful, upper-class, young, white woman could really ever truly love the likes of him.

With regards to Baldwin's *Another Country*, the main thing that troubled Uncle Charlie was the fact that Vivaldo, a white friend of Rufus, and Rufus's little sister, Ida, on the one hand, were permitted to develop their relationship, albeit with difficulty. But Rufus and Leona, Rufus's Southern, white girlfriend, on the other hand, were not. And Rufus, due to the internal and external tensions, became physically abusive, which eventually landed Leona in a mental institution.

"Why," Uncle Charlie asked Alex once when they were in Bristol, "despite all those infidelities, did Vivaldo and Ida's relationship seem to have some promise, at the end, where Rufus and Leona's relationship ended tragically?"

After breakfast, Alex thought about walking around to check out the notorious South-side of Chicago, but he decided that it was better to just stay at the hotel, in the event that something changed. When he arrived at the hotel, people were boarding one of the buses. When Alex got closer, he recognized some of the people in line from his church, so he instinctively ran to the bus and asked if his name was called. The deacon on duty politely asked Alex if he received a number, which he did. Then, the deacon asked Alex what his number was. After telling the deacon that his number was "349," the deacon chuckled a bit and suggested that Alex try to get "comfatable" because he would at least have to wait until "noon, tomorrah."

Besides responding to email from me and the 'kiddos,' Alex had to admit to himself that he felt somewhat alarmed about Pieter. For Alex had written to Pieter about his dream about Athena, the Three Furies, Stephen and Orestes, and Pieter had still not replied. It had been five weeks since Alex had last heard from Pieter. After finishing-up his correspondence, Alex read and listened to world news in his room. At about 6:40 pm, he walked back to the same diner, where he had breakfast, to have his dinner. While he was eating his fried chicken, rice and black beans, and cold slaw, he remembered that he would definitely have to reward his hack driver and the pianist for getting him on that bus.

That night, Alex went to bed early, partly because of the rough sleep on the bus the previous night. And partly because he had become bored, which was a strange experience for Alex, because he could always find something interesting or worthwhile to do. But there, at that hotel, he felt inhibited. He was afraid that if he did something like visit Uncle Charlie and his family in Joliet, he would miss his moment with the spirit and the medium. But after only a couple of hours sleep, Alex woke-up abruptly, again because of a nightmare, the self-same nightmare as the previous night on the bus, but this time, as the furies read-off the wide-ranging sentences of his crime, for the entirety of existence, Alex became more and more defiant, until he became in his outward appearance as hideous as he was on the inside. And this time, not only the Three Furies, but also Stephen and Orestes, even Athena herself were terrified of what Alex had become, or, perhaps, what he always had been.

At 7:25 a.m., while Alex was preparing to take a shower, there was a knock on the door. Without the morning pleasantries, the deacon who told Alex that he would have a long wait to see the spirit asked to see Alex's ticket. When Alex walked back to the door with his ticket in hand, the deacon practically snatched it out of Alex's hand. After confirming the number with a number that he pulled from his shirt pocket, the deacon looked at Alex and told him to hurry up and get dressed. "Why?" Alex asked.

"Brother, we don't have time fo' this nonsense!" the deacon erupted. "The angel and the prophet want to see you, now. An' you s ho' don'' wan' them to wait!"

"But you told me that I would have to wait until this afternoon, and I was going to take a shower," Alex said.

"Give me the strength, Lawd. Please give me the strength," the deacon almost whispered while looking at his watch. "Brother, you got one minute, then I'm gone. Whatever you decide to do in that minute is yo' business, and it starts now."

When Alex returned to the door, more or less dressed, the deacon was gone. Instantly closing the door and running toward the elevator, Alex wondered if he had locked the lock. On reaching the elevator, Alex started to panic in earnest because the deacon was nowhere to be seen, and his audience with the spirit and the medium felt like it was slipping away. Hoping to catch the deacon in the lobby, he pushed the button to descend, the elevator door opened instantly, and the deacon stood there smiling.

"I'm sorry, brother, but I couldn' resis.'"

In the lobby, Alex was met by a taxi driver who knew where to take Alex. After about ten minutes of weaving and bobbing through

Chicago's west-side streets, the taxi stopped, and the cab driver pointed to the building where Alex had to go. When Alex opened the door and started stepping out of the car, the cab driver yelled at him, "Yo, bro, where my money?" Alex started reaching for his bill fold but hesitated because he had no idea where he was. He didn't even know the name of his hotel, nor did he know what street it was on. So, he decided to convince the cab driver to wait for him. Alex asked him if he could wait for an hour, to play it safe. To guarantee that Alex wouldn't stiff him, the cab driver insisted that Alex give him the key to his room, and Alex would have to pay him $50.00, which Alex agreed to.

When Alex entered the building, a young woman who was seated on a metal folding chair looked up from her cell phone, smiled, and asked if he was 349. Alex said yes, and she rose up from her seat and told him to follow her. He followed her into a basement, where about forty people were patiently seated. As he walked past them, he was surprised that none of them seemed offended that he was jumping in front of the line. When the young woman reached a bright maroon colored curtain, she pulled it aside, opened the door behind it, and shouted, "here's 349." Then, she left.

When Alex entered the room, the solitary person in the room had her back toward him. But when he entered the room, that person turned around, smiled, and said, "Please, close the door, Alex."

"I didn't know that our numbers were associated with our names," Alex said, somewhat surprised.

"My name is Sheila, and they're not," she said.

"Then, how do you know my name?" Alex asked.

"You are Alexander Herbertus Madden, and Phoebe, the angel, has been expecting you for some time now," Sheila said.

Sheila's facial features were clearly those of a man, a black man. But her dress, gestures, breasts, fingernails, voice, and hair were all quite effeminate. And once she became animated while conversing with Alex, Alex couldn't help but notice how Sheila would toss her head with her hair flying all over the place. It seemed as though Sheila had to clear her face of hair every other second. Alex also noticed that Sheila looked every now and then at an old, wooden box with an old, rusted clasp and two old, rusted hinges. After the small talk had been exhausted, Sheila jumped right into it.

"How can we help you? Phoebe is asking" Sheila said.

"If she's been expecting me, she must know why I'm here," Alex said.

"Of course, we do!" Sheila exclaimed. "But we'd still rather hear you say it,"

This vaguely reminded Alex of something he had heard before, but he couldn't quite place it.

"When I was a child..." Alex started, but he was interrupted by Sheila's laughter. He observed how she kept looking at that old, wooden box as if they were sharing some kind of telepathic joke at Alex's expense.

"I'm so sorry, Alex," Sheila said. "Go ahead now. Please continue."

Wary of the fact that Sheila could, and probably would, laugh more, Alex decided to make it quick.

"Something I forgot happened in the church before it burned down, and I need to remember what it was," Alex blurted out.

"Of course," Sheila started laughing again while looking at the old, wooden box.

"I am truly sorry, Alex," Sheila said. "I really don't know what's come over me."

"I really need to remember what happened," Alex repeated.

Switching from laughter to a chilling seriousness almost instantly, Sheila looked sternly into Alex's eyes, pointed at him, and began to speak.

"You probably forgot it because it was too unbearable to remember," Sheila said without any hint of laughter. "Are you certain that you want to remember what happened that Sunday morning all those years ago?"

"Yes!" Alex said definitively. "It seems as though everything that I am about to lose, my wife, my kids, my sanity, are all tied up with that one event. It is oblivious to me, at least."

While looking at the wooden box, Sheila took a few steps toward Alex, and then started walking counter clockwise in a circle around him, always glancing pensively, now at the box, and now at Alex. After having made five circles around Alex, Sheila returned to where she had stood formerly, stopped, and started to speak again.

"There is something very curious about you Alexander Herbertus Madden." Phoebe said, speaking through Sheila. "You are a seer, much like my Sheila, but you deny yourself the gift of sight. Huh, and I now know why. You are an utter abomination."

"Yes," Alex replied, "that's what I am, an abomination. I am poison for everything I touch, for everything I love."

"Yes, I see," Phoebe concurred, "but someone is protecting you, someone extremely powerful, your very own personal daimon, perhaps."

Then, this time, Phoebe took a few steps toward Alex and walked around him, this time clockwise five times. Then, she moved back to where she had formerly stood, and she was Sheila again.

"It has been done," Sheila said.

"What has been done?" Alex asked.

"Within 24 hours," Sheila added, "before you reach Charleston, what you seek to remember will be made known to you."

"Thank you," Alex said somewhat relieved. "How much do I owe you?"

Again, Sheila returned to her laughter.

"We don't ever charge children," she replied

Scoffing at her remark, "I'm 43-years-old!" Alex exclaimed.

"No, you're not," Sheila said coldly. "You are two, five, seven. Ten, thirteen, sixteen…"

Before she could continue, Alex interrupted her.

"Okay, okay, okay, I get the message!" Alex shouted.

But the reason why he yelled at her was because he had a glimmer of the traumas he experienced at each age, except for when he was seven and thirteen, and he did not like what he had seen and felt.

As it seemed as though there was nothing else to do but leave, Alex thanked both Phoebe and Sheila and said good-bye. But before he got to the door, Sheila asked him a question.

"Alex, what about the other boy?" Sheila asked.

Wanting only to leave that building as soon as possible, Alex had to ask how old he was.

"He turned thirteen five weeks ago," Sheila blurted out cheerfully, almost as if she had been wanting to say that all day.

"I … I don't think I could handle facing both of them at the same time," Alex eventually admitted.

While looking at the old, wooden box, "You won't have to," Sheila replied. "The seven-year-old boy will return to you before you reach Charleston, and Phoebe says that something will happen a few days after you arrive in Charleston that will trigger the thirteen-year-old to return to you."

When Sheila looked at Alex, she noticed that his thoughts were elsewhere, "Alex, what is it? What do you see?"

Alex did not respond.

Looking at the old, wooden box, and then turning toward Alex, "Take it, Alex! Take it! Phoebe says take it!" Sheila exclaimed.

"I did," Alex replied as a huge smile broke all over his face.

"That's right! That's right!" Sheila exclaimed. "Phoebe did say that you could see. But remember, Alex. You have not taken it yet, and until you actually take it and in time, the thirteen-year-old boy won't be able to return to you. But most importantly, Alex, if you do not take it in time, he will be lost to you forever. We hope you understand."

"I do," Alex responded, "and I thank you both again."

As Alex was leaving, Sheila turned toward the old, wooden box, and she was smiling.

When Alex stepped back into the cab, he noticed that he had been gone for about thirty-five minutes. "Where to?" the cab driver asked, but Alex couldn't hear him because he was still with the angel and the prophet in his mind wondering about all sorts of things like if the angel had ever possessed the prophet in front of other clients. And for some inexplicable reason, Alex couldn't help but wonder if his mother had ever spoken to the angel by way of one of the previous prophets. Perhaps that was why the angel was expecting him and wanted him to jump the line. When Alex awoke from his revelry, the cab driver was saying, "That'll be fi'ty dolla's." Still not fully aware of where he was, Alex stepped out of the cab, and stood there absorbed in his thoughts. He probably would have stood there till kingdom come if it weren't for the hand that touched his shoulder.

"Are you alright, brother?" the accompanying voice asked.

Alex turned and saw that it was Rev. Montague.

"Yes, I'm fine," Alex replied.

As Alex looked around to get his bearings, he realized that he was standing in front of his hotel while a bus was loading the last group to pay the angel and the prophet a visit.

"Can I offer you a cup of coffee, brother?" Rev. Montague asked. "You really look like you could use one."

Glancing at Rev. Montague from a slanted view, Alex sensed that he wanted something, but what could it be?

"Sure," Alex said, "there's a half-way decent diner a couple blocks away from here."

As they first started walking, there was a very uncomfortable silence, so Rev. Montague took it upon himself to start the conversation.

"Brother, I don't want to know your business," Rev. Montague started, "but were the angel and the prophet able to take care of you?"

"Yes," Alex responded. "I think so."

"I'm glad to hear it," Rev. Montague said. "Then, I guess we won't be seeing you anymore at church?"

Looking at the minister, trying to gauge his reaction, Alex told him that he would be leaving Charleston in a few days.

"I'm mighty sorry to hear that," the minister said. "I was starting to get used to seeing you sitting on my bench every Sunday after service."

They both smiled at each other.

"Thank you," Alex said, "but I really do have to be moving on."

"Of course, brother, of course," Rev. Montague said with a tone of understanding. "You've probably been curious about why I changed my mind about letting you come on the trip?"

"I briefly thought about it, and then I came to the conclusion that you had to get those three brothers on the bus," Alex replied.

"No, that wasn't it," the minister confessed. The church had the funds to help the brothers out. No, that wasn't it."

With this news, Rev. Montague did pique Alex's interest, and although it seemed as though the minister was going to tell him, perhaps out of some duty, Alex tried to give the minister a way out of telling him.

"Rev. Montague, I am here, and I got what I needed. I don't need anything else," Alex said.

When Rev. Montague started to speak, Alex reiterated that he didn't need to know why the minister changed his mind.

"But Brother Madden, have you thought that maybe I need to tell you?" Rev. Montague asked.

By this time, they had reached the diner, and the minister held the door open for Alex to enter first. When Alex stopped at a table and started to take off his jacket, the minister asked if they could sit at another table that was further away from other patrons. Alex, of course, agreed. After they got settled and ordered their coffees and slices of blueberry pie, the minister started.

"Brother Jones was a deacon in the church long before I arrived," the minister started. "When I was appointed the church's chief minister, he was in his fifth marriage. Except for his first wife, the other three all died. His fifth wife, Sister Mary Lou Jones, was fourteen years younger than her husband. He was 52, and she was 38. He already had three grown children. It was her first marriage. They both seemed happy about the arrangement, so I never worried about them."

Rev. Montague stopped talking when the waitress brought their coffee, pie, and water. When she left, he continued.

"After about, I think it was two years after I arrived," the minister continued, "Brother Jones had an accident at his work. He operated some special kind of forklift, and while he was working a double shift, and he didn't sleep well the night before... To make a long," the minister interrupted his own chain of thought, "gruesome story short, his forklift somehow fell off of the platform. And because there either was no seatbelt or he wasn't wearing it, he ended up getting his right pelvis crushed, which meant internal bleeding. His lower spine was damaged as well. Between several insurances, workman's comp., and eventually early retirement, financially, he and his wife were provided for."

Then, the waitress came by to top off their coffee and asked if everything was all right. When she left, the minister resumed.

"I have to admit, I wondered if Sister Jones would stay with him, and she did. But after about five months, she came to me after service one Sunday and asked if she and I could talk. So, we made an appointment for that Tuesday at 10:00 am."

When the minister paused to add sugar and cream to his coffee, having an idea of where this was all headed, Alex, again, told the minister that he didn't have to tell him. Rev. Montague looked at Alex, smiled half-heartedly and told Alex that he had already practically told him. So, he may as well finish.

"When we met that Tuesday in my office," the minister continued, "Sister Jones couldn't say enough about how loving a provider Brother Jones was, and that she loved his sense of humor. She also told me about how sensual he used to be. He gave her full-body massages on the weekends, and he massaged her feet every night before she went to bed. I still remember her telling me, 'Nothin' was betta' then them foot massages.' At first, it seemed like she just needed to go down memory lane, so I listened. But then, the whole thing abruptly turned. She started telling me how there won't be any more full-body massages, no more foot massages, no more sex. I was trying to tell her that she had to pray to God for the strength to endure, but she wasn't listening and hollered, 'Ever!'

At this point, the minister's eyes began to water, and a few tears began to fall.

"Brother, I was at a loss," Rev. Montague confessed. "And I had a problem with that feeling of helplessness. So, I meant to grab her shoulders and tell her that prayer is the only way out, but I grabbed her... I accidently reached with the intention of sternly commending her to prayer. But Brother Madden," the minister dropped off.

At this point, the minister's floodgates had opened up completely. Alex, no longer thinking about himself, called Rev. Montague, "Brother," telling him that he was "almost there," coaxing the minister to continue.

"I accidentally reached for her breasts, and she grabbed my hand, holding it there, on her breasts, telling me that there was only one thing that I could do to help her."

Alex thought that the minister was finished with his confession, but, no, he had more to say.

"Three years earlier, my wife, from one day to the next, left me, leaving behind a note telling me that she was not happy being my wife because I was too cold, too strict, and no fun. I'll tell you Brother. I was devastated. And after the hurt started to become more-or-less tolerable, after about eight months, I didn't think I would ever be able to trust any woman again to have feelings for them. But there I was with my hand firmly grasping Sister Jones's breast. Then, she released my hands to probe my crotch. Brother, I was erect. I didn't believe that that could ever happen again. But there I was with her firmly grasping me with her hand. We committed adultery then and seven-teen other times."

Again, thinking that that was the end of the confession, Alex was going to say something to the effect of 'Say 100 Ave Marias,' but he remembered that the minister was not Catholic.

"After the eighth time, I told Sister Jones that we had to tell Brother Jones. She told me that she already did. She told him after the third time, when he asked if talking with me was doing any good. She told me that he was clearly hurt, but she told me that he said, 'Better him than anybody else.' I saw him in church every

Sunday, shaking his hand, and I never asked for his forgiveness. And we kept on doing it."

When Alex asked Rev. Montague when he married his present wife, the minister told him that her name used to be 'Jones'.

"About five months later, Brother Jones died from an overdose of pain pills. Over time, he was complaining that the prescribed amount of pain medicine wasn't effective enough, so he started taking more. One day, he over did it."

After about a minute of silence, the minister continued. "After six months, we got married, believing we were safe. But we were still sinners, even in marriage, because we never came clean, at least I didn't."

Suddenly realizing where this was leading, "Roger, the pianist, knew about it," Alex blurted it out.

"Yes, Roger knew, but he never said a thing until you wanted to come with us to Chicago. I thought he was going to black-mail me for money, but all he wanted was for you to be on the bus to Chi-Town. But he wouldn't tell me why. Do you know why? Can you tell me, please?"

"I told Roger that when I first heard him play the piano, it was as though he had totally forgotten about the audience. I told him that watching and listening to him play that ragtime reminded me of Beethoven when he was deaf. When he was deaf, Beethoven still needed to feel the music, so he pressed his ear on the piano to feel the vibrations of the keys striking the strings."

"I see," the minister said. "No matter, next Sunday after I give my sermon, my last sermon, my wife and I will stand together and make our confession to the congregation and leave."

Not believing what he was hearing, Alex scoffed at him and asked if he were insane.

A bit taken aback, the minister asked Alex for clarification.

"Brother Montague," Alex started, "you obviously have not thought this through. You are a shepherd, and from what I've been able to see these past seven and a half weeks, a damned good one at that…"

"But my sin is compounded, brother. It's compounded," Rev. Montague repeated. "And I'm a man of the cloth,"

"Brother, you're not Jesus!" Alex exclaimed. "You are of flesh and blood, just like everybody else. It's a given that we will fall square on our faces, but the trick is that we pick ourselves up, brush ourselves off, and like a leading black intellectual I once met says, 'Fail better.' I'm not finished yet!" Alex shouted because it looked like Rev. Montague was about to interrupt him. "You have over four hundred people in your congregation, and they look-up to you to show them leadership through thick and thin. I've seen how they revere you, brother. You have to know that it will break many of their hearts if you mention this to them, and then disappear out of their lives, making it virtually impossible for your replacement to make any headway with them. No, please don't tell them. Don't tell anyone."

8
Alex's Recollection

While Alex and Rev. Montague were walking back to the hotel, Alex informed the minister that he would not return to Charleston on the bus. And before he left the minister to his flock, some of whom were waiting for him, Alex begged Rev. Montague to at least ask Roger what he thought about the minister and his wife "coming clean" in front of the congregation. But when Alex entered the hotel lobby, he decided to phone Roger, and he told him what he and Rev. Montague had talked about, and asked Roger to dissuade the minister from making such a public confession. Before they hung up, Roger thanked Alex for calling him.

When Alex went to his room, he went right to his computer, got on the Internet, and started looking up flights. Once he found the flight that he liked, Alex took out his credit card and tried to pay for it. But it wouldn't work. So, he tried again, and again, but it just wouldn't work. Getting nervous because he knew the bus he was on was about to leave and not having any other way of getting back to Charleston, he tried booking a ticket with another online travel agent, with no luck. As a result, Alex rushed to pack all of his clothing and ran to the elevator. Fortunately, the elevator came right away and only had to stop once to pick up a family of four, the mother, the father, and two boys. Then, Alex stepped into the lobby. Going to the reception, he interrupted the young lady behind the desk who was on the phone and asked if he was required to checkout. A bit annoyed, she asked if he was with the church group from Charleston, SC. When he answered, "Yes," she informed him that they had already checked out. Without thanking her, he ran with his luggage outside, and he saw Rev. Montague standing impatiently outside of the last bus. As he ran toward the bus, Rev. Montague's demeanor relaxed.

"No need to run brother," Rev. Montague said. "We still got to wait for Brother and Sister Thompson to come down."

Trying to catch his breath, Alex gasped, "Hello Rev. Montague, do you still have room for me?"

"We always have room for all our brothers and sisters," Rev. Montague replied, "especially when he's a wandering pilgrim such as yourself."

Just before Alex could get on the bus, Rev. Montague grabbed his right shoulder.

"I see you going behind my back, Brother Madden," Rev. Montague said.

"I had to," Alex replied. "I'm already drowning in guilt and shame. I really don't need to add anymore to what I already have."

"Well," Rev. Montague said, almost as if acquiescing, "if it makes you feel any better, Roger convinced me to talk to him about it before I take it to the congregation."

"Excuse my French Rev. Montague," Alex responded somewhat relieved, "but I am damn glad to hear that!"

As soon as Alex got on the bus, Brother and Sister Thompson exited the hotel, walking toward the bus with the newly hired porter and the hotel manager carrying their bags. Alex assumed he'd be sitting next to the same old, flatulent gentleman he sat with on the way to Chicago. But, for some unknown reason, the gentleman was nowhere to be seen on the bus. So, Alex sat totally alone, and he loved it.

Since no one had brought any food or drinks, the bus driver had to stop at a chicken restaurant. Although southern fried chicken, was their specialty, they boasted of having over 250 different recipes for chicken. Despite the fact but the waitresses made a great effort to push some of them more exotic chicken recipes, as far as Alex could see, everyone ordered fried chicken. Besides the four-piece fried chicken meal that came with collard greens and black beans with rice, Alex also ordered a slice of sweet potato pie. And after his meal, Alex walked over to the gas station to buy 2 Liters of water and a 10-ounce container of deluxe mixed nuts to tie him over until he reached Charleston.

A few minutes after Alex reboarded the bus, he started wondering when the memory would reveal itself to him. And he started feeling a little bit anxious because he had absolutely no idea of what to expect. He decided to take out his laptop to listen to a little classical music, Corelli, to try and relax, and after a while, he did fall asleep.

Until he woke up to go to the restroom in the back of the bus, Alex had slept very soundly. But after he returned to his seat, a heavy uneasiness overcame him, and the sleep that came to him was rough, full with terrible nightmares. Just before dawn, shortly before the sun poked itself above the horizon, Alex woke up after having experienced a battery of various nightmares.

Those four nightmares were particularly poignant for Alex. In fact, they were all quite harrowing, posing almost an existential threat of sorts because they seemingly inhibited Alex's breathing. In one of those nightmares, my grandfather was beating Alex without let up while Alex was calling out to my grandmother for her protection. For Alex, being beaten so viciously by his father was not all that unexpected in itself because Alex always felt as though my grandfather held some kind of resentment toward Alex, as if he would have preferred it if he and my grandmother had not had Alex. But the truly harrowing aspect of the nightmare came when my grandmother came, looked on while my grandfather kept beating Alex and she did nothing, said nothing. And after a few minutes, she turned her back and left the room.

In the second nightmare, Alex was one of the three little pigs, again, but this time, he was the one who built his house out of straw, which ended in his being eaten by the lion man.

In the third nightmare, while Alex is sleeping, he is awakened by heavy, frantic knocking on his front door. When he finally comes down to open it, there I am with disheveled clothes and hair, screaming at the top of my lungs, demanding to know why he never came for me. He attempts to slam the door in my face, but I stop him with my foot. Then, I tell him how the DSS have taken all of us—not only Misun, but also me, Johnny, Sarah, Tammy, Lucy, and Sim-Sim—away from our Kaka, who died of grief.

The fourth nightmare, though, was particularly taxing on Alex because it troubled him the most, so much so that he anticipated that it would somehow pertain to the lost memory that would soon be revealed to him.

This nightmare revolved around Alex trying desperately to get his father, my grandfather, to accept a letter that my grandfather Marcus consistently refused to look at, let alone touch, a letter that clearly had the name Marcus Madden on it. In refusing the letter, my grandfather would tell Alex, "No, it's not for me, it's for you. She mixed up our names." Again, and again, my grandfather reiterated those words, until nine-year-old Alex believed them. But Alex's name was not Marcus.

Once Alex was able to calm himself down, he reflected on those four nightmares, trying to unravel some hidden meaning. And although he searched and searched, there was no meaning to be found, except.

'What if there are multiple universes, and what if there are multiple Alexs?' Alex thought to himself, desperate to pound some sense into those horrific nightmares. 'What if there's a universe where my mother is indifferent towards me? And what becomes of that Alex? Is he the same Alex who gets Thunder at her worst, where she actually does jump up and down on his grave, screaming at the top of her lungs like a mad woman? And, of course, without Thunder, there are no Roya or kiddos. And I thought that I was a loser! Yeah, that must explain the loser *Three Little Pig* nightmare. In my version, I built my house out of bricks and mortar. I was the winner little pig, but there's a real loser me, somewhere, who dreams of himself building his house out of straw, and he gets eaten on account of his bad judgement.'

After having contemplated a while on those nightmares, Alex began to experience something akin to sublimity because he no longer felt damned. He began to believe that he would fly through his ordeals. He based this on the fact that although he did not find the minister who would be organizing the trip to Chicago, nor did he get on the bus by means of his own actions, he figured that he had something that drew the driver Mickey to him. He felt the same way about Roger, that Roger was drawn to him. Alex concluded that it was his luck.

The calming effects of such thoughts were soothing on Alex's mind and heart, to the extent that sleep would now come easily to him. But just before he could drift away into Zeds Ville, it dawned on him that the fourth nightmare wasn't a dream at all. It actually happened. It was a past, forgotten memory that had resurfaced to his consciousness.

In this more somber state, Alex figured that they were all connected somehow to that one memory that he asked the medium and the spirit to reawaken in him. Initially, Alex tried to remember the contexts of all four nightmares. But attempting the exercise brought along with it a swelter of fear. So, after Alex managed to calm himself down, he decided to try and remember the context of only one nightmare, the one about the letter.

The first thing that he recalled was that his mother, my grandmother, no longer lived with him and my grandfather. Alex tried desperately to reconstruct more of the context, but all he could remember was the letter and his conversations with his father regarding the letter. Alex remembered even handing his father the letter during dinner one time and my grandfather pushing it away, refusing to take it, refusing even to look at it, repeating that she wrote it to Alex and not to him. And Alex remembered presenting the letter to his father again a few days later, but on this occasion my grandfather became so annoyed that he smacked Alex and told him never to mention that letter or my grandmother to him again. Crying, Alex grabbed the letter from the floor, went to his bedroom, closed his door, and sat on his bed. After a while, he dried his eyes. With the letter still in his hand, he looked at it for a long time, fighting an urge to attempt giving it to my grandfather one more time because he was more afraid of finding out what was in the letter than he was of my grandfather hitting him again.

While seated upright and listening to the snoring of the others seated around him, Alex tried to remember what was in the letter, but while his ten year old self held it closed, he couldn't . So, Alex tried to rush his 10-year-old self to open the letter, but it didn't work either. When an elderly woman and her daughter woke up, Alex remembered that he had to go to the restroom. He quickly went before it would be occupied nonstop. While Alex was washing his hands, he saw his 10-year-old self open the letter, and its contents flooded his mind. Alex remembered that his mother, my grandmother, apologized for not being more understanding with regard to his need to leave the United States and immigrate to Africa. She also apologized for emptying the bank account. Further, she apologized for taking Alex and running off to her great-aunt in North Charleston, SC. And finally, Alex remembered his mother writing that she would like to have a reconciliation. She didn't actually write the word 'reconciliation,' but that's the word that popped-up in Alex's mind. She actually wrote that she would like to start-over and that she would follow him anywhere in the world where he wanted to go. Walking back to his seat, the adult Alex knew that his father knew that the letter was for him, and he even knew that his father knew what my grandmother had written in the letter. When Alex tried to focus on the envelop, besides the two names, his mother's and his father's, he saw Crownsville, Md. on the top right corner. And then, he saw 'Post Restante' smack dab in the middle of the envelope. Under it, the word 'Gulu' popped-up.

In his mind, Alex confused Gulu with Gullah, but Alex knew that his father came from Virginia and didn't have a strong connection with the Deep South. Still, Alex had to ask himself 'where is Gulu? What is Gulu?'

At around 7:30 am, the bus pulled into a lot that had several fast-food restaurants. A line to get off the bus had already formed even before the bus actually parked in the lot. So, Alex decided to wait until everyone had gotten off before he would leave his seat. He had only planned to get a small coffee, but once he entered the restaurant, he looked at what people were eating and changed his mind. He was going to order a big breakfast. It took a while for them to get their breakfasts, because the restaurant was somewhat understaffed. The assistant manager informed them that a couple employees had called in sick and that they were not able to find replacements. A deacon responded by thanking her for letting them know what was happening. When Alex finally got his breakfast, he wolfed it down because he feared that the bus driver would rush them in order to make-up for the lost time. Besides, Alex was hoping that the bus would arrive in time for him to make it to Jerry's presentation. But the bus driver never came around. In fact, it took another forty-five minutes after Alex had finished eating his breakfast before the bus left the lot.

While Alex was waiting near the bus, he heard a familiar voice say, "Good morning, Brother." Wondering if the speaker was talking to him, Alex turned around and saw the brother who sat next to him on the trip to Chicago walking towards him.

"Hello," Alex started, "I didn't see you on the bus."

"We on the other bus," the brother replied. "It' parked in the back. I saw you when you left the res'rant and thought I'd give you a holla."

"Thank you," Alex said.

Alex wanted to ask him a few other questions such as if he knew how far we were from Charleston? And if he thought we could get there before 9:00? But as he was about to ask these questions, a massive convulsion took firm hold of his stomach, and everything that he had just eaten and drunk protruded upward, and flew out forcefully from his mouth as well as his nostrils.

"Don' fight it, Brothe'! Don' fight it!" the brother shouted. "Jus' le' it come on through."

Once the vomiting had subsided, the brother said, "That looks like food poisoning to me. But don't worry none. I knows 'xac'ly what you gotta do."

While still bent over, Alex wanted to tell him to shut the hell up because he needed to focus on himself, but he couldn't while the brother kept talking.

"Yes, indeed! I knows 'xac'ly wha' tyou gotta do!" the brother repeated.

Alex tried to wave at him to stop talking, but he paid Alex no mind.

"You gotta drink a who' lot o' milk and a who' lot o' wate'," he finally said. "That'll be fi' dolla's."

Right as when the brother said, "fi' dolla's," Alex, looking inward at the not-so-long, awaited memory, started to cry.

"Aw! Damn, Brother! You don' have t' go cryin' on me!" the elderly brother said embarrassed. "Da's all righ'! Da's all righ'! You don' haf' t' gi' me no fi' dolla's. Here, here's fi' dolla's," the elderly brother said, slamming four wrinkled one-dollar bills and some change, which did not quite add up to five dollars, into Alex's hand. Then, he walked quickly to his bus.

When the bus parked across the street from Rev. Montague's church, it was 10:22. It was too late to catch Jerry's presentation. After Alex collected his luggage and said his farewells to

Rev. Montague and the brothers and sisters who shared their food with him on the way to Chicago, he made his way to the major intersection down the street, hailed a cab, and went to the house. Alex opened the door to an empty house. As he pushed the door open to enter into the house, there was a bit of resistance coming from the floor because of the mail. There were quite a few letters and cards. While picking up the mail, Alex noticed that one of the letters had Richmond written on the top righthand corner. There were other letters covering the name and street address, but Alex thought of Eugene. And it was from Eugene. Alex became glad thinking, hoping that Eugene was reunited with his wife and kids. After closing the front door and tossing the mail on the coffee table, Alex went up to his room, unpacked, undressed, and went to sleep.

At around 6:00 pm, Alex woke up to the sound of voices and the smell of food, and Alex was hungry. He knew that his landlady's mother was cooking because she is a far better cook than her daughter, and Alex also knew that his landlady would not be in before 8:30 pm. While dressing himself, Alex thought of what he could say to his landlady's mother to convince her to give him some food. When Alex entered the kitchen, Jerry, his siblings, and his grandmother had finished eating, but they had not yet left the table.

"Hey, Jerry," Alex started, "how did your presentation go?"

"None o' your motha', fuckin' business," Jerry replied as he excused himself and left the kitchen.

"Ooo! I guess you done pissed him off big time by nat goin' to his presentation," Jerry's grandmother said.

"Yes, I know, I know," Alex said. "I'll have to find some way of making it up to him."

"Well, you betta' do it quick," Jerry's grandmother said.

"Why do you say that?" Alex asked.

"Mary seem to think that you'll be moving on soon?" the landlady's mother replied. "Are you?"

"Yes, I will be leaving in a couple days," Alex confessed. "Ms. Rose, I know that you are angry with me, but I am married. That's why I couldn't do anything."

"Where's yo' wife?" the landlady's mother asked.

"She's out of the country," Alex replied.

"Do you have any kids?" she asked.

"Yes, we have four children," Alex answered.

"Woo! Four! I guess you weren't playin' when you were hittin' that!" she exclaimed. "Well, I believe in the sanctity of marriage, too. So, I guess you can fix yourse'f a plate, but leave enough for Mary."

"Thank you, Ms. Rose," Alex said as he walked to the cabinet to get a plate. "Ms. Rose, did Jerry happen to say anything about his presentation?"

"No, he didn't say anything about it, but he did call to ask me to pick-up Jonathan and Angela from school because he was going to be late," Ms. Rose said.

After Alex had eaten, he returned to his bedroom and phoned Roger. Roger was at the church, but they agreed to meet at the church bar at 8:00 pm. When Alex arrived, it was 7:50 pm. As the bartender came over to clean the table, he asked Alex if he needed a drink. Alex said "Yes," but he wanted to wait for Roger. While Alex was waiting, a man and woman were sitting next to each other at the piano, toying with the keys and giggling incessantly. It annoyed Alex because they would play a few musical notes, then stop. And then, they would do it again, but this time with a different song, and again stop. While looking at them with what have been bordering on contempt, it dawned on Alex that this was their foreplay, which totally brightened Alex's entire attitude towards them. And with that, he could turn to his early morning ... let's just call it a bombshell.

At 8:07, Roger texted Alex, who was seven-years-old, that he wouldn't be there until a little past 8:30. Alex was too engrossed in the memory to have noticed the doorbell tone on his phone. The first thing that he remembered was that his mother was firmly holding his hand as they were both seated at the church, listening to the sermon.

Alex could even recall the reverend's name,
Jackson, and what he wore, a blue, pin-striped,
three-piece suit with a red tie that had ducks.
They at least looked like white ducks to Alex.
The sermon was on the "Prodigal Son." Alex
began to feel the warmth of being in that church,
the one that had burned down, because of the
intermittent "Hallelujahs" and "Amens,"
culminating into the call and response of the
gospel music and choir. As Alex was reliving
that sermon, the music, and the singing, he now
knew why he actually looked forward to going to
church every Sunday morning. It was the most
potent dose of love that he had ever been hit
with, and would be the most potent dose that he
would ever be hit with, ever. The term that came
to his mouth was, "CATHARSIS." The feeling
was so pure that he wished for a second that he
could believe in the Christian image of God. For
a while, he wanted to! But then, a commotion
coming from the back of the church shook him
out of his stupor. A couple of the deacons came
and quickly ushered Alex and his mother to the
front of the church, onto the podium where the
reverend was standing, still giving his sermon,
and then through a door that was hidden by
plastic flowers. The door led down a spiral
staircase to the basement. Just before Alex
reached the door, he looked back and saw his
father. As he crossed over the threshold of the
door, he heard the long-anticipated scream.

"Lawd have Mercy! He got a gun!"

As the seven-year-old Alex stumbled down
the stairs, the adult Alex wondered if his father
had pistoled any of the brothers who were trying
to protect him and his mother. Before he started
falling down the stairs, he felt someone lacking a
delicate touch taking hold of him, lifting him up
horizontally, throwing him in his mother's arms
and stuffing them both in the room where the old,
wooden box with the rusted clasp and hinges was
kept when it wasn't being consulted. The door
was closed and locked behind them. It never
occurred to anyone to turn the lights on, not even
his mother. In a matter of minutes, Alex's father
was banging and kicking on the door, hollering.

"Mildred, Mildred, you betta open this damn
door!"

The adult Alex, incredulous as to what he was
seeing, saw his mother open the door. My
grandfather burst in, looked at her, looked at
Alex, and raised his hand that held the gun, and
struck her with it on her cheek bone. She fell to
the ground crying with blood covering the left
side of her face and sky-blue blouse. Feeling
himself being grabbed by the scruff of the neck,
Alex felt how his seven-year-old self resisting
against his father's grip in vain. Placing Alex
right in front of his mother, who was still laying
on the floor, Alex's looked at him.

"Kick he'!" my grandfather demanded. "Kick
the bitch!"

"No!" Young Alex screamed.

Alex had made up his mind that he was not
going to do it, and the adult Alex felt so proud of
him. But something happened. 'What was it?' the
adult Alex asked himself. 'What? What?'

"Alex," someone said.

Alex thought it was his father at first, and he
was about to say, "No!" again. But there was a
firm tug at his pants leg. Alex looked down and
there his mother was, still holding his pants leg,
looking up at him.

"Go ahead. It's alright. Kick me. You won'
hurt me," my grandmother said as she looked up
past Alex's head.

But young Alex was defiant.

"What I say, boy!" she screamed.

Still young Alex refused. Then, Alex heard a
slight click behind his head.

"God, no! Not my baby!" my grandmother
screamed and cried as she looked at Alex.

The seven-year-old Alex never knew what
was really happening, but seeing his mother cry
like that was too much for him to bear. But the
adult Alex knew all too well what was
happening. When his mother released his pants
leg, she closed her eyes and put her hands over
her ears. The adult Alex was thinking, 'Kick her!
Kick her, damn it!' He thought these thoughts
because he did not want his mother to see the
man who she loved kill her only child. The adult
Alex felt immense relief and unfathomable
shame and guilt when he started kicking his
mother as if he had gone mad, in her head, in her

back, in her face, in her mouth, in her breasts, in her stomach. After a few seconds of what seemed to the adult Alex as an eternity, his father whisked him away, and Alex never saw her again.

9

That Elusive Ass Whoopin'

"Hey, Al, Al!" Roger repeated. "Sorry I'm late. You wanna beer?"

"What! Oh, Yeah!" Alex replied as he returned entirely to the present.

Roger returned to the table with a large beer and a martini.

"I didn't know that you went for that fancy stuff," Alex said somewhat surprised.

"Man, Al," Roger started, "there's this new French violinist at the conservatorium that's a little sweet on me. We've only been out a few times, but she's so fine, Al, that I think I gotta marry he'."

"What?" Alex shouted. "Did I hear you correctly? You just met her, and you already want to marry her?"

"I know, man. It's crazy. It's too crazy," Roger repeated. "But when she talks to me, she has this way of looking at me, right into my eyes to make sure I'm payin' attention, like it really matters to her that I'm really listening. I loves me the fuck out o' that!"

"Is she why you're drinking martinis?" Alex asked.

"You know it, baby!" Roger replied. "It's her drink. But enough about me and my newly-found poison of choice. What about you and Chi-town? Did it work out for you?"

"Thanks for asking," Alex said. "Yes, it worked out, and it's still working itself out."

"You gonna be okay, I hope," Roger said.

"I hope so, too," Alex admitted, not quite sure if he would be.

Wanting to evade the images that resurfaced, Alex changed the topic.

"Have you been able to talk with the Rev.?" Alex asked.

"Naw, he didn't come to church today. But I should see him t'marr', though," Roger said with some certainty. "Did he actually tell you that he and his wife were hittin' the big 'A', and hard?"

"The big 'A'?" Alex said in a questioning manner.

"A-D-U-L-T-E-R-Y," Roger elaborated.

"Oh, that. Yes, he did," Alex answered.

"My hero," Roger said smiling.

"But please don't let him confess it to the whole church," Alex said.

"Don't worry, Al. He won't," Roger said confidently.

"How can you possibly know that?" Alex asked.

After telling Alex that it was his turn to buy the drinks, Alex returned with two martinis. Taking his drink and thanking Alex, Roger proceeded in telling Alex that after one of the weekly meetings between Rev. Montague and the deacons, Rev. Montague had to run right after the meeting, but Brother Jones made the other deacons and Roger stay because he needed to tell them something. Although Roger was not a deacon, he took part in those meetings because he was responsible for the band, the choir, the musical equipment, and the sound system. Brother Jones told them that his wife confessed to him that she and Rev. Montague were committing adultery. Brother Jones went on to tell them not to judge Rev. Montague, because he didn't. And finally, Brother Jones told then that when he's dead, Rev. Montague would "no doubt marry my wife," and that will make it all "clean again," because "I will be in heaven, and I will beg God to please make it clean." Brother Jones made each one of them promise not to judge Rev. Montague, and they all did.

Alex felt satisfied that Rev. Montague might be put at ease knowing that Brother Jones did not hold any ill-will towards him, and that Rev. Montague could finally talk to someone about it, to, as he says, "come clean."

"Did you like those martinis, Al?" Roger asked.

"I think you have to be newly in love to like them," Alex laughed, which caused Roger also to laugh.

"I'm gonna miss you, man" Roger admitted. "Won't be nobody to tell me how much I love my music."

"If it weren't for you and my driver, I wouldn't have made it on that bus," Alex said. "I will never be able to thank either of you properly."

"Just keep drinking these martinis, and you'll be thanking me plen'y," Roger laughed. "You know, Al, I'm startin' to like these things. It's just a pity that I gotta have me seven of 'em befo' I can say dat."

"How would you describe the intensity of your hangovers?" Alex asked, also laughing. "Small, medium, or large?"

"Al, Al," Roger repeated, "I think you're drunk."

"Yeah," Alex agreed, "I knew there was something wrong with how I assed that question."

"Damn! Al," Roger exclaimed, "you betta' stop while you behin'. Yo! Nancy, call Peabody an' ass 'im to give us a ride home."

Alex was dropped off first, and when he entered the house, he made all kinds of noises. He thought his landlady would come down and chew his head off, but she didn't. Before Alex went upstairs to his room, he noticed that the pile of letters on the coffee table had not been touched.

The next day, Alex woke up with a mild hangover, mild because he drank two cups of water after he brushed his teeth the previous night. After he showered and shaved, he went downstairs to an empty house and made himself some oatmeal. After he ate his breakfast, he washed and rinsed all of the items he had used and returned to the living-room, where he sat on the sofa. He took a sheet of folded paper and made a to-do list to tie-up the remaining loose ends before he left Charleston. On his list he had to pay Mr. Mickey, settle-up with Ms. Mary, Jerry, Face-time Roya and the kiddos, face-time me and my Kaka, and book a ticket to Maine, which reminded him of his credit card not working in Chicago.

Although Alex was still preoccupied by his new-found memories, especially the one in which his father held the gun to his head and Alex kicking his own mother, Alex decided to go out one last time to enjoy the Charleston cuisine and to catch a movie. For dinner, he returned to Candy and Elaine's restaurant and enjoyed a seafood medley, and, of course, peach cobbler.

When Alex returned to the house, a little after eight in the evening, his landlady was sitting on the living-room sofa going through the mail. On seeing Alex, she got up. Went to the kitchen, slammed the back door, and it sounded like she bolted it. Returning to the living-room, she went straight for the front door, closed it and locked it. Then, she walked to the coffee table, taking off her jewelry and placing it all on the coffee table.

"Before I give you this ass whooppin,'" the landlady started, "I need to know one thing. Did you want Eugene fo' yo'self, or did you want to have me f' yo'self?"

"Come again," Alex said confused.

"I just read a letter from Eugene, you know, that big head I was ridin' on the regular," the landlady said, "and he says that you tol' him to go back t' his wife and chidlin's. Did you do that?"

"Yes, I did Ms. Mary," Alex admitted.

"Alex, what do I do, first thing, every mother-fuckin' Sunday mornin'?" the landlady asked.

"You cook pancakes," Alex replied.

"Das' right," the landlady agreed, "I make pancakes for my babies, so they know their Mama loves them. Now, do you think that I actually want to wake-up at 6:00 in the a.m. on a Sunday mornin'? Well, I'll tell you. HELL No! But I have to because tha's the only time I have t' spen' quality time with my babies because I have to work 60-plus hours a week, every week, to keep a roof over their pretty, little heads, and give them 3 squares a day, every day."

The landlady paused, waiting for Alex to say something, but he stayed silent, so she continued.

"Have you ever wondered how I can do it, week-in, week-out?" she asked. "I didn't think so, so I will break it down f' you. I treat myself every Saturday night with some good food, some liquor, and a big head, the big head that you chased away. With that man, I could bust me fo', sometimes even fi' nuts a Saturday night, enough t' keep me goin' fo' a week. But you sent 'im away."

"I'm sorry Ms. Mary," Alex said.

"No, you ain't, no' yet, bu' tyou gonna be after this ass whoopin,'" she replied. "You gonna be!"

"Ms. Mary," I don't want to fight you," Alex said as she moved in closer to him.

"You ain't gotta fight," she said. "All you gotta do is take this ass whoopin', and then, I'm gonna kick yo' ass out o' my house."

Alex stepped away from her, and she smiled.

"There's nowheia t' go, Alex," she said. "Everything's locked down, and there's just you and me."

Although the landlady relished the thought of beating Alex, because she never has the opportunity to share her deepest thoughts with anyone, and she had an undivided audience with Alex, she decided to share them with him, before she would beat him.

"You know, Alex," the landlady started, "sometimes, I think the world is crazy. Or is it that I'm crazy? I want you to decide, then I'll kick yo' ass. It seems t' me that words are more important to people than the actions that suppose t' back up the words. For instance, In the Constitution, it says that I got three rights. What's that word I'm lookin' f'? Three somethin' rights?"

"Inalienable," Alex said.

"Tha's right, three inalienable rights," she said.

"There are actually more," Alex added.

"Really?" the landlady said astounded. "Isn't it funny that nobody talks about them either? I mean nobody has ever bothered to ask what this country would look like if we really believed that everyone had a right to 'life, liberty, and the pursuit of happiness.'"

The teacher in Alex began to smile. It was as if he could see the wonder and discovery in his landlady being explored and revealed.

"Do I really have a right to life?" the landlady asked. "Do my babies have a right to life? How can they have a right t' life if their Mama has to work 60-plus hours a week, every week, and never have time to be with 'em, hum?"

She wanted Alex to say something, but he remained silent, but he continued smiling at her. So, she continued.

"Am I free to not work 60-plus hours a week, every week and spend that time with my babies instead? Wouldn't that benefit this country if at least one of the parents could stay home full-time and take care of the childrens? Say somethin', now!"

"Of course, it would! Alex exclaimed.

"Thank you, finally, he speaks," she said. "And as far as pursuing my happiness is concerned, you can't pursue your happiness or the happiness of your childrens when you gotta work 60-plus hours a week, every week. Believe me. I know!"

"You are right, Ms. Mary," Alex said. "What most of us do, if we can, is arrange our lives, to the best of our ability, so that we will never fall victim to the spiral of social, political, and economic injustice that plagues this society. Living in America means always being on the defensive. Even the well to do can't really ever relax."

"So, I'm not crazy?' the landlady asked.

"Not by any means," Alex replied. "And yes, words are more important than deeds. There seems to be some kind of emotional satisfaction in just hearing words, despite the fact that they may be empty. I guess that's why politicians, for example, can fall short on their promises time and time again, ad nauseum, until we are sick of it. And we never consider other measures we could take such as recall, which means at any point, if the people are not happy with a politician because he or she is slacking on promises made, we can kick them out."

"If they did that, politicians would do what we wanted," the landlady interjected.

"Oh, yeah," Alex agreed, "especially if they wanted to keep their position."

"Thank you, f' listening to me, Alex," the landlady said. "And now, I'm gonna kick yo' ass."

As the landlady moved in closer to Alex, he side stepped and raised his guard.

"So, you are gonna fight back," the landlady smiled. "This should be interestin.'"

"No, I will not fight you," Alex said.

The landlady swung at him, but Alex backed away beyond her reach. She tried rushing him a few times, but he side-stepped out of her way, always with his guard raised. Then, she moved toward him, causing him to back away from her until she thought she had him cornered leaving nowhere for him to escape to. Then, she rushed him with her arms swinging at his face. Alex simply lifted his foot up to about his landlady's mid-section, not kicking her, but holding her at a distance. Then, he wrapped his arms around hers so tightly that she could neither move them nor free them. And he wrapped his right leg around her right leg in such a way that she could not do much with that either. After about a minute of trying to free herself, her frustration was palpable.

"I don't understand this," she said. "I should be finishing up whoopin' yo' ass by now."

Then, she tried biting him, but she couldn't get close enough to anything to bite. So, there they stood. Then, she got the idea to let herself drop to the floor in the hope that Alex would have to let her go. But Alex was strong enough to support her weight and lower to the floor in a controlled manner. After a few minutes, it seemed that the landlady had given up because she changed the subject completely.

"I works 60-plus hours a week, every damned week, " the landlady said once again. "And I let out three rooms, so I can pay the mortgage on time every month, every damned month. My kids get three plus healthy squares every damned day, too. You've seen me, how I operate. Okay, I'm a little strict, I admit that, like making you go to church and all, when I don't even go my own self. I know, I know. But when it comes to raising my kids, I am hardly ever here because I have to work at a job I hate like hell. Alex, I am doing everything right, ain't I?"

"Of course, you are," Alex said.

And still, I won't be able to save my babies," the landlady confessed. "I know I'm losing Jerry to the gangs, I know. And when he's totally lost, there won't be much hope for the other two."

Again, she paused hoping that Alex would say something, anything, but he remained silent.

"And I won't be able to bare seeing my baby girl being abused by some mother fucker."

Again, she paused, not so much waiting for a response from Alex, but gathering the nerve to say what's been on her mind.

"Then, you came here," the landlady continued, "and I found out somethin' I di'n't never realize about Jerry. You know what that is? He wonts to do good in school. The day he got the grade for his report, he called Mama and asked her to pick up Angela and Jonathan from school. I didn't know he did that until Mama tol' me. Do you know that that boy came to my job and asked to see me. He ain't never done that before. So, when they tol' me that my son wanted to see me, I thought that somethin' really bad happened. So, I stopped what I was doin' and hurried up to see him. When he started talkin', the only thing he could say was 'Mama.' He must 'a said 'Mama' at least six times. He was makin' me so worried that I wanted to grab him and smack the shit out of him, so he would start sayin' somethin' sens'ble. Shit, I was thinkin' that one of my babies got hurt. Then, he stopped tryin' t' talk and opened up his back pack and took out some paper. He handed it to me and on it was written a big, fat, red 'A+'. You should 'a seen dat boy smile, Alex. Didn't you see that he cared when you was workin' wit' 'im? Didn't you?"

"Of course, I did!" Alex replied.

"Then, help me!" she begged. "Help me save my boy from the gangs and the drugs, please! I'll... I'll give you all you' rent money back!"

When she offered to give Alex double what he paid for rent, Alex realized that saving her children from poverty was foremost on her mind. And Alex couldn't help thinking about what Pieter had once told him. During one of their sessions, Pieter told Alex that 99% of all mental health issues stem from people not having a healthy network of people whom they can speak and listen to. And one way to make sure that everyone is well covered is to have at least one mentor, some peers, and at least one mentee. Alex was thinking seriously about that. And for the first time in Alex's life, he acknowledged that Pieter wasn't quite the quack that he had always taken him to be. And Alex decided that he would tell Pieter that when he sees him.

Alex was able to checkoff everything on his to-do list except book his flight. For he couldn't leave before that one event took place that would allow him to reconnect with the memory of his 13-year-old self. It took three days before it happened. Earlier that evening, Alex was eating dinner with his driver and his girlfriend, who were formally announcing their engagement, and they wanted Alex and a couple other friends to celebrate the occasion with them. Such a celebration demanded drink, and a lot of it. And by the time that Alex had left, he had quite a buzz on him. And it should go without mentioning that Alex was not in peak form for what was to follow.

When Alex arrived at the house, it was 9:48 pm. His landlady wasn't home because she went to the parent-teacher conferences for her two younger children. So, she traded her day shift for the night shift with a colleague. She would get home to wake her children up for school. As Alex stood at the door, fumbling with his keys, a feeling of portentous rapture snuck up on him, as it were. The feeling reminded him of something he had felt recently, but Alex couldn't immediately place where he had felt it. However, it did have a sobering effect on him.

When Alex opened the door, he saw two people in the living room, a boy and a girl. The boy was standing up over her, and she was on her knees, sobbing. When it finally dawned on Alex what the boy held pointed at the girl's head, and remembering what the prophet and the angel had told him, moving quickly, Alex did manage to take the gun in time. As Alex looked at the gun, which was secure in his hands, the rapturous trickle that he had previously experienced opened its floodgates. Anyone looking at him would swear that he was having a seizure of going into a comatose state. As Alex was coming back to the extra-mental world, he heard a hand clapping. Glancing at where the boy and girl were, Alex noticed that the girl was no longer kneeling on the floor, and as he scanned the rest of the room, he surmised that she had left. Yet, the boy from whom he had taken the gun was not clapping. In the corner behind the boy, Alex could faintly see the movement of hands and feet walking toward the boy and Alex, Alex knew who it was.

"I jus' cain' tell you how happy I am that you did that," Jerry's gangbanger friend, Alphonso, said. "You just fucked up the solemnity of our little initiation here. And f' that, I will have t' keel yir black ass."

"You forget," Alex started, "I have the gun."

"Go 'ead, shoot me, bitch,if you got the balls," Alphonso replied.

Alex aimed at his right thigh and pulled the trigger.

"I be god damned!" Alphonso exclaimed. "That son ' bitch would 'a shot my ass f' real!"

Alphonso moved in closer on Alex throwing a flurry of powerful spin kicks to intimidate Alex.

"Is that tea-kwon-do?" Alex asked as if he were afraid.

"Yes," was the reply, but it didn't come from Alphonso. It came from a voice that Alex recognized. It was Jerry.

"You know, dickhead," Alphonso continued, "Afte' Iz kills you, Um a gonna dump yo' dead ass in the trunk o' my car and me and the fellas goin' make a trip to the Bayou, t' see my cousins and 'em. We go'n t' chop yo' dead ass up in nice, small pieces and feed you to the gators. And I will feed 'em yo' balls f' las'. And that won't be the end of it because we go'n hang around fo' a couple o' days to see the gators shit you out. Then, Iz gonna put a couple gator turds of you in a bottle, close it tight, and keep it as a reminder of you."

Then, suddenly, Alphonso rushed for Alex by throwing another flurry of more directed dynamic kicks. Alex quickly grabbed a lamp and backed out of reach of those kicks.

"Wha' tyou go'n do wit' de chicken-shit lamp?" Alphonso asked.

Right as Alphonso started speaking to Alex, Alex threw the lamp at Alphonso, who caught it. As he stood there holding the lamp thinking about what he would do with it, Alex ran to him and kicked him square in his testicles, chopped him in his throat, and swept his feet off the ground, causing Alphonso to fall hard on the floor. As Alphonso groveled on the floor, desperately trying to breathe, Alex walked around him, sporadically kicking him in the head, the back, the ribs, the hamstrings, until Jerry pushed Alex away from him.

"He can't breathe!" Jerry yelled.

"I don't give a shit!" Alex yelled back.

"Mama go'n be mad if she find dead people in her livin' room!" Jerry said.

"What the fuck!" Alex exclaimed. "You weren't thinking of that shit a couple minutes ago. There's only one way that I'm going to let this piece of shit live!"

As Jerry remained quiet, Alex resumed kicking Alphonso.

"Okay, what is it?" Jerry asked.

Alex stopped kicking Alphonso, looked at Jerry for a few seconds and told Jerry that he would have to leave the drugs and gangs.

"Okay, Alex! Okay!" Jerry acquiesced.

Believing that Alphonso would seek revenge, Alex knew he would have to fabricate a story that would oblige Alphonso to leave North Charleston at least for the foreseeable future.

"Shit, the L.T. is going to be pissed," Alex said.

"What's the L.T.?" Jerry asked.

"That's short for lieutenant," Alex replied.

"You a pig?" Alphonso asked.

"No, I'm an informer," Alex replied. "I had a little hustle going on with counterfeit checks. I was going to cash one more check and then leave

Dodge, leave town. But they caught me before I could leave. I was looking at 16 years in the pin. Then, some DEA agents told me that they can reduce my time if I work for them. So, I've been working as an informer for six years now."

"Why is you here?" Jerry asked.

"To get information about the gangs and the drug scene here," Alex replied. "But I have a bit of a dilemma."

"What does that mean?" Jerry asked

"You, Jerry," Alex replied. "If I turn this piece of shit into the LT, he's going to get you implicated. And earlier on, I wouldn't care, but now that I got to know you and your mother, I don't want you to go to juvie. Because from there, you will probably end up in prison."

Then, Alex addressed Alphonso directly, who was still on the ground grasping his groin area.

"So, I guess I have to make a deal with you, Shorty. You give me the names, phone numbers of all the members and the names of your drug and weapons dealers, I'll let you go. That's it. Take it, or leave it."

"You got some paper, Jerry?" Alphonso asked. "Afte' I give you this, how much time will you give me to leave?"

"How much do you need?" Alex asked.

"24 hours," Alphonso said.

Alex laughed, "I'll give you three, then I'll turn everything over to the L.T."

"Where am I suppose t' go?" Alphonso asked.

"You have money saved up, don't you," Alex asked.

"Yeah, I got almos' $67,000.00," Alphonso said.

"Shit, man! You can start a new life anywhere with that!" Alex yelled.

Looking at Alphonso, Alex could see that he was at a loss.

"Go to Alaska, man," Alex said. "No one will follow you there. Go to a place called St. Mary an get yourself an Eskimo woman. And you better be faithful to her because everybody in Alaska is a republican. And definitely don't do any of that gangbanging and drug bullshit up there because those republicans will shoot you on the spot if you try to introduce that shit to their children. Oh, yeah, how much of that $67,000.00 you got on you now?"

"I got about 800 dollas," Alphonso replied.

"I need it. Give it to me!" Alex demanded while holding out his right hand. "All right, you have three hours, and the clock starts ticking now."

Alphonso shot out of the house. Turning to Jerry, Alex shouted at him, telling him to get his "ass" to bed, and Jerry did as he was told. Alex went to bed as well, but sleep would not come to him. Initially, Alex didn't know why he was so restless, but at about 1:00 am he realized what the problem was. He was finished with N. Charleston. He wanted to leave, the sooner the better. He was somewhat relieved when it was decided that he was going to leave. But instead of jumping out of his bed and packing, Alex sat up and wondered about what he was going to do with Jerry. After a few minutes, Pieter's voice managed to ring through, "She's an absolute godsend, Alex." Alex was starting to accept that he needed to connect more with people, and not only on his terms.

10
Northward Bound

While Alex was packing his clothes, there was a knock at his bedroom door. It was Jerry. It seems that Jerry was worried about the 'L.T.', so he couldn't sleep. Alex asked Jerry if he had an I.D., a picture I.D. Jerry had a social security card and his school I.D. Alex told him to wash up, dress himself, and pack five boxers, five T-shirts, five nice shirts, three pairs of nice pants, and five pairs of socks. Alex also told him to take "a very warm sweater, a thick jacket, a hat, and a pair of gloves. But Jerry didn't have a thick jacket, nor did he have gloves.

"Is we goin' somewhere?" Jerry asked.

"We're going to pay the L.T. a visit," Alex responded. "He's a little pissed that I let the gangbanger go."

Alex called his driver, who took them to the bus terminal. Before they left, Alex wrote a note for the landlady, explaining where he was taking Jerry and why. Alex also left her his cell phone number and his home phone number. In the note, he also informed her that he would contact Jerry's social studies teacher and ask her to relay to him Jerry's homework. So, Jerry had to bring his school books as well.

"Why is you, a police informe', buggin' so much about my homework?" Jerry asked.

Alex just smiled.

When they stood in line at the ticket counter, Jerry asked Alex a flurry of questions that all included the L.T. Alex started regretting ever fabricating that narrative. But when Jerry asked how far they were going, Alex told him that they were headed north, and the they were going "almost all the way." Jerry wondered what that meant. At one point, he wondered if they would go to Canada, which he asked. Alex repeated "almost," and then Alex added that they will end up being about 50 miles shy of the Canadian border.

"The L.T. lives that far north?" Jerry asked.

"Yup," Alex said, barely with a straight face.

Alex and Jerry arrived at the bus terminal at 6:40 am. Their bus was scheduled to leave at 8:45 am. After Alex bought the tickets, he gave Jerry's his and told him he'd better keep it safe. Looking at the tickets, Jerry became quite animated.

"Shit, we goin' to Boston?" Jerry asked. "New York! We goin' t' New York."

"We're not going to New York or Boston," Alex said. "We will just be passing through."

"Do you think we'll see 'Gene in Richmond?" Alex asked.

"I don't think so," Alex said. "Richmond is a pretty big city."

"If we do, I'm gonna fuck 'im up," Jerry said.

"No, you won't!" Alex insisted.

Jerry clearly had something more to say on the matter, but he said nothing more about Eugene or Richmond. When they were finally on the bus, the first stirrings of hunger hit Alex, and Alex wondered if Jerry wanted to eat something. Alex apologized for not asking him if he wanted to have some breakfast. So, when they arrived in Myrtle Beach, Alex made a point of going to a large buffet restaurant that he had read about. Fortunately, the restaurant Alex had read about was only a 15-minute taxi ride from the bus stop. When they arrived at the restaurant, Jerry was hurrying to get his food, sit down, and eat it to make it back to the bus before it left. Alex sat down about five minutes after Jerry, who had already finished and about ready to go for seconds.

"Why are you in such a hurry to get heartburn?" Alex asked.

"I don't want to miss the bus," Jerry replied.

"Jerry, we still have more than two-hours before our bus leaves," Alex explained. "Relax, man, and enjoy your meal for a change. We will probably be back on the bus at least forty-five minutes before it departs. So, please, stop wolfing this stuff down like there won't be any more food tomorrow."

After about an hour of riding north on the bus from Myrtle Beach, Jerry dosed off, presumably from a full stomach and boredom. Alex was reading off of his eBook Reader, but after a while, he looked briefly at Jerry, and then Alex

remembered the entire encounter with Jerry's
mother, from her locking all the doors to prevent
Alex's escape, to taking off her rings, to their
entangled bodies on the floor. Then Alex
wondered about how this trip would end, how he
would want it to end, and perhaps how he needed
it to end. He returned to what he was reading on
his eBook reader, and just before Alex was going
to get up to go to the bathroom, Jerry stirred,
probably from a dream, then Alex vaguely
recalled an article that he had once read in a
major newspaper. In this article, Maya Angelou
wrote of how James Baldwin introduced her to
his mother and offered his mother a new daughter
in Maya Angelou. In particular, Alex was
searching for two poignant similes that
encapsulated how she felt about James Baldwin
as her brother. But they would not immediately
come back to him.

In Florence, SC, two young Bohemian-dressed
women got on the bus and sat behind Alex and
Jerry. Jerry was clearly fascinated by them. Later,
he told Alex that he had never seen "black
hippies" before. Half-jokingly, Alex told him that
he was missing out and that he should go to
California the first chance he gets. When Jerry
asked if Los Angeles was a good place to go to,
Alex confessed that he hadn't spent much time in
Los Angeles, although Santa Barbara was
expensive, Alex told him that he definitely had to
see it. But if he wanted to meet real Bohemians,
he had to go to Santa Cruz, in particular, UC

Santa Cruz, the university. After a while these
two women started listening to music. Despite
the fact that they were using earphones, Jerry and
Alex could still hear their music pretty clearly.
They first listened to the group America. When
"A Horse with no Name" was being played, Alex
sang along.

"You like dis Hillbilly music?" Jerry scoffed.

"This group is called America, and yes I like
them quite a bit," Alex said. "They're practically
up there with Crosby, Stills, Nash, and Young."

After America, the young women listened to
some Janice Joplin. Alex asked Jerry to listen to
her voice. Then he asked Jerry to guess if she
was black or white. When Jerry said, White,"
Alex smiled and told Jerry that she was white,
but all of her singing role models were black
Blues and Jazz female singers. Then, these young
women listened to Simon and Garfunkel. While
they listened to "Scarborough Fair," Alex sang so
loudly that the two young women heard him and
sang the lyrics with him. Then, "America" came,
and several other passengers sang along as well.

Unfortunately, the two young women got off
in Raleigh, NC. They arrived in Raleigh at 4: 50
pm. Because the stopover would last for three
hours, Alex decided to phone Jerry's mother and
explained where they were going and why. Alex
also informed her that Jerry would still be doing
his school work. Fearing that she would be angry,
but she wasn't. Indeed, she even suggested that

she write a letter giving Jerry formal permission to travel with Alex. So, Alex gave her is address.

"Maine, wheia de hell is dat?" Jerry's mother asked.

After the call, Alex asked Jerry if he was hungry. Jerry suggested that they go to. A rib joint called 'Love that Oink, Oink.' Alex found the name funny, and he agreed to go there. The restaurant was downtown, which was about ten minutes from the bus terminal. The restaurant had a bright, colorful décor, and the music you heard was jazz, for the most part, with a smidgen of blues. The owner, Big Sarah, was a big, boisterous, light-skinned, chain-smoking woman whose voice was so incredibly sweet that it seemed as though everything she said, absolutely every syllable, was being sung.

When they got back on the bus, unfortunately, the two young women had been replaced by two young, black men who were on their way to Richmond, VA., and they were going there for one reason, and one reason alone.

"They goin' t' push rock." Jerry whispered to Alex.

Indeed, not long after the bus had departed Raleigh, one of the young men was boasting about the fact that this was his seventeenth trip to Richmond and that he hadn't been caught, and that he would never get caught selling crack. The first time he said it, Alex basically ignored him, but the young man kept on, boasting about how much money he was going to make and how much "pussy" he was going to get, Alex noticed that Jerry was listening, and intently. Not only hearing again what Jerry's mother had told him as they were entangled on the floor and the gains that he at least thought he had made with Jerry, Alex knew he had to do something. But what?

"Stop it! Just stop it!" Alex yelled.

"Who you hollerin' at, dude?" One of the young men yelled back. "I see I'm gonna have t' bust yo' ass up."

"You are not going to bust up shit!" Alex exclaimed. "You are going to shut the fuck up and learn about the great setup."

The young man was going to stand up, but his friend held him back.

"Come on man, if you fight this dude, the police go'n come an' we go'n git busted," the friend said. "I don' wanna go to the pin, do you? Then jus' sit and listen t' this mothe' fucke' and git it over wit', so we cin go 'bout ourn bu'iness. You feelin' me?"

"Okay, man, what you got t' say?" the first friend asked.

"It's all a set up!" Alex started. "Do you know what the 13th Amendment says?"

"Wha's dat," the friend asked.

"It's the Amendment that abolished slavery." Alex replied. "It made slavery illegal. Do you know what the second part of the 13th Amendment says?"

"Naw man, what does it say?" the first young man asked?

"It says that this doesn't affect hard labor in prison," Alex explained.

"So, what, man?" the original young man sighed.

"The point that I am trying to make," Alex said a tad bit exasperated, "is that in the same breath, as they finally got rid of slavery, they remind us that hard labor in prison is still a viable option for limiting black bodies."

Alex waited for the lightbulbs to light up, but they didn't, not yet, anyway. So, he continued.

"Okay, let me ask you this, what percentage of the population in the United States do black people make up?" Alex asked.

Both young men shrugged their shoulders with an air as though they were waiting for Alex to give them the answer.

"We make up between ten and twelve percent of the American population," Alex said. "And do you guys happen to know about how much of the prison population in this country that we make up?"

"I don't know no numbe's, but I know it's mostly us," a black woman interjected who was sitting across from Alex.

"More than ninety percent," Alex said.

"Shit! You know what dude is sayin?'" the young man who held his friend back asked. "He sayin' the prisons in this country is actually the continuation of slavery, right?" he asked Alex.

"Have you heard of Angela Davis?" Alex asked.

"Man, you think we stupid!" the young man who had an altercation with Alex said.

"I'm sorry," Alex said. "She calls it the 'prison industrial complex', which implies that it is an industry, a business, forcing inmates to work for next to nothing. And James Baldwin said, correctly, that we are guilty simply because we are black. So, ultimately, it doesn't matter if we actually do something wrong. They even have private prisons that have black prisoners picking cotton in a getup that would remind anybody of the good, old days of slavery."

"Look, man," the young man that Alex had an altercation with said, "I know it's all one big set-up against young black men in this country. But I'm not goin' t' starve. I'm not goin' t' live unde' a bridge, and I'm sure as hell not goin' to work for nobody's minimum, fuckin' wage, where you gotta work 80-hours a week t' make it. Fuck that!"

"But there is a way out!" Alex exclaimed.

"F' all o' us?" the young man asked cynically. "Bull shit!"

That ended the conversation. Both young men turned away from Alex and continued their own conversation but privately, in a whisper. Despite that, Alex still had some things that he wanted to say, some more things that he wanted Jerry to hear, but the opportunity to say them had passed. All that Alex could do was wait for, or perhaps, if he is lucky, create the next opportunity where he could continue the conversation.

When they arrived in Richmond, it was 11:04 pm, and they both were asleep. It was the hustle and bustle of passengers getting off the bus that woke Alex up because several of them accidentally bumped into him as they stumbled to the front of the bus. Despite all that, it was the bus driver who yelled at him and Jerry to get off the bus. As they made their way to the front of the bus, Alex heard the bus driver swear under his breath. Alex suddenly turned toward him and could instantly see that the driver wasn't swearing at him or Jerry. He was preoccupied with other distant matters. An hour later, they boarded another bus that took them to Wilmington, DE, which they slept through, and then they traveled further to New York City. Finally, Alex was familiar with his surroundings. They arrived in the City at 6:55 am. When Jerry realized where he was, he asked Alex for the name of that part of New York City that's in all of the movies that are filmed in New York City. Not knowing exactly what Jerry meant, Alex went down the list.

"The Empire State Building, The Chrysler Building, Radio City Music Hall, The Statue of Liberty, Broadway."

Jerry said, "No," to each one. He added that, "it's a street, and when you there, you know you in the City."

"Times Square," Alex blurted out with confidence.

"Yeah, tha's it!" Jerry said smiling.

"Do you want to go there?" Alex asked.

"Hell yeah!" Jerry exclaimed.

"Get your shit and let's go," Alex said.

They exited Port Authority on 42nd Street and were able to grab a cab right away.

When the cab arrived, Alex looked to Jerry to ask him if this was what he meant, but he could see that it was. Jerry asked if he could get out of the cab.

"Sure, knock yourself out," Alex said, repeating something his father often said.

As Jerry stood dazzled by the people's comings and goings and interactions, the passing, tooting vehicles, and his scaling the facades of the overshadowing buildings, Alex made an observation.

'So, Jerry is a dreamer,' Alex thought.

"I'm going to live here!" Jerry said after getting back into the cab.

"Good choice," Alex said, "New York is one of the great cities of the world."

"Is it your favorite, too," Jerry asked.

"New York is definitely on my top ten list, but Berlin in Germany *ist meine lieblings* Stadt," Alex said. "I said that Berlin is my favorite city."

"Why is Berlin your favorite city?" Jerry asked.

"There are many reasons, but the top two are that I feel freest there," Alex said, "and that's the first place where I had an insane amount of sex in a very short space of time."

"I'm gonna live here!" Jerry repeated.

"Well, make sure you have a constant stream of some serious paper coming in," Alex said, "because New York is one of the most expensive cities in the world. And please don't do it by being a pimp, a dealer, or a thief."

At 12:07, their bus arrived at the South Station terminal in Boston. After they collected the luggage, they walked directly to the Northern New England Gopher ticket booth. Alex was hoping that there was time to go to China Town to his favorite Taiwanese restaurant, but the next bus would depart at 1:00 pm, and the next one that would make a stop in Augusta will leave at 4:15 pm and arrive in Augusta at 7:15 pm, which would be very dark and a little late because from Augusta, it would still take an hour and twenty minutes to get to the house in Bozeman. As far as food went, they settled on steak and cheese subs.

As the bus sped its way farther north, the amount of snow on the ground next to the highway increased and expanded farther and farther away from the highway until everywhere was covered under a few inches of snow. As the bus approached the border between New Hampshire and Maine, Alex told Jerry to watch out for the Piscataqua River Bridge.

"Now, we are in Maine," Alex said when they crossed the bridge.

"So, Massachusetts and Maine are next to each other," Jerry said.

"No," Alex replied, "we rode through a little stretch of New Hampshire."

"Tha's whe'e Earnest Everett wen' t' school," Jerry added.

And as the bus pressed deeper into Maine, Jerry started noticing the increased density of the trees.

"Wha' do you call I' when you got no space t' move or breathe, like when you on a elevator tha's full?" Jerry asked.

"Claustrophobic," Alex replied. "When we get to the house, write it down in your vocabulary book."

"How do you spell it?" Jerry asked.

"Look it up!" Alex shouted.

"What am I go'n t' look it up wit'?" Jerry asked.

"I have all kinds of dictionaries at the house," Alex said. "The reason why I want you to look it up is because you will have better chances of remember it if you look it up as opposed to just being given the answer."

Looking at Alex curiously, a rather doubtful expression washed across Jerry's face.

"I have another theory," Jerry said. "I think you full o' shit, and you don't know how t' spell it."

Alex, of course, knew what Jerry was up to.

"Okay, I know that game, but I'm not falling for it," Alex said. "I'll tell you what I'll do, though. I'll take my trusty pen here and this trusty piece of paper, and spell the word. Then, when we are at the house, you can check and see if I'm right."

"What do I git if you spelled it wrong?" Jerry asked.

"We will both learn how to spell claustrophobia correctly," Alex said.

"I'd rathe' git some money," Jerry said.

11
Home Sweet Home, Again

When they arrived in Augusta, it was 6:52 pm.
First, Alex needed to get his SUV jump started,
which took almost an hour because most of the
people he asked didn't have any jumper cables.
Also, they stopped in Skowhegan to do some
shopping. After they entered the house, a division
of labor was established. They decided that Alex
would put away the groceries, and Jerry would
get the fires in the two main woodstoves going.
But it turned out that Jerry's fire-making skills
left a lot to be desired. So, when Alex had put the
food away, the house was just as cold as when
they had arrived.

"Man, the way you were bragging about your
fire-making skills made me think that you were
probably a hotshot arsonist who was wanted in
all fifty states in a previous life," Alex said with
some disappointment.

"I couldn't find any fire-starter fluid," Jerry
said.

"Oh, my fucking God!" Alex exclaimed.
"Don't you ever, never, ner, ever use that shit to
start a fire inside."

"I used a lot o' pape', but the wood wouldn't
burn," Jerry said.

"Okay, okay," Alex repeated, "my bad, I
didn't tell you about the kindling and the birch
bark. Come on, I'll show you where they are."

"Wha's kindlin'?" Jerry asked.

"It's long, thin pieces of wood," Alex replied. "They catch quickly, and we use birch bark because it has a lot of energy that takes a while to burn, so there's enough time for the kindling to catch fire. Then, the larger pieces of wood will burn nicely."

"Was you born in the country or the city?" Jerry asked.

"I was born in Baltimore," Alex replied. "It's a city of more than 500,00 people,"

"Did we pass through it?" Jerry asked.

"No, we didn't, but you should know that," Alex replied.

"Oh! Snap!" Jerry exclaimed, "is this your family?" taking the picture in his hands.

"Yes," Alex replied.

"Damn! You really got four kids?" Jerry asked in amazement.

Alex didn't answer the question because to him the answer was obvious, but he did wrest it out of Jerry's hands and returned it where it was above the fireplace.

"What will you want for breakfast," Alex asked, "porridge or an omelet?"

"Is porridge like oatmeal?" Jerry asked.

"Yes," Alex replied.

"Fuck that!" Jerry exclaimed. "Give me a omelet."

After making Jerry's bed in the boys' bedroom, Alex dug out several pairs of boots from the vestibule closet and told Jerry to see if there's a pair that fit him. Fortunately, there was a pair that fit Jerry, and when Jerry asked if they were "going to make a snowman or something," Alex laughed and remembered all the snowmen and all the snowball fights he had with the kiddos.

"If you want to make a snowman, knock yourself out," Alex replied, "but I was thinking more about walking to the part of the river where the rapids are. And we can check-out all the tracks of the animals that live up here."

"Oh, yeah, are all the animals on the poster here?" Jerry asked.

"All of them, except the wolves and mountain lions," Alex replied. "Well, that's not totally true. There are probably a few of each. Sometimes you hear about a pack of wolves crossing into Maine from Canada. Also, there are probably a few mountain lions, but the loggers, who would be the ones most likely to see them or the evidence that they lived in a certain place, would never report it, because if it were known that mountain lions were present in a certain part of the forest, the loggers would have to stop cutting down the trees, which means they would lose work."

"What about the lynxes and bobcats?" Jerry asked.

"Yes, it seems as though we have a lot of them," Alex replied, "and the even interbreed."

"Have you ever seen them?" Jerry asked.

"No, not in the wild, but I have seen a few bobcats, lynxes, and a mountain lion in cages not so far from here," Alex replied.

"Can we go there?" Jerry asked.

"Yes, we can go when it's warmer," Alex replied, "but I have to warn you that the animals are in old-school, barred cages. Some people have a problem with that."

"Can you see any animals here?" Jerry asked.

"Oh, God yes!" Alex exclaimed. "I regularly see chipmunks, voles, muskrats, skunks, porcupines, beavers, bald eagles, hawks, ospreys, owls. I once saw a huge barn owl at the top of one of those trees in front of the house, and of course there are all kinds of fish in the river. There's even a guy who has buffaloes around here."

It was both surprising and refreshing for Alex to see that Jerry was interested in wildlife and nature. In contrast to most of his inner-city students, Jerry became visibly animated while listening to Alex talk about the local wildlife.

At 7:00 am, Alex woke-up Jerry and told him to hurry up and get dressed because the house was cold, so he had to start the fires in the two woodstoves. When Jerry came downstairs, he saw that the dining room table was being set, so he sat at the table.

"What the hell are you doing?" Alex shouted.

"Ain't we eantin' breakfas'?'" Jerry asked.

"The woodstoves have to be lit first, and I mean roaring," Alex replied.

Jerry did manage to start the fires and get them "roaring," but he had to use a lot of birch bark and kindling to get there. Nonetheless, Alex commended him on being a true pyromaniac.

"Why is dis fire or'nge, when the fire from our gas range is blue?" Jerry asked while he was serving himself the omelet and sausage links."

"I'm not sure, but I do know that blue flames burn more oxygen, which makes them hotter than orange flames," Alex replies.

"So, i's de temp'rature," Jerry stated.

"It also depends on the fuel," Alex added. "You should look it up."

After breakfast, Alex opened the living-room curtains, which hid the sliding doors that open to the back deck and to the backyard. As Alex looked to the tree line, looking for deer or turkeys, he saw a gray-green tent that was pitch in his back yard on the snow. Initially, it made Alex think of Pieter's tent, the one Alex had set alite. He even wondered for a second if Pieter were inside of it, but he quickly dismissed the idea. Armed with a bowl of hot porridge, honey, a table spoon, a thermos full of coffee, and a cup, Alex tapped on the tent. After having tapped on the tent, Alex shouted, "Hello, hello," but still, there was no reply. So, he opened the tent. There was a sleeping bag, a backpack, a few items of clothing, some pots and pans, a gas stove, and some gas bottles, but the occupant had left. Looking for tracks, Alex saw that he or she, probably a he, from the smells and the mess, had gone into the forest. Alex wondered if he was a hunter or an escaped criminal. Alex dismissed the latter choice, though, because it would be safer for an escaped criminal to camp-out in the forest and not in the open. Not knowing when he'd return, Alex left his goods behind for this unannounced visitor and walked back to the house.

"You know who it is?" Jerry asked.

"No," Alex replied.

"Did 'e come in on skis?" Jerry asked seriously.

"No, I didn't see any ski tracks," Alex smiled. "Why do you ask that?"

"He might be a illegal immigrant from Canada," Jerry replied. "They got all kinds o' illegal immigrants in my school."

"Are you a xenophobe?" Alex asked.

"Wha's dat?" Jerry asked

"Someone who hates people from other countries and cultures," Alex replied.

"Do I hate!" Jerry scoffed. "My bes' frien' in school is from Guam. His name is Ricky."

At that moment, there was a knock at the door.

"Watch out, Alex!" Jerry exclaimed as Alex walked to the front door. "He might have a gun."

There was a big, strapping, blond-haired, blue-eyed man at the door, who smiled and started speaking Finnish. Alex knew it was Finnish because he once had a Finnish girl friend who lived in Lapland, Finland about 150 miles north of the Artic Circle. Alex was astonished of the fact that he still remembered some Finnish because he hadn't been there for over twenty years.

This gentleman's name was Jussi, not as in 'juicy,' but the 'J' has the 'Y' sound. To understand in detail what Jussi was saying, Alex asked him to speak English. Jussi started by saying that he was an analysand of Dr. Pieter Aziz. But when Alex heard Jussi say "Dohtori Pieter Aziz," he started laughing uncontrollably. In fact, it took Alex a good ten minutes to get his laughter under control. Jussi was clearly annoyed, but he was a man of great patience, so he waited for the laughter to subside. Jussi continued by telling Alex that he had a session scheduled with Pieter--Jussi stopped referring to Pieter as 'Dohteri--but Pieter was a no show, which worried Jussi because Pieter stressed on him that he wouldn't make any progress if he missed sessions. As a result, Jussi booked a flight to Quebec City, made his way to the U.S.-Canada border and crossed it. When Alex heard that, he thought about Jerry, and smiled. Jerry was listening in on their conversation, and every now and then, he would ask Jussi how to say various things in Finnish, such as I love you, where are you from in Finland, and do you like ribs? Jussi's first response was "*Mina rakastan sinua*. The second response was "*Mista olette ko Suomisa*? And the last one was a bit problematic for Jussi because he didn't know what ribs were. So, he replaced ribs with "*poro*," which means reindeer.

At around lunch time, while Alex was making some sandwiches, Jussi asked Alex how was it that he knew Finnish, for Finland is a small country. Because Alex was confident that he could say it in Finnish, he did, but he failed miserably. While trying to explain to Jussi, Alex said, "*Mina olin ollut yksse soumalaiset tytto.*" Although Alex thought he was saying that he had a Finnish girlfriend, he was actually saying that he had been a Finnish girl. You should have seen Jussi's face just before he cracked up laughing. Jussi kept saying "*Milloin? Milloin?*"

But Alex wasn't familiar with the Finnish word "*milloin*," so he asked Jussi what it meant. While laughing hysterically, Jussi barely managed to speak.

"I asked you when."

"Oh, when I had the Finnish girlfriend?" Alex asked.

"*Ei!*" Jussi exclaimed.

'*Ei*' means 'No.' It's pronounced by saying the interjection 'hey' without the 'H.'

"No, I ask when you was Finnish girl," Jussi said, still laughing.

Realizing what he had done, Alex asked Jusssi how to say, "I had a Finnish girlfriend."

"*Minulla oli suomalainen tyttöystävä.*"

Alex was very curious as to why Jussi needed a psychoanalyst, but Alex made a point of not asking Jussi about it, but Jerry was far too nosey as well as direct to sit on a question

"You look all right," Jerry started. "Why you need to see a shrink?"

Jussi was clearly not familiar with the term shrink, so Alex restated the question, replacing 'shrink' with "Dohtori Pieter Aziz." And that time, Alex managed not to laugh. Jussi looked at Alex and Jerry for a couple of seconds, probably sizing them up. And apparently after coming to the conclusion that he could trust them, he said what had to be everything.

After Jussi had done his tour in military service, he joined the French Foreign legion, mostly in Francophone African countries. When Jerry asked him if he had killed anyone, Jussi was forthright, "Yes." Alex asked him if that was his difficulty. Jussi made it very clear that he had no problem whatsoever to kill bad people who hurt women, children, or the weak. Later, Alex found out that "the weak" meant the elderly, the handicapped--both mentally and physically--and the abject poor. Jussi spoke a lot about his experiences in France and in Africa while he was in the foreign legion, and based on the kinds of missions that he preferred, close combat, Alex realized quickly that Jussi was probably quite efficient in killing people. And from that point on, Alex regarded him as being an 'Achilles,' but while Jussi spoke of his exploits in Africa, and some of it was immensely macabre, he clearly had no problem with the horrific dances he had had with death.

But when he started talking about the Former
Yugoslavia, both his tone and demeanor changed.
The first time that Jussi had heard about the
conflicts in the Former Yugoslavia, he was on the
outskirts of Bangui in The Central African
Republic. He had just finished training a group of
experienced local soldiers "in advanced hand-to-
hand, and feet, combat." A Swedish colleague
named Magnus, whom he had fought alongside
in Mali and who was also an advanced hand-to-
hand combat trainer, brought up the Croatian
struggle for independence from the Former
Yugoslavia, which, for all intents and purposes,
was dominated by Serbia. Magnus's real interest
in the conflict was the fact that he had a Croatian
girlfriend, whom he was going to see. When Jussi
asked if she was in The Central African
Republic, Magnus laughed and said, "Of course
not, she lives in Split, Croatia." Jussi told Alex
and Jerry that there was something in the way
that he smiled that showed that something was
up, but before Jussi could say another word,
Magnus asked him to come with him. Jussi was
taken a bit aback by that sudden and out-of-the-
blue question. And there was silence for a few
minutes between them. Then, Jussi started
speaking. He reminded Magnus that most people
see them as mercenaries, whores. But Jussi
stressed that he was not a whore, that his chief
motivation was not money. Jussi then added that
he joined the Legion not because of some great
love of France or of French values but simply

because he was a warrior, and the French government afforded him the opportunity to lead the life of a warrior, "no more, no less."

"Jussi, you've been doing France's bidding in Africa for four years," Magnus said, "and I've been here for six. Are we really making a difference here?"

"I am warrior," Jussi replied, "and a honorable one. I have never killed the innocent, no women, no children, and none of the weak."

"That's all fine and good," Magnus started, "but what about the hundreds of men that we've trained?"

Jussi could not respond to that, because he knew first hand that many of them did, through debriefings and boastings. Indeed, several of the men whom he had trained boasted about raping the captured wives, daughters, sisters, and mothers of enemies.

"But that's not me," Jussi cried.

"Of course, it is us!" Magnus insisted. "Of course, it is us! That's why I am getting out of this hell trap."

"The Legion will not let you leave before your tour is finished," Jussi interjected."

"No, but they won't chase after me into a war zone either." Magnus retorted. "There's a transport flying to Benin and then to Madagascar. From there, I will make my way to Morocco, and then to the Balkans. You should come with me."

"I don't know if you've noticed," Jussi said, "but our brothers in the Legion take what we do most seriously. They would rather die than return empty-handed. And I for one am not willing to kill a brother. But I wish you well, and stay in touch, by the proper channels, of course," with that, Jussi wanted to make sure that no one in the French Foreign Legion could find out that they were in correspondence.

About 10 months later, Jussi was at the end of his tour in the French Foreign Legion, and because he was not going to be promoted as an officer, because he wasn't French, he was hesitant to renew, but he had no other options available to him, not until he received his biweekly letter from Magnus. In the letter, Magnus was telling Jussi about Operation Storm, which was an offensive that many senior officers believed would cinch Croatia's independence. Magnus had been promoted to 2nd Lieutenant and responsible for training snipers. Because the offensive was a few months away, and many of the recruits were in desperate need of proper training, Magnus literally begged Jussi to come. He promised Jussi that he could get out after the offensive if he wanted. At this point, Jussi was very much tempted by Magnus's offer, not only because the Croatian war for independence looked as though the decisive end was in sight, but also because of the comradery between the soldiers who came from all over the world. It came across to Jussi as being quite romantic, reminding him of the stories his grandfather told him when he was a young man fighting with the

anarchists in the Spanish Civil War against
Franco and the Germans. Jussi's grandfather was
such a staunch opponent of fascism, that he
couldn't stomach Finland's decision to fight
alongside the Germans to rid themselves of the
Russian yoke. So, he went to Poland to fight
against Russian occupation. From that letter grew
the notion of the Croatian war with Serbia being
the modern-day version of the Spanish Civil War,
where it was, supposedly, clear-cut which side
was right and good, and which side was wrong
and evil. So, Jussi wrote back to Magnus that he
was coming. And although Jussi was received
warmly by the Croatian high command, he was
not taken-on, initially, as an instructor, but as a
combatant. As the Croatian command were
taking stock in the men and resources that they
had at their disposal, they were obliged to move
Jussi four times, before they found a unit that
could fully appreciate a warrior of Jussi's caliber.
It consisted mostly of upper-class Croatian men
and a hand-full of foreign-born soldiers who
were also looking for their very own Spanish
Civil War.

After a little less than a month of training,
Jussi's unit took advantage of a few days leave, a
couple of weeks before the offensive would
commence. As Magnus was also able to get leave
for three days, they met up in Zagreb. When they
met at the designated hotel bar, Magnus had
brought his now pregnant wife Mischa. Jussi had,
of course, seen her a few times before, and she

was as full of patriotic fervor as she had been on the other occasions. Her manner of expressing her patriotism came across to Jussi as comical because it was so incredibly absolute and beyond suspect. Indeed, she reminded Jussi of his many brothers in the French Foreign Legion. During their meal, the two brothers had so much to talk about, but because they would not start drinking until after the meal, much of what they had to say was superficial in nature. But once the alcohol started to flow freely, the mood took on a more somber note, at least for Jussi. On the one hand, Jussi was impressed with the degree of commitment, organization, and comradery he witnessed on the field during the mock maneuvers, but all of that contrasted markedly with the barroom discussions that took place during the evening. For many of the competent soldiers he practiced with turned out to be misogynists, xenophobes, homophobes, and a few of them were even open fascists. Particularly for that reason Jussi was seriously considering abandoning his unit and leaving Croatia. Mischa, Magnus's wife, became so enraged that she quickly moved toward Jussi to smack him but Magnus caught her before she could strike at Jussi. Pulling her behind him, he apologized to Jussi for his wife's behavior, and then backed away with Mischa still behind him. After having backed up about three meters from Jussi, Magnus stopped and looked at him.

"Jussi, my brother," Magnus said, "there are only two choices for men like us. Either we fight the battles that they tell us to fight, or we fight the battles that we choose to fight ourselves, but fight we must."

Jussi decided to stay with his unit, at least until Operation Storm was completed, which turned out to be a big mistake. For only three days into the operation, after 5 hours on intense of house the house fighting, what was left of Jussi's unit was relieved. They were ordered to go to a designated camp, eat, and rest to be ready to return to the field by 04:00. When Jussi finally managed to get his food, he didn't feel like eating in the mess tent, so he ate as he walked to his tent, which could accommodate 12 men. Jussi had taken a crash course in Croatian, so he could follow a bit of the language. While standing outside of his tent, finishing off the rest of his meal, Jussi noticed many men walking towards the latrines almost simultaneously, almost as if they had all gotten a bad case of *ripuli*, diarrhea, which made Jussi chuckle. But on further examination, the men were not going to the latrine. There were going beyond the latrine, into the forest. Jussi then thought he heard one of the soldiers tell his companion, *"Dobili sui ih, dobili sui ih."* "They got them, they got them." After a few seconds, Jussi found himself running behind the other soldiers who were running toward the forest. Jussi justified his own running by making sure that his Croatian brothers would treat the captured Serbs humanely, according to the Geneva Convention. But after having ran about a kilometer and a half, there were no Serbians to be found anywhere. So, where were they running to? Then, at about two kilometers from their camp, Jussi found his Croatian brothers huddled around several trees. Suddenly, someone shouted, "*Spali ih*!" "Burn them." Jussi followed the eyes of his Croatian brothers higher up in the trees and saw three bodies, hanging. The bodies belonged to non-combatants. Ind fact, it looked like they were a family. Looking above at other trees, he found more bodies hanging. After walking and inspecting other trees, he counted twelve bodies, and yes, several of them were kids. One may have even been handicapped. Wondering what they could have possible done to deserve such a death, Jussi asked what did they do? At first, he didn't understand the reply that he was given, because of the laughter that followed. The two words that stood out, though, were "*Roden*" and "*Cigani*." Jussi knew that "*Roden*" meant born, but he had no idea what "*Cigani*" meant. After repeating the word "*Cigani*" a few times, it resonated somehow with him, but he didn't know how, at least not right away. After a couple of minutes, the word "*Zigeuner*" popped into his head from the blue. Jussi knew that "*Ziguener*" is the German word for Roma people, otherwise known as Gypsies. Engulfed in sheer horror, he finally understood what was being said--their crime was that they were born Roma.

The Goddess Returns

The tears were already running down Jussi's face when he told Alex and Jerry that he was running behind the Croatian soldiers, but now the tears were streaming so profusely that he couldn't continue with his narrative. Not knowing how to comfort Jussi, Jerry stood up and said that he was going to the woodshed to make more kindling. Alex also wished that he could walk away, but the words of the shaman with the feathers in his hat came floating through Alex's living-room, "And you have to be able to help people heal themselves." After Jussi calmed down somewhat, he told Alex that by the time he had arrived, two high-ranking officers were on the scene ordering men to cut the bodies down" carefully," and an investigation of sorts was started. So, Jussi knew that this heinous crime was by no means representative of the entire Croatian armed forces. Yet, the knowledge that some of the men he was fighting alongside, some of his comrades, were fascists was a devastating blow for him

With regard to Jussi, Alex, ashamedly, felt utterly useless, and he felt somewhat relieved when Jussi said that he would go for a run to Solon and back, which was about ten miles round trip. Alex took the opportunity to check up on Jerry, and surprisingly, there was no blood on any of the kindling.

"You're a better man than I am," Alex said.

"How you mean?" Jerry asked still busy with the kindling.

"When I first started chopping wood and making kindling, especially when I made kindling, it was a real blood bath," Alex said.

"You didn't use gloves?" Jerry asked, still busy with the kindling.

"No, I'm like you, I have to feel the wood with my fingers," Alex replied.

"How's 'e doin?'" Jerry asked, changing closer to the real subject.

"Jussi, he went for a jog," Alex replied.

"I'm sorry I left. I…" Jerry dropped off.

"Don', don't worry about that Jerry," Alex tried to reassure him.

"I still feel stupid 'cuz I'm the one who got him talkin,'" Jerry admitted.

"Really, man, don't worry about that," Alex tried to say in a more reassuring tone. "Everybody has some shit that they have to wade through, everybody. And those who have people around them that love them and care about them have the best chances of getting through their shit."

"Do you care about him, or do you think i's his own problem? Jerry asked.

"Why?" Alex asked.

"You jus' met 'im," Jerry added.

"Well, Jerry, I just met you, too," Alex started, not knowing where this would lead to. "I could leave you to your drug dealing, gang-banging, and likely early death thinking, 'oh, that's his problem.'"

Alex paused because he was trying to recall that simile that Maya Angelou used to describe what a brother was with regard to James Baldwin. Alex was a bit angry with himself because he had every intention of looking the letter up, but he hadn't.

"So, when are we goin' to talk to the L.T.?" Jerry asked.

"There is no L.T.," Alex confessed.

"Then, why am I here?" Jerry asked.

Before answering the question, Alex looked, inwardly, one more time for the simile, and there it was: "brothers…are as necessary as air and as precious as love."

"Jerry, I once had a philosophy professor, Professor Nauta," Alex resumed with some degree of resolve. "During one of our classes, while deviating a bit from two other philosophers, Adam Smith and Emanuel Kant, said that you can't only use people for your own personal benefit. You must also allow yourself to be used by them, so that they can also reach their goals and aspirations. I interfered in your life, and I benefitted greatly from it."

"You mean when you took the gun off o' me?" Jerry asked.

"Yes," Alex said.

"I hear dat!" Jerry exclaimed.

"What do you mean?" Alex asked.

"You should 'a seen yo' face when you took it," Jerry said laughing. "You looked like you done busted the mother of all nuts when you took dat gun off me, like dat was somethin' you needed t' do all yo' life."

Remembering that moment and what he felt when he had the gun in his hand and imagining what Jerry had seen on his face, Alex began to laugh as well.

After a minute or two after their collective laughter had subsided, somewhat, Alex continued.

"Jerry, I'm going to ask you a question. But I want you to think about it a while before you answer it."

"What is it?" Jerry asked.

After telling Jerry that he had made enough kindling, they both returned to the dining room. Looking at the woodstove in the dining room and seeing only ambers, Alex returned to the vestibule and brought a few pieces of wood into the dining room. After he threw the two pieces of wood into the woodstove, he sat down.

Looking at Jerry and trying to muster up the courage to pose his question, Alex realized that he had to just jump into it.

"Will—you—be—my—brother?" Alex managed to ask. "Don't answer it yet, because I have to explain what it will mean. It means that you will have to give up the gang banging. You will have to give up the drugs. You will always and consistently strive to get 'A+s' in school. You will learn to speak at least two foreign languages. And of course, you will go to college and earn at least a master's degree."

"Did Mama ask you to do this?" Jerry asked.

"Yes, she did," Alex conceded, "but I'm doing this primarily because I interfered in your life and I benefitted from it."

On repeating that, Alex scanned Jerry's body language and could find no visible signs of revulsion.

"Will it also mean that I can't fuck anymore?" Jerry asked, "because I ain't promisin' dat."

"Got damn!" Alex exclaimed. "Are you doing that already, at 14?"

"Al, you don' know jus' how pushy junior and senior girls can be," Jerrry confessed. "And they don' take no no's fo' a answe'."

"No, you don't have to give that up," Alex replied, "but I see that I will have to buy you a wad load of rubber johnnies."

In the evening, Alex took Jerry and Jussi out to dinner at the only restaurant, a family restaurant, in Bozeman because he didn't feel like cooking. When they returned from the restaurant, both Jerry and Alex sat with Jussi and listened to Jussi as he spoke of his experiences in Croatia and how he met Pieter and their sessions together. That night, just before Alex turned in, he had a strange inkling to check his email, and there was indeed a very welcomed post regarding Pieter. The email was sent by a Nancy Nbulu, a nurse in a clinic in Tanzania. She had written that Pieter had contracted malaria for the third time. She added that his condition for the moment was stable, but he was in need of better treatment which they could not provide, nor did they have the resources to move him to another facility. After establishing where approximately the clinic was, and determining it's time zone—it was eight hours ahead--Alex set his alarm for 1:30 am, so he'd have ample time to make all the necessary phone calls. Then, he went to sleep.

Shortly after he had fallen asleep, Alex was summoned again to the Goddess Mother's throne room, where, again, the other goddesses were present, and, of course, /Caggen's vacant throne next to her own.

"Congratulations, Everyman," the Goddess Mother said almost as soon as his presence was announced, "We never would have thought in a million years that you would ever have made it thus far. And here you are."

Alex thanked the Goddess Mother, looked at the two panthers, which were sitting quietly, and then raised his hand to ask if he could speak further. After permission was granted to him, he begged profusely for forgiveness for raising the question if She was Inanna, the Sumerian Goddess of Heaven and Earth. Although it was clear from her body language that she didn't much care for Alex's groveling, she listened patiently without cutting him off.

"No, Everyman, you are here fair and square, as you say," She replied. "This is the third and final 'Ordeals'. All you have to do is answer this final question, and you will be home free, as you say. You will then be free to train Thunder. Are you so far as to begin?"

"Yes, your Grand Worshipfulness," Alex responded. "I am ready."

"Who are We?" the Goddess Mother asked.

While considering his reply, Alex remembered the "Wife of Bath's Tale," sensing how analogous his present position was to the rapist knight who had to find out what women wanted most of all. The analogy laid in the fact that both of their predicaments were pressing matters of life and death.

"You are the Goddess Mother," Alex started. "Everything that was came through you. Everything that is comes through you. And all that will be will come through you. Because of you, everything that is is related: people, plants, animals, insects, stars, minerals, spirits, everything is related to everything else. And through you, we become cognizant of our relationship with all that has ever existed and will exist. Through consciousness in you, everything is alive and everything is connected, even the atom as well as the electron. Through us, your children, you learn more and more about yourself. You are our mother. You are my mother."

Surprisingly, Alex was quite confident that he had nailed it. And as he looked upon the other goddesses and then to the Great Mother, yes, they were all quite pleased. After congratulating Alex for successfully "maneuvering: his way through the 'Ordeals', Alex woke up to the sound of his alarm. After a few minutes of feeling rather pleased with himself, he heard the familiar sound of thousands of tiny feet and legs scuffling and shuffling under his bed.

"So, I see that you made it in one piece," /Caggen said as soon as his human avatar had settled.

"Why wouldn't I?" Alex said full of himself.

"Alex, these are supposed to be 'Ordeals,' 'Ordeals'," /Caggen repeated, somewhat annoyed. "That entails that there is a requisite demand for excruciating woe. And as I look upon you. There is none to be found."

"I guess I passed with flying colors," Alex said. "I guess my having read all those books on panpsychism has stood me in good stead."

"Did Coti see this as the second or the third 'Ordeals'?" /Caggen asked.

"The Great Mother congratulated me on making it to the third ordeal," Alex replied.

"What exactly did she say?" /Caggen asked.

"The Great Mother said She never would have thought that I would make it in her presence for a third time," Alex answered as honestly as he could.

"Alex!" /Caggen said in a tone that was meant to set off alarm bells, "I hate being the one who has to dash delusions of grandeur. However, I genuinely believe that this excessive amount of confidence that you are harboring is misleading and a ruse that Coti has crafted for you."

"Why would the Great Mother do something like that?" Alex asked as he sat up on his bed.

"Alex, as I mentioned earlier, you are my surrogate," /Caggen said. "She has suffered greatly at my hands, just as women have suffered greatly because of what men have put them through over the millennia. The reason why she calls these tests, 'Ordeals', is because there must, by definition, be a rather intense portion of torment, distress, agony, and misery on your part, which as of yet, I have not seen."

"Are you saying that she doesn't want me to succeed?" Alex asked.

"No, not at all!" /Caggen exclaimed. "Ultimately, she does want you to succeed, but in the process, she will need to see you suffer to her satisfaction, which, if I know my wife, means that the true pain that she has in store for you will be utterly, bitterly galling. It is quite likely that it will drive you mad."

"Which is what the gods, and goddesses, do to those they wish to destroy," Alex retorted.

"Alex, this is a very grave matter!" /Caggen exclaimed.

Alex brushed it off, though, and changed the subject by asking /Caggen when he would teach Alex how to cure people. In frustration and disgust, /Caggen vanished without the customary disassembling into thousands of small, black and green praying mantises.

***

Jussi's arrival into Alex and Jerry's lives reminded Alex of John Ford's play, *The Queen*. He told me when we were together in Crete with Marjan and Sana'a when he was thinking about what Jussi's mother had to go through with his polyamorous father. I think it was because of the degree of sexual suggestiveness of Greek culture. After leafing through it, Alex understood why the relationship between /Caggen and the Goddess Mother made him think of it.

The Queen opens with a group of officers who, after having taken part in a failed insurrection, are being given a reprieve by the queen of Aragon. But their leader, General Alphonso, wasn't so lucky., at least not until the queen comes to Alphonso, only seconds before his execution, demanding that he apologizes for his actions and promise never to do it again. The queen really wants to pardon him. But Alphonso rejects her offer outright, which seems to be some kind of a twisted turn-on for the queen— something that only a guy could imagine— because the queen not only pardons Alphonso, but she also insists that they get married, which, of course, would make Alphonso king and head of state. Oh, yeah, I almost forgot to tell you why Alphonso started the insurrection—it was because the queen, the supreme leader of Aragon, was female. In other words, he was trying to save Aragon fron "ruin." Alex refers to him as being "a stone-cold, in-your-face misogynist. He even had the nerve—after becoming the king—to tell the queen that they should be completely separated for an entire week, so that he can work on his negative attitude toward her for being a woman—"⁇I be a married bachelor one se'nnight. You cannot but conceive." The queen, of course, had something far more physically vigorous in mind. But, because she was an 'obedient' wife, she gives him what he wants.

After a month, Alphonso had not made any efforts to see the queen, so she sent two members of her court to find out why. When they ask Alphonso about it, he replies with the following_ "⁇If she intend to keep her in our favour, Let us not see her." In other words, Alphonso is saying that if she wants him to continue liking her, she should stay away from him.

By this time, the queen is feeling quite miserable and dejected because, although she has held up her part of the deal with Alphonso, he has not held up his end— "⁇I yield to you, my lord, my crown, my heart, ⁇My people, my obedience. In exchange, What I demand is love." That love was not forthcoming from Alphonso.

Things even turned for the worst when the queen comes to see Alphonso herself, while her men were still with him, asking Alphonso the following—"⁇Wherein, my gracious lord, have I offended? Wherein have I transgressed against thy laws…." Alphonso's reply was obsessively cruel. Not only does he call her a whore—"⁇But that she might with safety of her honour Mix

with some hot-veined lecher, whose prone lust
⬚Should feed the rank impostume of desires,
And get a race of bastards, to whose birth I
should be thought the dad." But he also says the
following—"⬚See me no more, never. From this
time forth I hate thy sex. Of all thy sex, thee
worst." In other words, he is admitting that he
hates the female sex in general and hers
especially.

After a while, Alphonso's conviction that the
queen is 'loose' grows to the point where he
believes that she is having an affair with
Petruchi, one of her trusted advisors. Of course,
Muretto, Alphonso's most trusted advisor, fuels
the flames, regarding the queen's infidelity, kind
of like Iago, mostly because he knows that's
what Alphonso wants to hear. But from time to
time, he tells Alphonso, indirectly, how he truly
sees the queen, as a beautiful, chaste, and loving
woman.

All the while, the queen continues to love
Alphonso wholeheartedly. She even goes so far
as to order her trusted men not to move against
Alphonso.

The suspicions Alphonso harbors regarding
his wife and Petruchi pushes him to the point
where he orders the queen's execution, and the
only thing that could save her is a champion who
will fight for her honor. If the champion wins, the
queen will be considered chaste and free, but if
he loses, she dies. The funny thing is that
Alphonso starts to see the queen's beauty, and he

is in conflict. There are moments when he thinks that she is a ravishing beauty and chaste, and there are other moments when he thinks that she is as guilty as sin.

On the day of the queen's scheduled execution, not one, but three champions came to fight for her honor—Velasco (another trusted lord and advisor), Petruchi, and Muretto. Muretto, is finally able to talk sense into Alphonso, who finally sees the queen as the true person that she has always been.

Alex, along with most of the queen's chief advisers, believes that the queen should not have stayed Alphonso's execution and be rid of him, once and for all. Two days later, Alex did become more conciliatory towards Alphonso, partly because he, Alex, had always been conciliatory when it came to his relationship with /Caggen. And for Alex, /Caggen and Alphonso became bedfellows, so to speak.

"The Great Mother should have destroyed /Caggen a long time ago," Alex once told me, "just as the queen of Aragon should have followed through with Alphonso's execution. But maybe that's thinking too much like a man because the feminine principle is not about law, order, or punishment. It's more about love, compassion, understanding, patience, and forgiveness." In fact, the queen of Aragon even says this in Act I— ⬚"When law craves justice, mercy should grant life."

***

Although it was early, too early, at least for Jerry, and realizing that he had missed his alarm to call Africa, Alex washed himself, got dressed, and made his way to make milk coffee. When he entered the kitchen, Jussi was standing at the sink looking out at something through the window.

"Morning Jussi," Alex said. "Would you like to have a milk coffee?"

"What is that?" Jussi asked.

"It's two-thirds milk and one-third water with coffee, instant coffee," Alex replied.

"*Ei kiittos*," Jussi responded. "Can I have very black coffee?" Jussi asked.

"Of course," Alex answered. "Would you also like to share a cheese and champignon omelet?" Alex asked while waving the mushrooms and cheese.

Jussi declined the omelet and asked if there was any porridge. Alex looked and found some oats. While handling the oats, Alex changed his mind and returned the eggs, cheese, and mushrooms to the refrigerator. He then took out a pot to cook the oats.

"Are you lactose intolerant, or something like that?" Alex asked.

"*Ei*!" Jussi exclaimed. "I just don't like milk."

As a result of that, Alex took out a second pot, one for Jussi to cook his porridge, and another for Alex to make his own.

The Goddess Returns

After breakfast, Alex checked his email, again hoping for some news from Pieter. But there was nothing about Pieter, which made Alex feel even more uneasy. But at around 10:20 am, there was a knock at the door. Alex was chopping wood, so Jussi opened the door. It was the postwoman. She had a registered letter that required a signature. Jussi signed and took all of the mail to Alex who was now loading the wheelbarrow to load the wood into the various wood racks. After Alex had filled the woodracks, he turned his attention toward the post. Leafing the the post, a stamp of part of an elephant caught Alex's attention, so he pulled it to the front. Although the sender's name didn't ring any bells—it wasn't either of the three contacts that Pieter had left behind for Alex--the return address was Arusha, Tanzania. The letter was written by a Sister Catherine Mbele who informed Alex that Pieter had indeed contracted malaria, for a third time, and that his chances of making it didn't look hopeful. The letter was dated November 14, which was eleven days ago. As the letter was written on letterhead, there was a phone number. Needless to say that Alex dreaded making the call, but he had to do it all the same. After browsing the time differential between Arusha, Tanzania and Bozeman, Maine—Arusha was eight hours ahead--Alex decided to phone the clinic and hoped for some good news. Although Sister Mbele did not pick up the phone, the orderly who answered Alex's call did know Pieter, and he assured Alex that

Pieter's condition, although fragile, was stable. Alex was relieved to hear those words, but he was wary of false hopes, false news, and the strong possibility that they were talking about two very different people, so he asked the orderly if there were any possibility that he could speak with Pieter. Half surprised, again, Alex was quite pleased to hear the orderly say, "of course." After a few seconds of contemplating how it could be done, he gave Alex his personal cell number and asked him to call back in twenty minutes.

When Alex called, it was Pieter who answered the phone.

"Alex, is that you?" Pieter asked in a rather uncharacteristically distressed voice.

"Yeah! Piet!" Alex exclaimed. "It's me, man."

"You mean 'It is I,'" Pieter retorted.

Alex was already beginning to regret asking the orderly if it were possible to speak with Pieter directly And as Pieter started explaining that the term 'is' is a form of the verb 'to be,' which is a linking verb, linking the subject in front of the linking verb with the adjective behind the linking verb, Alex wondered what in hell possessed him to need to come in contact with Pieter.

"Man! Do you want me to come and pick your 'arse' up, or not?" Alex asked thoroughly annoyed.

"Please do!" Pieter exclaimed. "The food here is atrocious, a-tro-cious," Pieter enunciated.

Then, Pieter suddenly started speaking Afrikaans. After Alex reminded Pieter that He didn't speak Afrikaans, Pieter started speaking Dutch with a heavy, Afrikaans accent. Because the orderly was gracious enough to allow Pieter to use his phone, Alex made a point of keeping the call brief. Besides getting the details of how to get to Pieter, Alex informed him that Jussi was there, and Pieter insisted that he come with Alex because, according to Pieter, at least, Jussi was at a crucial phase of his treatment. After Alex asked Pieter if he could hold on for about a week, Pieter asked why it would take so long. That's when Alex told him about Jerry and that he would have to take Jerry back home first.

"Well, I suppose I'll just have to endure this persecution for another week," Pieter said glumly.

Alex said, "Bye," and hung-up. Afterward, he went to the vestibule and called Jerry, asking him to get dressed and come down stairs. Five minutes later, Jerry entered the dining room where Alex and Jussi were already seated.

"What up?" Jerry asked.

"Do you have any picture I.D.," Alex asked.

"Only my school card," Jerry replied.

"Do you have any other I.D. on you?" Alex asked.

"I got my social securidy card, and I got my work permit," Jerry responded as he took them out of his pants pocket.

"Is your work permit still valid?" Alex asked.

"Wha's de da'e t'day?" Jerry asked.

"The 25th of November," Alex replied.

"Why?" Jerry asked.

"My roommate is sick, and I have to go get him," Alex explained.

"Jussi's shrink doctor?" Jerry asked.

"Yeah," Alex replied. "I'm sorry Jerry, but we are going to have to do a rain check for Christmas."

"Tha's a'right," Jerry said. "I'm glad that I go' t' come this far north and see y' house, but you cain't cook worth shit, Alex."

As soon as Jerry had said that, Jussi started laughing and walked over to Jerry to shake his hand. Realizing that it was true that he couldn't cook, Alex started laughing himself.

"How do you feel about flying?" Alex asked.

"Who, me?" Jerry asked. "You askin' me?"

"Yeah, you," Alex replied.

Jerry was clearly apprehensive, so Alex gave him the spiel that flying was safer than riding in a car. But that didn't quite resonate with Jerry, so Alex brought something else to Jerry's attention.

"Jerry, if you decide to take me up on my offer, there would be times when I would be abroad, in other countries," Alex said. "That means that there will be times when you would have to fly, alone, to hook-up with me. So, if you are planning on accepting it, you should take advantage of being able to fly with me now, so later you would already be used to it."

"Do I have time t' think about it?" Jerry asked.

"I'm very sorry, Jerry, but no, there is no time because we have to book the tickets right away," Alex said regrettably, while holding his cell phone, waiting for Jerry's response.

After Jerry had consented, Alex also asked Jussi if his passport was still valid. Jussi smiled at Alex and nodded, asking Alex if he wanted to see it.

"It's just that from what you told us, you must be used to crossing borders without asking anyone's permission," Alex explained.

Jussi stood up, took his passport out of his pouch, which was hanging from his neck, and handed it to Alex. When Jussi handed it to him, it was open on the page that revealed a red stamp and a visa of the United States. Alex did inspect Jussi's date of expiration and his passport would still be valid for another three and a half years. After Alex had booked the tickets, he returned Jussi's passport to him. Jussi asked Alex if he had paid for all the tickets. When Alex admitted that he had, Jussi asked why because he could pay for himself.

"First, because Pieter told me that you had to come for your session," Alex said. "And second because I get most of my money from my wife, who got her money from her father, who, for all intents and purposes, stole it, not unlike most of the world's millionaires, billionaires and trillionaires. My wife and I at least put it to some good use this way. If that's all right?"

"*Olet hullu, mutta pidän sinusta.*"

241

"Yeah, my wife also says I'm crazy, and I like you, too," Alex replied.

After printing out the e-tickets and handing them out, Alex informed both Jerry and Jussi that they would be leaving at 2:00 am. He also informed them that he would be ordering pizza for dinner. Loud cheers roared from both Jussi and Jerry.

At 1:00 am, Alex woke up, went to the bathroom, and proceeded to wake up Jerry. Alex then went to wake up Jussi, but Jussi's bed was made, his sleeping bag was rolledup, and his rucksack was packed. There was no sign of Jussi, though. While Alex was shaving, he smelled the coffee, and as Jerry went down the stairs, Alex heard him shout excitedly.

"Tha' smells li'e buttered toast!"

They ended up leaving at 2:22 am because Jussi had forgotten to pack his tent, which was still standing in Alex's backyard.

They arrived at the Portland airport at 4:32 am. The customer-service attendant was reluctant to issue Jerry a boarding pass because of his not having a governmen-issued I.D. with a photo. But when the shift supervisor got involved, she couldn't keep her eyes off of Jussi. Then, she started talking to him, asking him about his relationship with Alex and Jerry. Jussi simply told her the truth that they were going to Charleston, SC to drop Jerry off at his home, which his I.D. could confirm, and then he and Alex would go to pick up a friend who had contracted malaria. Jerry also reminded Alex to show her the letter from his mother. Fortunately, the three of them were able to board the plane, but not before the three of them handed over their phone numbers.

"Was dat smooth or what! Jerry exclaimed. "She asked f' all our numbe's jus' t' git Jussi's."

Jussi started laughing. When Alex asked him what was so funny, Jusssi told him that once he leaves America, he would not be using that Sim card anymore. So, that supervisor will be very angry with Alex and Jerry when she finds out that her plan to get in contact with Jussi failed.

Before he had gone to bed the previous night, Jerry called his mother to tell her that he would be back home, "tomorrow." He also asked her to ask cousin Mickey if he could pick them up at 10:30 am and to get his money.

When they arrived at the Charleston airport, Mickey was there waiting. When he saw them, the driver greeted them warmly, hugging Jerry, Alex, and Jussi, after Alex told Jussi in Finnish that their driver was his friend.

"*Han on minun ystävä.*"

Surprisingly, the landlady was there to open the door when they arrived at the house. After she kissed and hugged Jerry, she looked at Jussi and then at Alex and became visibly worried.

"Alex, do you know how to say a threesome in French?" the landlady asked.

"Menage trois," Alex replied.

"Tha's righ'," she concurred. "Jerry, did they make you take part in a what he just said?"

"Wha's dat?" Jerry asked.

"A threesome," the landlady replied.

"An' what is dat supposed t' be?" Jerry asked, somewhat annoyed.

"Damn!" Jerry's mother exclaimed, "dey don' teach you shit a' da' school! I's when three people, us'ally consentin' adults, ha' sex wit' each othe', all three togethe' a' the same time."

Jerry just rolled his eyes at her and went up to his room.

"I guess I'll take dat as a 'no,'" the landlady concluded.

Alex quickly settled with his driver, because they had to get back to the airport.

"So much?" Mickey asked when he opened the envelope that Alex had handed him.

"I would not have made it on the bus if it weren't for you, Mr. Mickey," Alex said.

"So, you di' make i' on de bus?" Mickey asked.

"Yes, I did," Alex replied.

"Di' you fin' wha' tyou was lookin' f'?" the driver asked.

"Yes, yes, I did," Alex replied.

"Is you okay?" the driver asked.

"No," Alex replied, "but, now, I at least know why I'm not okay."

"I' mighty sorry t' heia' dat," the driver said.

"Don't be," Alex responded.

When Alex extended his hand toward Mickey and said, "Thank you," Mickey threw his arms around Alex and hugged him very warmly.

"You still want me t' take you gen'emens to de airpor', righ'?" Mickey asked after the embrace.

"Of course," Alex replied.

12
The Crux of Jussi's Back Story

Alex and Jussi checked-in two hours and seventeen minutes before their flight's departure time. And while they were looking for their gate, Alex recieved a vibration on his phone. Although it was his landlady's phone number, the text was from Jerry, and it simply read, 'YES!'

After Alex and Jussi had found their gate and settled down, Alex called his former landlandy's number to speak with Jerry. Surprisingly, Jerry answered the phone.

"So, it's official now," Alex started. "We are brothers. I'm calling because I've been thinking about something."

"What up?" Jerry asked.

"Although we will be together during holidays and your school vacations, it will still be difficult for you to be the model scholar if you are doing it on your lonesome," Alex said

"It'll be aw righ'," Jerry responded."

"No, it won't!" Alex insisted. "Do you have three or four people around you who are serious about their education?"

"You mean i' my class?" Jerry asked.

"Or other ninth graders in your school who are serious students," Alex added.

"Yeah," Jerry answered, "one boy and three girls. DJ is the boy's name. He like boys, though."

"That doesn't matter," Alex said. "Many of my schoolmates are gay and lesbian. I even had a trans-gender professor. They were all wonderful people. Jerry, do you think they would be interested in starting a study group with you? There will also be tutors for you."

"Wha' tyou mean?" Jerry asked.

"You will have a math-science tutor, an English-history tutor, and an art tutor," Alex said. "Because my little brother has to earn A's and B's...Jerry, I just think it will be easier if you have a support group around you."

"I git it," Jerry said. "I'll ask 'em."

Just before they hung up, Jerry's mother got on the phone. She thanked Alex for what he will be doing for Jerry. When she asked him how to send him back his rent money, he told her to take her kids somewhere nice with it.

While hey were waiting for their flight to New York, which was the first leg of their itinerary to Kilamajaroo, Tanzania, the silence between Alex and Jussi felt unbareably awkward for Alex, so much so that he constantly thought of what the healer in Rapid City told him, 'I was told that you have to learn how to do four things--go to where the Great Spirit is, go to where the ancestors reside, make rain, and help people heal themselves.' Alex had no idea where to begin with Jussi, but he was curious as to what Pieter was doing that Jussi would come all the way from Europe to have his session. Alex thought to himself, 'Although Pieter may be a very capable quack, he is still just a quack and a bit of a flake. If he can help people heal themselves, surely I can do it.' So, Alex decided to investigate something that he was wondering about when Jussi first told him that he had fought for Croatian independence. He remembered that Josip Broz Tito was not only the president of Former Yugoslavia, but he was also the commander of the Partisan during WWII. Alex aalso knew that Tito was a communist, but he didn't know who controlled the Yugoslavian government. While he was looking it up, Alex found out that the Axis forces, Germany as well as Italy, were vying for influence in Yugoslavia, so they both invaded and annexed Yugoslavia in a matter of a couple of weeks, starting from April 1941. The Independent State of Croatia was established soon there after, and Ante Pavelic, the leader of the infamous Ustashe, came to lead it.

The Ustashe was a brutal, Croatian ultra-nationalist, fascist organization that, among other things, believed that Croatians were a Germanic people, not Slavic. As such, they took the handbook of their nazi brethren, nazi racial theory, and regarded Serbs, Jews, and Roma people as being subhuman, and did their damnedest to exterminate them, all of them. Besides the Germans, Italians, and later the Chetniks, Tito also had to fight the Ustashe, who were so horrifically brutal that senior German officers sent communiques to the German High Command complaining about Ustashe atrocities.

While Alex was taking all of this in, he kept taking glimpses of Jussi, wondering how he would respond when Alex informs him of this. At one point, Jussi returned his glance at Alex just as Alex looked at him.

"Alex, why you look at me so much?" Jussi asked.

Alex was taken aback by the candidness of the question. And although Alex did make an effort to find a plausible lie, there weren't any to be found. As a result. there was only the truth.

"Have you ever heard of Josip Broz Tito?" Alex asked.

"Of course!" Jussi exclaimed. "He was the president of Yugoslavia."

"What else do you know about him?" Alex asked.

"He was communist," Jussi added.

"Is that it?" Alex asked.

"I'm not communist," Jussi replied, shrugging his shoulders, as if Alex were insinuating that he should know more about a dead communist.

"During World War II, he was the leader of the Partisan," Alex said, wonderinging whether he should continue. "The Partisan resisted the Nazis, the Italians, and the Ustashe."

"What is Ustashe?" Jussi asked.

"They were the government in Croatia when Yugoslavia was occupied by Germany and Italy during World War II" Alex answered. "They were like the Vichy government in occupied France during World War II."

"They were Nazis?" Jussi asked terrified and alarmed.

"Yes, they were fascists," Alex replied, looking closely at Jussi, whose hands were now covering his face.

After a a couple of minutes, Jussi composed himself sufficiently enough to speak.

"Alex, did you just learn about this?" Jussi asked.

"I knew that Tito commanded the Partisan, the resistance, but I didn't know who he was fighting," Alex replied.

"You know this from history?" Jussi asked.

Alex gestured in the affirmative.

"That means I should know of this, too!" Jussi declared. "*Voi vittu!*"

Alex was shocked to hear *Voi vittu*,' because he remembered when his former Finnish girl friend had told him that it was the strongest cussing that could be done in Finnish. And because of the shocked expression around Alex's eyes, Jussi burst first into laughter. And then, he cried. That's when it dawned on Alex that Jussi had assumed that Alex was not familiar with 'voi vittu.' Although Alex's former Finnish girl friend could never pinpoint a worthy English equivalent, because of the way that people used it the handfull of times he'd heard it spoken, Alex considered it to be comparable to 'mother fuck,' but a hundred times more powerful. After about five minutes, Jussi started to pull himself together, but several times when he looked at Alex, he couldn't help laughing, which also brought along with it a few more tears. At one point, Jussi stood up and gestured to Alex that he was going to wash his face. A few minutes later, Jussi returned to his seat, and the first announcement that boarding would soon begin was made.

Once they were in their seats, Jussi started listening to older Finnish pop bands such as Eppu Normalli. Alex was reading from his eBook reader. After about an hour in flight, Jussi took out his ear buds and moved in a manner that at least suggested to Alex that he was going to stand up. But Jussi remained seated, and for a while, he stared ahead, looking at the back of the seat that was in front of him. After about fifteen minutes of this, Jussi started speaking.

"What other things did you read about those Croatian Nazis?" Jussi asked.

"The Ustashe?" Alex asked. "They killed hundreds of thousands of people."

"What people?" Jussi asked.

"They killed Jewish people, ethnic Serbian people, Roma people, and Croatian people who were against them," Alex replied.

"Alex, that is ethnic cleaning," Jussi said. "You speak German?"

"I try," Alex replied.

"Is Roma people the same as Ziguener people?" Jussi asked.

"Yes," Alex responded.

"*Perkele*!" Jussi exclaimed, then he looked at Alex to see if he knew this swear word as well.

Alex did know it, but he didn't want to see Jussi cry again, so Alex acted as though he hadn't heard anything. Jussi was a bit surprised that there was no reaction from Alex because 'perkele,' which means 'fuck,' is far more common than 'voi vittu.'

Jussi then started telling Alex about the time when he moved from his family's potato farm in Hämeenlinna in the south of Finland to his maternal grandparents' home in Kemi. This was around the time when his parents separated. Jussi added that although Kemi is more to the north of Finland, it doesn't quite reach the Artic Circle.

Initially, Jussi understood that his mother left his father because his father went crazy. It started after he, Jussi's father, whose name was Mauno, read a newspaper article about colorado bugs being found among imported goods on a ship that originated from Poland. After re-establishing the fact that all Finnish people can put away a decent amount of alcohol, adding that only the Irish can drink more, Jussi explained how, as those reports continued to trickle in, his father drank more and more heavily until Jussi's mother became fed up and left.

Jussi had an older sister, Sisko, but as she was already married when their parents separated, it was only he and his mother that moved in with his grandparents. Jussi, though, didn't like the move because he had no friends in Kemi. But he was able to make new friends quickly, and Kemi is where Jussi started to think seriously about making a career out of the military.

Kemi is also where he fell in love for the first time. In his folk art class, there was a Finnish-Roma girl who he was fond of. She wore the traditional Roma costume, which to Jussi, was very stylish. She and her clothes were impeccably clean, and she always smelled like roses. Jussi loved her long skirts and her long, braided, brown hair. Her name was Merja, and Jussi wanted desperately to talk to her. But she was shy and stayed aloof from everyone, including the other girls in the class.

On a couple of occasions, though, Jussi did see her leaving school at the end of the day with a Roma boy, who looked just like her, and a girl. Jussi found out that the boy was her twin brother, and the girl was of Tartar decent, a Turkic people, and her best friend.

Merja's brother's name was Olipekka, and he loved playing soccer. Although Jussi was into fishing and hunting, and couldn't see the point in chasing a ball up and down a field, since his experience of playing soccer never involved actually having possession of the ball, he decided to play to connect with Merja by means of her brother. But Olipekka was just as aloof as his twin sister, if not more so, which meant that Jussi would have to find another way to make contack with Merja.

The opportunity presented itself one day as Merja and Soraja, the girl from Tartar decent, were waiting for Olipekka. As Jussi had quit the soccer team, he made a point of being at their meeting spot in order to at least see Merja. While the girls were engaged in their own private conversation, three boys confronted them, and one of the boys knocked Merje's books out of her hands. The three boys walked away laughing. Before Merja and Soraja could kneel down to pick up the books and papers, Jussi spoke to them.

"No! They must pick them up!"

As Jusssi ran toward those boys, he wondered if he had frightened the girls more than the boys had done. Jussi told Alex about his frustration with the slow, simmering kind of anger that only the people from the northern parts can have. And as Jussi was taller, fitter, and very muscular, the three boys decided, wisely, that it would be in their best interest if they apologised to the girls, pick up their books and papers, and promise never to offend them again. After the boys had done so, Jussi asked the girls if they were satisfied, and they were.

Soraja, although she was the shyest of them all, was eager to keep Jussi around because she felt safer with him. So, Merja pushed Soraja to invite him to eat lunch with them. After a couple of weeks, they started seeing each other outside of school as well. And as Merja learned more about Jussi, the situation between his parents, his military aspirations, and his physical prowess, her feelings and thoughts gravitated more and more toward him. Merja's brother, Olipekka, did like Jussi, but he was all too aware of how his parents, especially his mother, would feel when she found out that her oldest daughter was seeing a 'Finnish' boy.' Olipekka tried to bring this fact to his sister's attention on several occasions, but Merja wouldn't listen. She couldn't listen, for she was in love. Ruing the day when his mother would find out about Jussi, Olipekka was becoming desperate because the family was central in his culture, and his mother was the kind of person who was brutally consistent. In other words, if she were to disown Merja verbally, because of her relationship with Jussi, for example, their mother would not relent, regardless of feeling regret for having said it.

So, Olipekka decided to warn Jussi about his mother. That was around the time when Jussi found out something new about his father. Besides being paranoid about the colorado bugs eating all of his potato plants, Jussi's mother told her son a piece of juicy news about his father when Jussi asked if it were possible that they return to the farm. After she told Jussi that there will definitely not be a reconciliation, she went on and explained why. She was quick to tell Jussi that his father's insanity was not the real reason why there wouldn't be a reconciliation because most people were crazy, if not everyone. The only difference is that some insane people can live well with their insanity and others can't. And Jussi's father could still function despite the specter of colorado bugs. So, that wasn't the real issue.

The 'real' issue, however, sprang up right after the last time that they had had made love. While his mother was recovering from a rather intensive orgasm, Jussi's father decided that that was the best time to inform his wife that he would like to have a more open relationship with her so that they could have sex with other people. Despite the anticlimax of her orgasm, i.e, killing it after the fact, she didn't want to make any hasty decisions. And two days later, when she initiated foreplay, Jussi's father committed a cardinal sin, coitus interruptus, when he again mentioned his desire to have multiple sexual partners while remaining married. To be clear, she didn't have that much of a problem with her husband's extra-marital fantasies, for she was well aware that men were the true freaks in the world. They have always been, and they will always be. Men can't help that they are twisted, they just can't. But it was his timing that irked her so, always around the time of coitus, union, as if he were insinuating something. She never told Jussi what that something was, of course.

It was around this time when Olipekka told Jussi about Romani culture in general and his mother in particular. By now, Jussi and Merja had developed a very sensuous relationship, having explored each other's bodies, as well as their own, quite extensively. At this stage of their relationship, sexual intercourse was imminent. But Jussi was troubled by what Olipekka had told him about his family, so much so that he had to talk to Merja about it.

"Is it possible that your parents would disown you for us being together?" Jussi asked.

"I don't care," Merja replied.

Because all of the relationships that Jussi knew of, except for his maternal grandparents, all ended in some form of separation, Jussi decided to end his relationship with Merja.

"Miksi?" Merja cried, which means 'why.'

"Boyfriends, lovers, and husbands come and go, but family has got to always be family, no matter what," Jussi replied.

Jussi told this to Alex because he regarded all Romani people as being part of Merja's family. As such, he would never hurt them. Still, Alex could not get to the root cause of Jussi's feelings of guilt.

13
Straight from the Horse's Mouth

When their plane arrived in New York, the purser called Alex's name over the loud speaker. Jussi couldn't see what was happening, but two men in suits came on board and escorted Alex off of the plane. Afterward, the rest of the passengers could disembark.

When Alex asked them questions, such as what is this about, and what will happen to his luggage, they remained silent. When they exited the airport, they told Alex to put his hands behind his back, and they cuffed him. And just before they got into the car that pulled up, they placed a black cloth sack over Alex's head. The trip was short and silent. When they got out of the car, Alex's hands remained cuffed, and his head remained covered. After walking into what sounded like a busy kitchen of a restaurant or hotel, they entered an elevator that went down. After about a minute, the sack was pulled off, the cuffs were removed, and one of Alex's captures told him to wait. Only Alex's two captures were in the space, which looked like a small conference room. After about ten minutes, the president of the United States entered the room. The president was on his cell phone when he entered the room but the call had ended by the time he was handed a file. However, before the president could open the file, one of the older gentlemen in his entourage walked up close to Alex.

"In Sumerian as well as in biblical mythologies, the gods, and God, made humans to do their work. We, the 0.1%, are the descendants of the gods. You have always worked for us, and you will always work for us," an elderly gentleman with white, short-cropped hair around his ears, much in the fashion of the Nazi esthetic said.

"Did that bastard really say that?" the president asked, looking incredulously at the man and the rest of his entourage.

"Yes, he did, Mr. President," several secret service men said in unison.

"Jason, Jason," the president repeated, trying to draw the man's attention, "what's' our motto, hunh? A compliant slave is a happy slave, and a happy slave is what?"

"A happy slave has no idea that he's a slave," Jason said.

"Hey, you had me worried there for a minute," the president said ostensibly relieved. "That's right, a happy slave has no idea that he's a slave. So shut the fuck up!"

Returning to his file, the president quickly leafed through the handful of pages, and then, he looked at Alex.

"So, another man who's trying to rid the world of patriarchy, masculine domination" the president said. "Why?"

"If you follow patriarchy to its logical conclusion, the human race will become extinct," Alex replied.

"The only reason why there is order in the world is because of white, western men. And, if push comes to shove, the powers that be will allow a man of color to hold the reigns, for a while. But a woman, hell no! Remember, even three million more votes can't win a woman a presidential election. In other words, fuck what the people want!"

"You have just conceded that there is no democracy, at least not in America," Alex said.

"How about that!" the president said, feigning astonishment. "Al, get with the program. It's not about democracy, nor has it ever been. If it were, then the franchise, the vote, would be sacrosanct. Do you happen to know how many tens of thousands of people were robbed of their vote in Florida alone? 'The hanging chet.' My God, that was a brilliant play!"

Alex started to speak, but the president cut him off.

"We found out a long time ago that most people don't really care about abstract things such as democracy, freedom, truth, justice, equality or the rest of it. Al, have you ever heard of *panem et circenses*?"

"Of course," Alex said, "bread and circuses."

"Most people are selfish and greedy, Al," the president added. "The powers that be realized a long time ago that as long as you have a system that allows them to continue being greedy and selfish, along with some smoke and mirrors, you can control them."

"Wow!" Alex exclaimed, "you are actually smart."

"Only smart!" the president exclaimed. "What other multi-billionaire president can convince tens of millions of poor, working-class stiffs as yourself that he has your best will at heart while he's taking their healthcare and food stamps from them? Who? I'm a goddamn genius!"

"Mr. President," an aide said.

"I got it," the president said. "Al, I like you, so if you promise to cease and desist with this Indian prophecy thing, which will supposedly lead to the downfall of patriarchy, I'll make this go away. Can you do that?"

"I don't want to end the masculine principle," Alex said.

"What do you want, then?" the president asked.

"I just want to temper the masculine principle with the feminine principle, to reach a balance between them."

"That means women would become our equals like in the Minoan civilization," the president said. "Then, we would have to compete with them on an equal footing."

"What's so bad about that?" Alex asked.

"Do you believe this guy!!" the president exclaimed. "Mr. English teacher, which are better students, boys or girls?"

"Girls are," Alex confessed.

"That's right, Al," the president concurred. "The only advantage we have over women is the psychology of our brute strength."

"You mean they fear us," Alex said.

"Alex, I don't want to kick a stuffed pig around the backyard with my sons while my wife and daughters are out closing the big deals in the marketplace and congress," the president said referring to something from ancient Greece.

"So, it's we who fear them," Alex said.

"Jason," the president continued, what's the name of that shithole, you know, the one where the president along with her entire cabinet are females? you know, where the men sit around in their underwear, looking at each other while they try to get drunk on that three percent beer? Hell no! Not here! Not in the good ole U.S. of A! Not on my watch! Not on my watch, goddammit!"

"New Zealand, Mr. President," a secret service agent said.

"New Zealand is definitely not a shithole!" Alex interjected.

"No, it's Finland!" Jason insisted. "The soft, easy way is not going to work with this one!"

"Neither is Finland!" Alex added. "They both are far more democratic than we ever will be!"

"You've given me no choice, Al," the president said in a regretful tone as he signaled his men.

At that moment, a loud, scurrying sound could be heard from behind the door of an adjacent room. The president told two of the secret-service men to check it out. But they could not open the door. They could turn the knob, but the door simply wouldn't open. Alex started smiling because he recognized the sound.

"Al, do you know what's behind door number one?" the president asked.

"Yes," Alex said, "I think I do."

"Would you care to enlighten the rest of us?" the president asked.

"It's Eshu Legba," Alex replied. "It's Elohim, it's Satan, it's Shiva, It's Dionisius. He's also known as /Caggen."

Jason started laughing, saying that Alex was mad. The mythologies had gone to his brain. Alex retorted by saying that the mythologies are true. Then, everyone except for Alex started laughing.

Alex then walked to the door and opened it. /Caggen was smiling from ear to ear. One of the secret-service men took out his gun and moved toward /Caggen while the other stepped in front of the president. The president pushed the secret-service agent out of his way and moved quickly to the other one.

"You better put that gun away," the president urged the other secret-service agent, "before you wind up shooting yourself in your own ass hole, Nick. Come on, put it away."

"Who is this?" another elderly gentleman asked uneasily.

"If I'm not mistaken," the president said, "this must be the Lord. Lord meet everyone, everyone meet the Lord."

He doesn't look anything like Max von Sydow," another billionaire in the president's entourage said.

"Of course not," the president responded. Before 8,500 years ago, there weren't any white people in Europe. Everyone was brown and black."

"Malarkey!" Jason exclaimed, "I'm not black.

"That's true," the president interjected. "You're probably not black, but you are brown. At least you come from brown people as do all of us."

"If that's true, when did people start turning white?" one of the secret-service agents asked.

"Somewhere around 8,500 years ago," Alex answered. "Somewhere in present-day Turkey. The first fair-skinned, blond-haired people was among the first people who took to agriculture, which was also around the time when women's bodies became a hot commodity, give or take a few thousand years."

That's all academic," the president said clearly annoyed. "After all these millennia, you grace us with your presence. What do we owe this honor?"

"Our covenant," /Caggen said.

"Would you like to amend it?" the president asked.

"I wish to terminate it," /Cagged said.

At that moment the president and his entire entourage looked at Alex.

"Lord, for millennia, we have ruled the world according to your precepts," the president said.

"And I have only been pleased with you," /Caggen replied.

"Then, if I may ask, Lord, why end the covenant now?" the president asked nervously.

"Edward, our covenant is killing everyone, and I include myself when I say everyone," /Caggen admitted. "You will cease and desist any further actions against Alex and his daughter Thunder."

/Caggen turned toward Alex and told him to be on his guard because he was convinced that the Goddess Mother was planning something big for him, and then he transformed into thousands of little, black and green praying mantises that made their way to the adjacent room, and the door closed of its own accord when the last mantis left the conference hall.

"So, I guess the gig is up boys, it's over," the president said in a defeated tone

"I guess you'll have to get used to kicking the stuffed pig around with your sons and grandsons," Alex said as he left.

14
Pieter and Alex Reunite

Forty minutes later, Alex was back at JFK, and
he found Jussi waiting at their gate. Jussi was so
relieved to see Alex that he walked up to Alex
and hugged him.

From JFK, they flew to Amsterdam, and from
there, they flew to Kilimanjaro, Tanzania.
Although they both slept during most of the flight
to Kilimanjaro, Jussi was curious about the
Ustashe, so much so that he wanted to know the
gory details. Alex was hoping that he could leave
it at mutilations, but Jussi didn't know what it
meant, So, Alex told him that they cut of
people's organs. Jussi gestured toward his private
parts. Alex nodded, and to drive it home, Alex
told Jussi that he had read that they cut the
breasts of Serbian women off.

"Were the Serbs the victim then?" Jussi asked
surprised.

"I'm not sure, but it seemed that way to me,"
Alex replied.

"Did they hang *Kaaleet*, I mean Roma
people?" Jussi asked.

"I don't know, but I wouldn't put it past
them," Alex replied. "I mean to say if they did, I
wouldn't be surprised."

Jussi needed to know if the Ustashe hung
people, Romani and Serbians, so he asked Alex if
he would find it out for him. But after a few

minutes, Jussi shouted, "*Jasenovac*!" A minute later, Jussi looked at Alex with tears in his eyes.

"*Jasenovac* was a Croatian-run concentration camp," Jussi said. "Most of their victims were Serbian people. And I was told that the Serbians were the bad guys. I should have known this."

"The Independent State of Croatia, as part of occupied Yugoslavia, committed genocide against Serbians, Jews, and Roma." Alex said. "That means that many were killed, forced to leave their homes and country, and they were forced to give up their religion."

"*Etninen puhdistus*!" Jussi exclaimed, alarmed in Finnish.

"What?" Alex asked.

"Ethnic cleaning," Jussi translated. "I should have known this."

For the remainder of their travel to Tanzania, they both were silent. But Alex couldn't help thinking just how far reaching /Caggen's actions had been and the fact that he will never really face a trial or be punished for creating and spreading patriarchy and its woes onto and throughout the world.

While reflecting on his time with the president and his entourage in that conference room, Alex wondered what that one iconic aspect of the patriarch was. After a few minutes, an answer came to him. He didn't know if it would be the definitive answer, but it did seem likely for the moment. It was the belief, the conviction, that whatever he thinks, regardless of how egregiously ensconced they are in the absolute unconscionable—the endless and meaningless wars, the continued saga of denying women the absolute right to their own bodies, revolving-door disenfranchisements, illegal revocations of citizenship, suspect misogyny, homophobia, the genocidal war on nature, xenophobia, etc.-- that it is right, and justifiably so.

When they arrived at the airport in Kilimanjaro, Tanzania, Jussi and Alex made their way through customs, baggage claim, and the car rental, where they rented a jeep. It was Jussi who insisted on getting a jeep, even before they exited the airplane. Surprisingly, Jussi had a functional GPS that actually got them to the clinic where Pieter was recuperating. When they arrived, Alex was a bit apprehensive because he was afraid that Pieter's condition had reversed. But that was by no means the case. Pieter was sitting up and drinking tea when Alex and Jussi walked through the clinic's doors.

"*Kayf a hal, habibi*?" Pieter shouted, smiling from ear to ear. "At last, I am saved!"

"We're not the ones who caught malaria, so we should be asking you how you are doing," Alex said, as he walked up to Pieter's bedside and hugged him warmly.

"My! My! My!" Pieter exclaimed. "Is that love or what!"

The head nurse came to Pieter's bedside and enquired about Alex and Jussi's relationship with Pieter. The way in which she pulled Alex aside brought back the previous ominous thoughts he entertained before he entered the clinic.

"Mr. Madden," the head nurse started, "there was a moment when we thought we were going to lose Dr. Botha, but he has pulled through. Yet, he is not yet out of the woods."

"What is it?" Alex asked anxiously.

"He will still need to take his medicines. Otherwise, he could very well die," the head nurse stressed.

"I will see to it that he takes his medicine," Alex said.

"And on time," the head nurse added.

"Yes, and on time," Alex repeated.

"If you can promise me this, then, I will release Dr. Botha to your care," the head nurse said.

Alex extended his hand toward the nurse, and they shook on it. As they returned to Pieter's bedside, the head nurse informed Piter that she had released him to Alex's care and that he must be diligent with regard to his medicines. After she said, "Godspeed," to Pieter, he tried to pinch her bottom one last time. But she knew how to gracefully evade this attempt without having to turn her back.

As Pieter was getting dressed, Jussi was collecting Pieter's things, and Alex collected Pieter's medicines, getting a sense of how often Pieter would need to take each one.

"Alex, when are your due to return to Maine?" Pieter asked.

"I bought a one-way ticket," Alex said. "Since, we'd be flying back together, I waited.

"Good!" Pieter exclaimed.

"Why is that good?" Alex asked.

"It's good because I still have one consignment of medicines to deliver," Pieter replied.

"Okay, where do we have to go?" Alex asked.

"You will be happy to know that it is around Lake Victoria," Pieter replied.

"Where exactly are we going?" Alex asked, stressing 'exactly'.

"The clinic is in Uganda," Pieter replied.

"Where in Uganda?" Alex asked drably while being re-introduced to life with his long-time roommate.

"We shall have to go to the Bidi-Bidi Refugee Settlement in north-western Uganda," Pieter replied.

"Oh! Shit!" Alex exclaimed. "Does this mean that we are going to have to deal with the Lord's Resistance Army?"

"We might," Pieter replied, "but don't worry. I'll protect you."

"Fuck that!" Alex exclaimed.

"I'm joking, Alex," Pieter said, laughing. "The Acholi-Pii Refugee Settlement was closed, and its inhabitants were moved to two new refugee settlements in western Uganda."

Alex wasn't laughing.

"If I see anyone that even remotely resembles Alice Lakwena or Joseph Kony, I will fuck you up!" Alex exclaimed.

At that moment, the orderly, who nursed Pieter beck to health, entered the room and addressed both Alex and Jussi, asking which of them had taken Pieter into his care. Alex gestured with his hand, and the orderly presented him with a bill with both hands and left.

"What the fuck is this?" Alex asked while looking at the bill, and then his eyes turned to Pieter.

"The lesser sum is the aggregate of my medical expenses," Pieter answered, "and the larger sum stems from the clinic for so graciously permitting me to use their reserve generator in order to keep my vital medicines cool."

"It's very considerate of them to have converted the shillings to dollars," Alex said sarcastically. "I realy hope these people accept plastic."

"They do, Alex," Pieter said. "They do."

Jussi assumed responsibility for navigating a route to the Bidi-Bidi Refugee Settlement, which housed, for the most part, South-Sudanese refugees. He also managed to secure the jeep to theback of the truck to tow it.

It took two and a half days for them to get to the Bidi-Bidi Refugee Settlement. The customs officials were claiming that Pieter's papers for transporting medicines weren't in order. Initially, Alex became angry with Pieter, but on closer examination, based on a checklist that the customs officials had provided, Alex realized that Pieter did, in fact, dot all of the necessary 'i's' and crossed all of the adjoining 't's.' Then, it dawned on Alex what was really happening.

"These fucks are corrupt!" Alex exclaimed. "They're expecting a bride."

"Yes, Alex, it is, indeed, better to be late than to have never arrive," Pieter concurred. "But we are not going to pay them a single, solitary, rand."

"Then, we may be here for some time," Alex said.

"It's about the principle of the thing, Alex!" Pieter added. "We are trying to deliver sorely needed medicines for hundreds of thousands of displaced people, and these officials are exploiting that fact. Shame on them!"

"We've already been here for almost four hours," Alex said. "This may turn out to be an entrenched war of attrition."

"No matter how long it takes, we shall prove victorious!" Pieter exclaimed.

"Pieter, I believe we will have to rethink that strategy," Alex said.

"Why?" Pieter demanded.

"Some of the medicines in the back require cooling, right?" Alex asked.

"Of course," Pieter replied.

"Then, there will be a point in time when we will have to recharge the batteries that are keeping the medicines cool," Alex said. "And I have a very funny feeling that these guys will not be so generous with their electricity," Alex said.

"So, are you suggesting that we pay them?" Pieter asked.

Before Alex could respond, Jussi jumped into the conversation and told Pieter that that's how much of Africa works. Although Alex agreed that the customs officials would have to be paid, he didn't want to give them money. So, he asked Pieter if he, by any chance, was carrying any contraband, such as alcohol or cigarettes or chocolate. Fortunately, Pieter did have a couple of bottles of whiskey and four cartons of cigarettes that were intended for "some relatives in South Africa."

Alex was about to say that they were not going to South Africa, but he suddenly remembered that at some point he was due to meet his 13-year-old self, and he remembered what Thunder's mother told him about a coyote man, a trickster being the only one who could bring him to the place where he was when he first became a man. And although it was inconceivable for that place to be in South Africa, or anywhere else in Africa, for that matter, Alex wasn't about to lose Pieter out of his sight. They ended up giving the two highest ranking customs officials each a carton of cigarettes, and they were immediately on their merry way. After a few hours of driving, Jussi decided that it was better to pitch a camp at a truck stop where there would be lots of people present all the time. Alex was also able to find a portable generator that could recharge the batteries, so the medicines could remain chilled. However, there was quite a bit of noise and even a fight, at one point. So, Jussi and Alex had a rough time staying asleep, but Pieter slept right through everything.

The next day, after they broke camp and ate their breakfast, they took off, moving ever closer to the Bidi-Bidi Refugee Settlement. Jussi wanted to drive the whole day, but Alex insisted on a division of labor. Jussi would drive till around noon, and Alex would drive till around nightfall, with breaks, of course. Shortly after they started on the road, Alex fell asleep. Jussi just smiled and kept driving. Since Pieter was fully awake, Jussi took advantage of the time that they had together to finally have his session.

At about 6:45 pm, Jussi woke up and asked Alex where they were. Alex was sure that he was still on the right road, but he wasn't sure about where they were because sometimes there was a lack of signs. When they finally got their collective bearings, it was Pieter who told them that they were only four hours away from the Bidi-Bidi Refugee Settlement. Instead of stopping for the night, they decided to drive through to Bidi-Bidi. They were all pretty excited that they would be at the Bidi-Bidi Refugee Settlement within the next few hours. For Pieter, it would mean Mission Accomplished. As long as Jussi was in Africa, he feared being apprehended by the Legion, who would undoubtedly leave no stone unturned to find Magnus. So, he wanted to get out of Africa as soon as possible. Alex knew that he was going to have to confront his 13-year-old self, so he wanted to get back to the United States as soon as possible to get it over with. But of course, the Bidi-Bidi Refugee Settlement was farther than Pieter had thought. It was actually six hours away. And as the gas stations were closed, it was good that Jussi also insisted on filling up the tanks and bringing along two reserve 20-liter jerry cans. Alex was so incredibly livid, that he pulled over and went for a ten minute walk around the truck. When he got back on, Jussi drove the rest of the way to Bidi-Bidi. They arrived at Bidi-Bidi at 2:00 am. Since Pieter and Alex were already sleeping, Jussi simply pulled over, turned the ignition off, and fell asleep at the wheel.

More times than not, Alex tends not to remember his dreams when he awakens, if the sleep was particularly rough. But on this occasion, not only could he remember every single dream that he had dreamt that night, but he also believed that they were all in some way significant in that they were all trying to tell him something. His unconscious was clearly trying to bring several things to the attention of his conscious self.

In one dream, there was his father, who was desperately trying to get away from something, something that was most terrifying to him. Alex tried to determine what it was that his father was running away from, but he was unable to see what it was. For Alex, the truly surprising aspect of that dream was that he, Alex, felt sorry for his father. He even had a need to help and protect his father.

In another dream, Alex was a child at home with his parents. After he dresses himself, he descends the stairs, and when he is halfway down the stairs, he smells toast. Along with the toast, Alex can see the butter and the strawberry jam, and he can already taste them in his mouth. But when he gets to the kitchen, neither the strawberry jam nor the butter is on the table. And although the toast is in the toaster, it is burnt to a very pungent and offensive crisp. Alex decides to look for his mother, but she is nowhere to be found in the apartment. So, he looks out of the window and after a while, he sees her coming out of a neighbor's home. Instead of returning home, she knocked on the next neighbor's door furiously. The door opens, she enters, and after a few minutes, she leaves that neighbor's home and knocks on another neighbor's door.

The third dream was one that Alex never would have expected to take place while he was in Africa. In this dream, he was looking at his 13-year-old self, who was looking for something above him, below him, behind him, around a boulder, in the water, and then he looked up, directly into dreaming Alex's eyes, smiled and gestured to him to come. Alex woke up startled, thought about the dream, and established that his 13-year-old self was somewhere here, in Uganda. And Alex was eager to meet him.

Alex first tapped on Pieter's shoulder, and then he tapped on Jussi's. Not knowing how it got there, the sharp edge if a hunting knife was pressing against Alex's throat. Pieter came to Alex's rescue by calmly calling Jussi's full name, "Jussi." Jussi then looked at where his knife was and apologized profusely to Alex. It turned out that Jussi had a nightmare. The French Foreign Legion commander was chasing him. Alex couldn't believe that the knife hadn't drawn any blood. He kept checking for blood, but it hadn't torn through the skin.

"Yes, you are definitely up there with Achilles," Alex said.

The Bidi-Bidi Refugee Settlement was vast. And it took a while before they found the clinic and a doctor to receive the medicines. At the clinic, there were three interns, four nurses, and two doctors, both of whom were with Doctors Without Borders. When Pieter found out the scope of the need, he became quite disappointed in his efforts because he had only brought enough medicine and supplies to treat a few thousand people, at most. But there were more than a quarter million refugees at Bidi-Bidi. The doctors as well as the interns were quite happy to receive such a generous cargo, But Pieter clearly felt dejected. Alex picked up on this and told Pieter that the next time he brings medical supplies to

Bidi-Bidi Refugee Settlements he will help him. Pieter quickly perked up and asked Alex if he would come with him. Alex assented vivaciously.

After the medicine had been delivered and the doctors provided a list of "sorely needed" medicines for the next time, Alex, Pieter, and Jussi spent a few hours walking through the refugee settlement, talking with several of the refugees. Jussi even played soccer with the kids. Alex was particularly amazed at the extent to which many of the refugees could speak English, not only the professionals, but also the teenagers as well as some of the kids.

They had planned on leaving at around 2:00 pm, but it took a while brfore the kids were willing to let Jussi go, for they enjoyed playing with Jussi immensely. Some of them would deliberately foul him by running into him. Jussi would fall dow and then it would turn into a big wrestling match, with some of the kids choosing to be against Jussi and others with him. After a few minutes of this, the soccer would resume, until someone else would deliberately run into Jussi.

Alex and Pieter successfully managed to get Jussi out of the game by telling the kids that if they wouldn't let Jussi go, they wouldn't let him come with them when they returned.

15
A Shaman Emerges

The plan was to drive from Moyo, where the Bidi-Bidi Refugee Settlement was, to Gulu via Adjuman.

'So, my father brought me here, to Uganda.' Alex thought to himself, now convinced that his thirteen-year-old self would come to him there.

In Gulu, they would catch a flight to Kampala, courtesy of the Doctors Without Borders. From Kampala, Pieter and Alex would eventually catch a flight to Cape Town, and Jussi would fly to Helsinki via London.

On the way to Gulu, all three of them were in pretty high spirits, so much so that they were singing various songs of The Beatles, Pink Floyd, and Simon and Garfunkel along the way. The only bit of bad luck that came their way was that the truck ran out of gas in Adjuman, about twenty miles away from the Gulu border. After Jussi emptied the two jerry cans into the gas tank, they looked for and found a gas station, filled the tank and the two jerry cans. They decided to turn back and take rooms at the hotel they had noticed a few miles back.

Although Alex didn't like the idea, Jussi insisted that they all spend the night in the same room because it would be safer. And Alex's worst fears came true. Not only did Pieter snore like a chainsaw, but he also farted, what Alex thought to be, nonstop. Jussi, however, didn't seem to mind. That night, Alex had several more dreams. The first was his 13-year-old self looking again at Alex, and gesturing toward Alex to come to him. The second dream or nightmare, depending on how you see it, was one of his recurring dreams in which Alex is in a clearing with other people. It starts raining only on him, and then the rain turns to blood. And again, the other people laugh at him. He woke up from both nightmares, but he was still able to fall back asleep on both occasions.

After finishing off the food that they had brought from the Bidi-Bidi Refugee Settlement, they continued on their way to Gulu City. While Jussi was driving, Pieter was talking with Jussi, and Alex was reflecting on his dreams. The thing that he was really concerned about was the fact that his 13-year-old self started coming to him while he was in Africa, in Uganda. Not being able to come up with a satisfactory answer for why his 13-year-old self would come to him at this time and place, Alex's eyes as well as his mind started to wander. But as soon as they crossed the Adjumani-Gulu border, a very subtle sense of familiarity took silent hold of him, which he did not notice at first.

When they arrived at the air strip in Gulu, two attendents of the air strip immediately approached them to ask if they had come from the Bidi-Bidi Refugee City. When Pieter acknowledged that they were, he was escorted to the manager of the strip, who was profusely sorry for having to inform Pieter that the medical transport that he and his companions were due to board for Entebbe is grounded until further notice. The manager couldn't tell Pieter what was wrong with the plane, nor did he know when it would be back in the air. The manager was more than happy to offer Pieter the use of his phone to make "alternative arrangements," though. Pieter was so flustered that he feared that he would have blood on his hands if the phone didn't work. But fortunately, for everyone concerned, the phone did work adequately. After calling the Bidi-Bidi Refugee Settlement twice and the sister NGO he collaborated with, he returned to Alex and Jussi with a Plan. They would drive south to Jaber, and then turn east to go to Lira. In Lira, they would return their rental jeep and trade their truck in for a jeep. Afterward, they would drive to Kampala, drop the jeep off at the headquarters of Doctors Without Borders, take a taxi van to the airport in Entebbe, and fly back home. When Pieter presented his plan to Alex and jussi, they both thought it was a good plan, but Alex didn't feel like traveling anymore that day, for he had an upset stomach. He suggested that they spend the night in a hotel in Gulu and leave early in the morning for Lira, and then Kampala.

By 4:00 pm, they were settled in their hotel room. Alex really wanted to have his own room, but because he felt sorry for Jussi sleeping through Pieter's flatulence alone, he acquiesced. All three of them immediately hit their beds and fell asleep. After an hour or so, Jussi woke up, and he was hungry. As Alex and Pieter were still sleeping, Jussi couldn't get food for himself without bringing something for them, but they were sleeping. However, Jussi was now becoming hangry, so he decided to wake up Pieter and Alex to ask them if they wanted anything to eat. But neither of them was hungry, so Jussi went out to see what Gulu had to offer in the way of its cuisine.

While Jussi was out, Alex asked Pieter about his bout with malaria. Alex also felt compelled to tell Pieter that he was terrified when he read the head nurse's letter that "things were not looking good." In response, Pieter looked at Alex, smiled, and started speaking.

"Alex, it's a shame that you are a 'wine, women, and song' kind of fellow, instead of a sex, drugs, and rock-n-roll' kind of fellow," Pieter said.

Alex immediately regretted having said anything about how he was worried.

Alex feared that an awkward silence would ensue, but Pieter had something else on his mind that he had to talk to Alex about.

Alex, I don't mind one bit that you consulted with my patient, Jussi. But I am curious as to what you told him," Pieter said.

"We talked about a lot of things," Alex responded. "Could you be a bit more specific?"

"I don't know if you are aware of this, but Jussi, not unlike so many other men and women, regarded the war in the former Yugoslavia as a righteous war," Pieter said.

"That's a contradiction in terms," Alex said.

"He regarded it as his Spanish Civil War," Pieter added.

"I'm sure there were some things that the anarchists did that they weren't proud of," Alex retorted. "Everyone knows that the fascists and the communists did all kinds of unconscionable things."

"The point I'm trying to make, Alex," Pieter said, "is that Jussi came to me because while he was fighting for Croatia's independence from Serbia, a few of his Croatian comrades lynched a Romani family. Has he talked to you about this?"

"Oh, that, yeah," Alex replied. "Well, I asked him if he knew anything about Tito. "He had heard of Tito and he knew that Tito was the leader of the Partisan, the resistance in Yugoslavia."

"What else did you say to him?" Pieter asked eagerly.

"He also knew that Tito, of course, was a communist," Alex replied. "Although I didn't know who was in control of the government in Yugoslavia, I knew it wasn't anyone left leaning. So, I checked it out. I found out that after Hitler and Mussolini had annexed Yugoslavia, the fascist Ante Pavelić and his barbarian butchers, the Ustashe took control of Croatia. The Ustashe were so incredibly ruthless that the Nazis in their communiques to the High Command, complained about just how barbaric the ustashe were."

"How did Jussi respond to all of this?" Pieter asked.

"He was shocked to find out that the Serbians were the victims of genocide..." Alex said.

"Was this at the hands of the Croatians?" Pieter asked.

"Yes," Alex replied, "yes, it was."

"I see," Pieter said. Then he stood up and started pacing the room.

"Jussi was shocked about that," Alex repeated, "and he then asked me if he should have known this. I wanted so much to find a way to avoid answering that question. But there was nothing else to do but tell him 'yes, you should have known.'"

"So, when you told him that," Pieter said, almost as if talking to himself while still pacing the room, "he finally accepted responsibility, brilliant."

"What's so brilliant?" Alex asked.

"For the longest time," Pieter began, "Jussi has been in conflict with himself. On the one hand, he acknowledges that those Croatian soldiers who lynched that Romani family were his brothers-in-arms, but because he didn't know that Croatia had a fascist past, and that some of his Croatian comrades still harbored fascist sentiments, he thinks that he shouldn't be held responsible. But on the other hand, he can't stop thinking that he is partly the blame simply because he fought with them. In other words, he feels as though he is guilty by association. And as a result, he can't stop thinking that he harmed a relative of his first girlfriend, a Finnish-Romani girl."

"That's why he kept saying, 'I should have known,'" Alex added.

"And the teacher just casually comes along, gives him a little history lesson, and voila, Jussi can now move on to the next phase of his recovery," Pieter said. "Just brilliant."

"Are you angry with me for interfering?" Alex asked.

"God forbid!" Pieter exclaimed, "No, Alex, I am grateful to you for helping both of us. However, I would like to ask a favor of you."

"And what would that be?" Alex asked somewhat apprehensively.

"As you have made progress with Jussi, where I couldn't, I would like to hand over his case to you," Pieter said.

"Why me?" Alex asked. "I know less psychoanalysis than you do. Of course, that's not saying much, but anyone listening would get my drift."

Pieter dismissed the slight, sat down across from Alex on the next bed, and took both of Alex's hands in his.

"Remember, I am a 'wine, women, and song' kind of guy," Alex reiterated.

"Alex, you are a teacher," Pieter started, "and you may not be aware of this, but by means of

your teaching, you have the capacity, the
patience, and the compassion to help people heal
themselves. That is a gift that you may not
squander."

"Thank you, Pieter," Alex said. "But I still
wouldn't know where to start."

"Think as a teacher, Alex." Pieter said. "What
would Alex, the teacher, do in this case."

While Alex was considering that question,
Jussi returned to the room. He and Pieter were
engaged in light conversation, but Alex was
silent for the remainder of the evening.

16
That Big-assed Pangi

Early the next morning, they woke up, washed, shaved, ate breakfast, and drove to Lira. In Lira, after returning their rental jeep to the local dealership, trading the truck in for the jeep went seamlessly, but because the jeep did not have its own jerry can, Jussi appropriated one of the truck's jerry cans and placed it in the back of the jeep. After they filled the jeep's tank, they were off. On this occasion, Pieter wanted to drive. Under normal circumstances, Alex wouldn't be caught dead in a car that Pieter was driving. But because they were in Africa, and he wanted to talk with Jussi, he didn't object. Before they set off, Jussi had shown Pieter on the map how to drive southwest to Aduku, and when they reached Apac, Jussi would take over the driving. The plan was to drive from Apac to the Kigumba- Kakoge Road. Then, they would go south to Kakoge, and from there it was more or less a straight shot to Kampala.

However, things didn't initially go as planned. When Pieter saw the sigh to Apala, which was northeast of Lira, he, for some strange reason, thought that was what Jussi had told him, so he took that turn. And because Jussi and Alex were engaged in deep conversation, they took no notice of the error. When they entered Apala City, Pieter announced it.

"We have finally arrived in Apala," Pieter said.

"*Ei oo...ei ole oikein*!" Jussi exclaimed, "*Perkele*!"

"Why did Jussi just say 'this isn't right' and 'fuck?'" Alex asked.

"I haven't the foggiest," Pieter replied.

"Dohtori Botha, you drove northeast, not southwest," Jussi explained. "We should be in Apac, not Apala, see," Jussi said as he showed Pieter the map.

It's okay, Pieter," Alex said. "It's an honest mistake. Let's let Jussi drive now."

Pieter moved over to the passenger seat, making way for Jussi to take the driver's seat. Jussi immediately turned the jeep around and drove off. After a few minutes, when everyone had settled down, Pieter tried to start a conversation with Jussi. Pieter was curious about what he and Alex had talked about earlier in the day. Initially, although Alex couldn't hear every single word of the conversation, he did know what they were talking about.

When they were at the Bidi-Bidi Refugee Settlement, Alex took notice of just how well Jussi interacted with those kids he was playing with during the soccer match.

Then, Alex entered into the conversation.

"Jussi," Alex started, "I couldn't help but notice how good you are with kids."

When Jussi heard that, it visibly caught him off guard. It was clearly something that he had never considered, but he acknowledged for the first time the credence of the statement.

"You once told me that the only thing you are good at is 'killing,'" Alex said. "I would beg to differ."

"I do like kids," Jussi admitted.

"Jussi, did you get the cap at the end of high school? Alex asked.

In Finland, when a person graduates from high school, they get a special cap, which kind of looks like a sea captain's cap. So, Alex was asking Jussi if he had completed high school, which Alex was not sure of because Jussi had taken the military option as a career.

"Yes, I do have the *ylioppilaslakki*, Jussi said. "*Miksi* … I mean why do you ask?"

Alex couldn't help but think of how lucky some kids would be having Jussi as a teacher.

"But I don't want to stay in Finland," Jussi said. "In Finland, we have everything. The kids there don't need me. Alex, I must to be needed."

"Those kids back in Bidi-Bidi, and kids all over the world like them, need you very much, Jussi," Alex said. "I only think that you should study to be a teacher in Finland because Finland has one of the best educational systems in the world, much better than in the United States, for example."

With regard to Jussi's military experiences in Croatia, Alex brought up Wilfred Owen and his poem *Dulce et Decorum Est*. After telling Jussi that in his opinion, Owen was the best of the

The Goddess Returns

WWI poets, Alex pulled up the poem on his phone. After he pulled it up, Alex handed his phone to Jussi and asked him to read. Jussi didn't know the Latin, so he asked Alex what it meant. After repeating the Latin, *Dulce et decorum est pro patria mori*," Alex translated it: "It is sweet and honorable to die for one's country." After a few minutes of perusing the poem, Jussi looked at Alex.

"War is not sweet," Jussi replied

"No, Jussi, war isn't sweet," Alex concurred. "Jussi, the reason why I shared this poem with you is because I would like you to do something. I would like you to take out the aspects of war that Owen puts in and replace them with the aspects of war that characterize what war is for you. Do you understand?"

Jussi used the example of the gas that Owen mentioned, telling Alex that since the role of gas is virtually nonexistent now, that he would take it out and replace it with something that has come up repeatedly in his own experience, such as harming non-combatants.

"Yes, make the poem relevant to your life as a soldier," Alex concurred.

When the jeep was about 15 kilometers from Lira, Alex started hearing the faint sound of drums. He started looking around because he felt as though he had heard them before. So, he was trying to figure out from where the sound was coming. But he couldn't establish that. He then asked Jussi and Pieter if they heard the drums.

They, however, did not. After a few minutes, on the side of the road, Alex saw a boy carry someone over his back and shoulder. Alex assumed that Jussi and Pieter would pull the jeep over to offer them a ride, but when they didn't Alex screamed at them to stop the jeep, which Jussi did. Just as Alex was about to chide them for not stopping, he looked back for the two people, but they weren't there. Both Jussi and Pieter looked back at Alex curiously.

"Didn't you guys see the people on the side of the road?" Alex asked.

"We haven't seen anyone, Alex," Pieter said.

Looking at Jussi, Jussi shook his head, and then he asked Alex if he were okay. Alex then asked them if they heard the drums. Again, they hadn't. As soon as they continued toward Lira, in his mind, Alex saw a boy wave at him. Alex quickly recognized the boy he saw when Jerry pointed the gun at the girl in his home. Then the boy gestured to Alex to come. Alex instantly recalled his time with the Angel and the Prophet in Chicago and shouted for Jussi to stop.

"For heaven's sake, Alex! Pieter exclaimed. "Between the drums and the ghosts, I would say that you are going mad. Have you done something to offend the gods?"

"I don't know," Alex murmured.

While looking around, Alex acknowledged to himself that he knew this place. Then, while looking at Pieter, Alex remembered what I had told him about something Mumma had once said to him: 'for you to get back to that place where you were when you first became a man, you will need a heyoka, a sacred clown, a practical joker, to guide you back there. He will be the only one who can get you back there."

Alex jumped out of the jeep and took off his shoes.

"I have been here before," Alex said. "After a few hundred meters, there is holy ground. If you want to come, you should leave your shoes here because you might lose them in the jungle."

"Alex, you have never said anything about having been in Africa," Pieter said, "not even when you were under hypnosis."

"I know, Pieter, I know," Alex repeated, as he walked into the thick, verdant canopy.

Despite the fact that Pieter was still quite weak from the malaria, he didn't want to miss anything, so he asked Jussi to come and help him catch-up with Alex. Pieter tried walking while grasping Jussi's shoulder, but they fell further and further behind Alex. So, he decided to carry Pieter, piggy-back style. And then, he told Pieter to hang-on tight, and Jussi started running. he had run about half a kilometer with Pieter on his back. He didn't stop because he was tired but because of everything he was seeing.

"Dohteri Botha, what are these things?" Jussi asked. "I have seen such things in other parts of Africa, but I don' know what they mean."

"Jussi, this is a liminal place," Pieter said.

But because Jussi was visibly not familiar with that term, Pieter was obliged to explain further.

"Jussi, this is a very, very special place," Pieter continued. "When it is time for the older children to become full members of the community, the tribe, they are brought to this 'nowhere place,' the boys separate from the girls. They are taught the rules that women and men must observe, and they must take part in all manner of rituals. During that time, they may not see their parents, nor may they return to the village. And finally, when it is over, they return to the community as full members, as adults."

"Does Alex have to go through that?" Jussi asked.

"It's strange that I had never noticed it before, but from some of the marks that Alex has on his face and body does suggest that he had already gone through his rite of passage," Pieter said.

"So why does he have to come back?" Jussi asked.

"I gather Alex has some unfinished business," Pieter replied.

When they caught up with Alex, they were all in a clearing. Fortunately, they were able to catch Alex as he was doing some kind of mime. They first saw Alex go through the motion as if he were taking something from someone, but there was no one there. Then, they saw Alex go through the motion as if he were pulling someone toward himself, and then into himself. Pieter then called to Alex, who looked at them, smiled, and walked over to them. Both Pieter and Jussi couldn't help noticing Alex's right hand. He held his hand as if he were carrying something in it, but it was empty.

"Are you able to tell us what is happening, Alex?" Pieter asked.

"When we were driving along the road here, I saw a boy trying to carry a girl on the side of the road," Alex said.

"That's why you wanted us to stop the first time," Jussi said.

"Yes," Alex replied. "My unconscious self was trying to tell that to my conscious self. And when I told you to stop the second time, I remembered that I had gone through my rite of passage here, and I had to see it again."

"*L'en so et pour so*i," Pieter said. "In Sartre's Existentialism, the consciousness must at times reflect on its past experiences."

Both Alex and Jussi looked at Pieter strangely. Realizing that neither one of them were impressed, Pieter gestured to Alex to continue. But Alex didn't continue to speak.

"What do you have in your hand?" Jussi asked.

"Oh, this," Alex said as he inspected his right hand. "It's an AK47. This is going to sound crazy to you, but I took it from my thirteen-year-old self."

"Did you use it?" Jussi asked.

"I don't remember the faces or any other images, but I still can sometimes feel my fingers squeezing the trigger along with the way the recoil jerked my arm around," Alex admitted. "I also her a girl's voice crying. And there are other voices, men's voices who are telling me to do it. One of them keeps saying, 'I'm gonna kill that white devil. I'm gonna kill that white devil.' And at one moment. He screams, 'And I'm gonna kill him now!'"

"Alex, they made you, a little boy, pull the trigger!" Pieter shouted.

"I knew it was wrong, Pieter," Alex confessed, "and besides, today saying '*befehl ist befehl*' just won't fly."

On the othersidde of the clearing, a woman who had difficulty walking started for the three men. Jussi was the one who noticed her first.

"A woman with a big-assed pangi is coming toward us," Jussi said.

"What's a big-assed pangi?" Alex asked. "Oh, shit! So, that's 'a big-assed pangi.' That has to be the biggest mother-fuckin' machete that I've ever seen!"

The woman was closing in on them, and Pieter had exerted a great deal of energy to hold on to Jussi to get there. He was too exhausted to do it again. The woman drew ever closer to them, and Jussi became anxious.

"I don't want to hurt her," Jussi said.

The Goddess Returns

Looking around and finding a nice-sized branch, Alex told Jussi and Pieter to go on ahead, and he would closely follow.

"She's probably pissed because we're trespassing on her land," Alex said. "As soon as we are off of her property, she will stop chasing us."

When they entered the jungle, Alex thought the woman had given up the chase, but when he turned and looked, she was still hot on their trail. After they had gone about one hundred and fifty meters, she was still in pursuit. 'She must be rich,' Alex thought. At about two hundred and fifty meters, when Alex looked behind himself, he saw that the woman had tripped and fallen. Alex relays this news to Pieter and Jussi as they moved steadily toward the road. Suddenly, there was this piercing shriek behind them, "Alex!" All three men stopped.

"Okay, dudes," Alex started, "I know that you don't hear the drums, and that's okay. It really is. But..."

"She said, 'Alex,'" Jussi blurted.

"Pieter, there's no point in Jussi and I sharing the same insanity alone," Alex said. "Why don't you come in on the fun, too?"

"Alex, I have to say that this is some spooky shit," Pieter said. "But, yes, I heard her call out your name as well."

When Alex turned around, he couldn't hear the woman moving. So, he assumed that she was still on the ground. He walked a couple of steps

in her direction and shouted, "I'n still here." Jussi
and Pieter were right behind him. Alex could
then hear some movement, and after a few
seconds, the woman reemerged. Before she could
make a step toward them, Jussi reminded Alex of
the pangi.

"We will leave if you do not throw the pangi
away," Alex said.

She tossed it right then and there and move as
best she could towards them. When she was
about three meters away from Alex and pointed
to his branch. Alex threw it away. As she
hobbled closer, she asked Alex to show her his
hands. He thought that that was a curious request,
but he did it with his palms up. She slapped his
palms hard and told him to turn his hands over.
He did, and with both of her hands, she pulled
Alex's right hand towards her. Then, she grabbed
Alex's head and examined his face and eyes
carefully. After a few more seconds, all of this
gave way to a murmur.

"Alex, you came back. You finally came
back."

There was something surprisingly familiar
about the sound of her voice. And a name was
forming on the tip of Alex's tongue, but it wasn't
yet ready to roll off.

"You remembe' me?" she asked him.

Still looking at her, Alex said "Yes."

She laughed and told him that he lies.

"Adongpiny, how could I forget you!" Alex
exclaimed. "You and your sisters were always

mean to me. Yet, when the death squad came to the village, I carried you to the clinic."

Adongpiny stopped laughing and turned away from Alex.

"When your American father brought you to us, you were just a boy who came from far away," Adongpiny said. "But Aber, our youngest sister, knew who you really were, our baby brother. She was born with magic, like our father's father and you. When she told us, we knew that it had to be true, but we were not ready to believe it. I am very sorry for making your time with us so difficult, Okeny Atim."

While his sister was speaking, more and more memories flooded into Alex's consciousness, and one memory in particular stood out.

"Do you remember the time when our mother ran out of the house looking for you?" Adongpiny asked.

"Yes," Alex replied, "I remember it very well."

"And when she found you, she held your head and looked deeply into your face, like I just did. And when she saw that you were hers, she embraced you tightly and kissed you all over your head and she cried. Do you remember?"

At this point, the tears were pouring down both of their eyes. After a few minutes, Alex collected himself, wiped his eyes, and continued speaking.

"Adongpiny, if I am your brother, and I don't doubt that, how did I end up with my American parents?" Alex asked.

"The last time our father took me to the mountain, he told me everything," Adongpiny said. "He told me that his father told him that you were coming and that you would be special. But you should not be born in Africa because you would die here. So, our father decided that you would be born in America. Our mother did not want to give you away, but she also didn't want you to die. She was always happy before she went to America, but when she came back, she was only ever sad, until the day she found her son again. And three days later, she was killed with the rest of our family."

"You called me 'Atim Oleng,'" Alex said, "but I remember you and our sisters calling me another name."

Adongpiny turned away from Alex and laughed.

"I am sorry, my baby brother. That was a very mean name we gave you."

"What was it?" Alex asked.

"*Kidega* means not wanted," Adongpiny said somewhat ashamed. "We thought your parents did not want you."

Alex had many more questions such as what were the names of their parents and sisters, but Adongpiny interrupted him, telling him the rest of what their father had told her the last time they were on the mountain.

The Goddess Returns

"Our father also told me that he, our mother, and our sisters would be killed, but you and I would survive," Adongpiny said. Our father's father told him this. That is why our father named me 'Adongpiny,' Survivor. He also told me that because it was important that I be here to receive you when you return, I could not marry or have children or let a man touch me in any way because if I did, I would die."

"HIV and AIDS," Alex blurted out. "Our grandfather knew HIV was coming in the early 70s?"

"No, he knew it in the 50s," Adongpiny said.

When Adongpiny said that, Alex remembered what I had told him about coming from two long lines of healers.

"What I don't understand," Alex started curiously, "is what was so important that you were denied love and children? Was it just to say, 'Hi' to me?"

"No, baby brother, it wasn't only to wave at you," Adongpiny said visibly annoyed. "And who said that I was denied love? I simply could not let a man touch me."

From the way that she said that, Alex understood that his sister had done whatever it took to keep men from touching her.

"Will I get to meet my sister-in-law?" Alex asked.

"Soon enough," Adongpiny laughed.

"How many knives are you carrying on your person?" Alex asked.

She smiled and returned to the previous subject.

"Alex, when we become big … do you remembe'?"

"Yes, of course," Alex replied.

"When we came back to the village, we danced as full members," Adongpiny said. "But the dance we all danced is not the true dance of our ancestors. Approximately seven hundred years ago. The tellers of our history teach us that famine and disease took many of our ancestors, and all of the few elders who knew the whole dance died. Many people knew parts and pieces of the dance but not the whole thing. Alex, that dance was the link between our living and our dead. For seven hundred years, that link has been broken."

"What does this have to do with me and you?" Alex asked.

"Everything, my baby brother!" Adongpiny exclaimed.

"Could you stop calling me that, please?" Alex asked.

"Only if you do what I say," Adongpiny laughed.

"What do I have to do?" Alex asked.

"You had to be kept safe because our father's father said that when you came back, you would know the dance, the whole dance of our ancestors," Adongpiny said. "Alex, listen carefully to what I am going to ask you. Do you know a dance that dead people taught you?"

The Goddess Returns

Alex's reflex was to reply in the negative, but he remembered /Caggen, turning left, and meeting the irritating man at that huge hut when he was walking through the land of the dead. Then, he remembered the women who taught him a dance. He looked at his biggest sister not knowing what to tell her. Again, she moved closer to him and took his head with both of her hands.

"Alex, did dead people teach you a dance?" Adongpiny asked once more.

"Yes," Alex replied.

Adongpiny screamed with joy and pulled Alex's head down to kiss his left cheek.

"But when I asked them if I was theirs, they said no," Alex added.

Looking alarmed, Adongpiny asked, "Why not?"

"They told me that I didn't come to them the right way," Alex replied.

"Then, why did they teach you the dance?" Adongpiny asked.

"Three older women taught me because they believed that I would meet their descendants. Then, I could teach them the dance," Alex replied.

Clearly relieved, Adongpiny reminded Alex when he first met their ancestors, he did not know who they were, and neither did they know who he was. But because he kept coming back, they saw that as a sign that he would meet their descendants, which was why they taught him their dance. But now, Alex knows who he is, and he knows the dance.

"Alex, my baby brother, oh, sorry, today, you will reunite our living with our dead!" Adongpiny declared.

"Whoa! Whoa! Whoa!" Alex exclaimed. I came to them three times, and each time I came, I came to them the wrong way," Alex said.

"Alex, look," Adongpiny said a tad disappointed, "our father's father said you would be the most powerful, except for one of your kids. But so far, I am not really impressed. How should you come to them?"

Alex remembered the call and response structure of the dance. The living first stomp their bare heals on the ground three times. Then, the dead by way of drums respond by banging on the drums three times. Afterward, the lead dancer stomps his or her right heal against the ground three times, followed again by three drumbeats.

At this point, Alex was stuck. He wasn't sure about how to proceed, and Adongpiny was becoming impatient with him. As he looked at his big sister, Pieter, and Jussi, Alex became more nervous. So, he closed his eyes, and looked for something, anything that could help him. The relaxing darkness allowed Alex to focus, and he remembered something that /Caggen had told him, "When in doubt, turn to your imagination." And finally, it came to Alex. He knew what to do. Finally, the lead dancer jumps as high as he or she can and comes crashing down through the roof and the ceiling of the dwelling of the dead, which is when the dead rise up to meet their living, and the living meet their dead.

"I got it!" Alex shouted.

Adongpiny went back to where she tossed her pangi and picked it up. Before she was out of sight, she told Alex to meet her back at the clearing. When he asked her why, she informed him that very many people in their tribe have only been waiting for this day. So, they all would need a wide, open space to dance. She was going back to the clearing to call them.

17
The Actual Collateral Ancestor

Unbeknownst to Alex, however, the Goddess Mother had observed everything that had transpired. For she was preparing the final 'Ordeals' for Alex. /Caggen was correct when he warned Alex to be on his guard. The first three 'Ordeals' were far too easy, as /Caggen had warned, but Alex paid him no mind. And now, Alex was going to walk right into a trap that he could never have anticipated, one that could very well kill him.

When Alex walked back to Pieter and Jussi, they both looked at him with totally new eyes.

"Look at me," Pieter said astonished. "Here I am thinking that I knew you, but, Alex, or Atim, or Oleng, or whatever your name is, you are a complete mystery."

"Pieter, try to look at it from my perspective," Alex said. "I am still a complete mystery to myself."

Before they made it back to the clearing, drums were being played.

"Now, I can hear your precious drums," Pieter said.

"Minä myös," Jussi said nodding his head and smiling.

"Fucking finally!" Alex exclaimed.

When they got back to the clearing, several dozen people had already collected themselves, and when they saw Alex, Pieter, and Jussi, they

306

cheered heartily. Some children wanted to go over to them, but the adults would not allow it. The adults were eager to get the dance underway before someone changed his or her mind. A couple teenage girls did bring them some water, which was cold, surprisingly. A couple concerns arose in Alex's mind, so he set out to find Adongpiny as more and more people were constantly streaming in. When Alex found her, the riddle of the drummer was solved.

"So, you were the secret drummer," Alex said.

"It is our tradition that if someone leads something for the village, his or her family members must help," Adongpiny said. Alex, did the girls bring you and your friends water?"

Yes," Alex replied. "Thank you."

"Good, good," Adongpiny repeated, meaning very good. Alex, you go over there and start practicing the dance slowly, so the others can learn it first. When everyone is here, I will come over to you to tell you to start."

Alex wanted to ask her an important question, but he decided to wait until Adongpiny would come over to him.

While Alex was walking over to that part of the clearing where he would start dancing, he had an eerie feeling, as though something were missing, as if he had overlooked something. By the time that he had arrived at the spot, he still didn't know what it was. But when his mind started to drift, he made an effort to refocus, and he thought of /Caggen. Then, it came to him. It was his mother, the one that had adopted him, my adopted grandmother. /Caggen had told Alex that she was wandering, looking for his adopted father, my adopted grandfather. Although Alex had no intension of looking for his father, he had to find his mother and bring her to his biological parents, where she could find rest. Although Alex had absolutely no idea of how he should go about looking for his mother, he turned to his imagination, and the idea came to him to look like her by taking on her features as he remembered them with a little more age on top of what he remembered. The first half-dozen times brought him to women who **favored** my adopted grandmother but they were not her. So, he was proud of getting the idea of assuming her form and shape, but he was disappointed by the fact that he couldn't get them exactly right. Then, he thought to include her character and temperament which in his mind were as reliable not to ever change like the North Star. And it worked. He found himself walking beside a woman who still had step in her gait, as though she were on a mission. However, Alex was not totally certain that she was his mother, for her back was a bit bent, and her hair was unkept, wild, and totally gray. As he was looking at her, Alex couldn't help but think of the Old English poem *The Wanderer,* which is about a warrior that survived his lord. In exchange for riches and a home in his lord's hall, the warriors swear an oath that they will fight to the death. The warrior of *The*

Wanderer broke his oath, so no other hall will take him on, and he must wander alone for the rest of his days.

"Mama," Alex said, "is it you?"

"Who's there?" she asked, startled, holding her walking stick as if she were prepared to strike out with it.

Hearing her voice and observing her movements, Alex knew it was, indeed, his mother.

"Mama, it's me, Alex."

Still with the stick at the ready, she moved closer to Alex to try and recognize him.

"Oh, Lawd!" my grandmother shouted, "Alex, are you dead, too?"

"No, ma'am, I'm not dead yet," Alex replied.

"Then, what are you doing here?" my grandmother asked.

"I was looking for you to take you to a safe place," Alex said.

"Ah, that's so sweet of you, baby, but I have to find your father," my grandmother said.

Alex really didn't want to find his father, and he was considering how he could convince his mother to be taken to his biological parents without having to include his father. Alex came up with an idea.

"Mama, I think you haven't been able to find Pops because he doesn't want you, or anyone else, to find him," Alex said.

"I don't remember askin' you f' yo' 'pinion!" my grandmother erupted.

"I'm sorry Mama," Alex said.

But what Alex said about his father not wanting to be found struck a chord with her. And because Alex was able to find her, she figured that Alex could find his father as well.

"Alex, Lawd knows that I'm tired o' this endless walkin'," Alex's mother said, "so, I'll tell you what I'll do. You can take me to this safe place of yourn if you promise to fin' yo' father and bring him to me there. Alex, I know that you hate your father, so, I know you don't want to look for him. But for you to get what you want; I have to get what I want. Do we have a understandin'?"

Alex looked for other possible options, but he knew that he would not be able to change her mind, so he had to agree to her conditions.

"These people ain't dead, Alex," Alex's mother said as she scanned the people who were collecting in the open area.

"I know," Alex replied. "In a bit, my biological parents will be here, and you can stay with them."

"Are they dead or alive?" Alex's mother asked.

"They died a long time ago," Alex explained.

"Are you angry with us for not telling you that you were adopted?" my grandmother asked.

"No, not at all," Alex replied. "It looks like it had to happen that way."

"What do you mean?" Alex's mother asked.

"Mama, is it okay if I tell you later, because besides bringing Pops here, I also have to dance?" Alex asked.

"Sure, go ahead, do what you gotta do, but remember, if I don' see my man soon, I'm gonna keep lookin' fo' him myse'f," Alex's mother said.

Alex disappeared, but after a few seconds, he came back.

"Oh, no, he didn't just come back without my man and think that I'm gonna just stay here!" my grandmother declared.

Alex gestured to her to be a bit patient. Then, he took on his father's features. Knowing that he was forgetting something, he looked around for a clue. While glancing at his mother, he remembered, and disappeared again.

However, neither Alex, nor his mother were the only ones who had been looking for Alex's father that day. For the Goddess Mother had been anticipating this day for some time now, for it was time for Alex's final 'Ordeals'. Alex should have listened to /Caggen when he had told Alex that the previous 'Ordeals' were far too easy, and that the Goddess Mother was a bit of a trickster in her own right.

When Alex found his father, he found a man with a gray scruffy beard, bald headed, and even more surprisingly, he was blind in both eyes. On closer examination, Alex realized something alarming.

'Shit, he blinded himself,' Alex thought.

The ironic thing, besides walking quite quickly, was that he regularly stopped and turned to determine if anyone was following him. After a while, Alex realized that his father was listening for sounds of others following him. He was not using his eyes.

"Who's there? Leave me alone!" my grandfather screamed as he cowered away from the direction the sounds of Alex's movements were coming.

"Hey, Pops! It's me, Alex," Alex said.

"Alex, Alex," my grandfather repeated, "is that you? I can't see."

Alex wanted to ask my grandfather why he blinded himself, but he remembered that his mother would only wait so long. So, Alex decided to ask him later.

"Pops, before you ask me, no, I'm not dead," Alex said "I know how to travel through the underworld. And I'm here to take you to a nice safe place. Mama's already there waiting for you."

"Oh, no, son, I can't go with you," Alex's father said.

"Why the hell not!" Alex exclaimed.

"Alex, we raised you better dan dat, now!" my grandfather stressed.

"I'm sorry, I'm sorry," Alex said, "But I was only able to convince Mama to stay there because I promised to bring you there as well."

"Alex, son, I've known that Mama has been looking for me for some time now…"

The Goddess Returns

"So, why have you been avoiding her?" Alex interrupted.

"Because of the shame, Alex, the shame that I have had to die with and relive, not remember, but relive every single day of my death," Alex's father said.

The memories of everything my grandfather had done were starting to resurface in Alex's mind, but Alex resisted them, because the most important thing right now was getting back to that open clearing.

At that very moment, Hermes entered the Goddess Mother's throne room. Bowing his head first toward the Goddess mother and then to all the other goddesses who were also present during Alex's previous 'Ordeals', Hermes then returned his gaze toward the Goddess Mother. She gestured to him to place the item that he had brought there to its predetermined spot. Thinking that he would be permitted to observe this final 'Ordeals', Hermes stayed and watched the interaction between Alex and his father after Hermes had put the item in its spot. But after about a minute, he felt as though he were the only one who was observing said interaction, for all of the goddesses, not including the Goddess Mother, though, were looking at him. While looking around at them, he smiled, bowed, and moved to exit the throne room. But the Goddess Mother looked disapprovingly at all the other goddesses and commanded Hermes to remain in the throne room. Then, all eyes returned to Alex, my grandfather, and the object that Hermes had brought to the scene.

Before Hermes had come on the meta-side of the scene, Alex could easily put aside the memories of the pain that my grandfather had brought to bear on Alex, and the pain that my grandfather had brought to bear on my grandmother. Yet, when it came to the pain that my grandfather had forced Alex to bring to bear on my grandmother took somewhat more effort to put aside, but Alex did eventually do it without feeling any ill will or anger toward his father. At one point, Alex even felt proud of himself that he had managed to do it.

But a few minutes after Hermes's arrival into the throne room, everything had taken a turn for the worse. As Alex was trying to convince his father to come with him to join Alex's mother, his wife, a massive swell of anger was building inside of Alex, and he was becoming disoriented, for what he was actually saying was in diabolically sharp contrast to what he wanted to say, and he believed them both. After a few minutes, Alex had fully regressed to his seven-year-old self. The cause of this was the green, flaming sword that Hermes had installed seven meters away from the father and son. The green, flaming sword was like the Sirens that Odysseus had wagered to listen to. The green, flaming sword sang to Alex a song, the lyrics of which demanded that the blood of the father would have to be poured on the ground from a sword that was wielded by the son. Yes, PATRICIDE!!! Alex, seven-year-old Alex, understood that to be the only way that he and his mother could ever find peace.

It was at this point when /Caggen came to me, fearing Alex was in trouble.

"Thunder, wakey, wakey!" /Caggen exclaimed loudly.

"You lied to me," I said as my astral-self emerged from my body. "You are not my collateral ancestor."

"Thunder, darling, I know, and I do apologize for that. However, right now, I fear that Alex is in mortal danger," /Caggen quickly said.

"I also know a couple of your darker secrets. In this book called *Tricksters and Trancers* by Mathias Guenter, I learned that you were the first shaman, heyoka and that you allowed your people, Bushmen, to be massacred. Wait! In what danger? Where is he?" I asked.

"Yes, everything you have stated vis-à-vis myself is accurate," Caggen admitted, almost forgetting about Alex. "I am the original shaman, and every shaman after myself partakes of myself. And the Bushmen you mentioned, my people, were rather egalitarian when it came to the relationships between the sexes, which I encouraged. However, when I shed everything feminine, including being the original shaman, my people could not follow me. So, I abandoned them and left them to their own devices. Despite that disappointment, the Indo-European tribes, advancing from the north, along with the Semitic tribes, advancing from the south, both embraced my patriarchy whole-heartedly and spread it throughout the world, which, by the by, reached and decimated my people."

"Okay, Wow! We can talk about this later," I said. "You said that Alex is in danger. What danger?"

"Of course, of course," /Caggen repeated, remembering the present emergency. "I finally found the time to teach Alex rain-making. Yet, when I attempted to fetch him, I could not do it."

Why not?" I asked.

"The Goddess Mother would not permit me," /Caggen replied. "I told him that his 'Ordeals' were not complete."

"But I thought…"

"Thunder, there is no time for this!" /Caggen shouted. " I cannot help him, but the Goddess Mother has not blocked you, so go!"

"I see him," I said.

"Be gone, already!" Caggen shouted, again.

"Bye," I said and left.

When I arrived, Alex was almost within reach of the green, flaming sword. I, too, could hear the things it was telling Alex, childish things, petty things, almost ancient things. At first, it was difficult for me to believe that Alex was under the influence of such words because what I was hearing didn't belong to a list of actual events experience by any particular child, but the words came across to me as if they were the linguistic component of an archetype, in Alex's instance, the archetype of the Devouring Father. Nevertheless, seeing that Alex was drawing nearer to the green, flaming sword, I quickly jumped in front of him, trying to draw his attention away from it and onto myself.

"Hey, Alex," I started, "why don't we take grandad to grandma and you introduce me to everyone?"

But, not surprisingly, Alex only demanded that I move out of his way. With that tone, I saw right away that he was not in his usual frame of mind.

In the meantime, on the meta side, several goddesses became physically alarmed that I had interfered in Alex's 'Ordeals,' and they gestured to Hermes to remove me. Begrudgingly, Hermes started moving towards me, but before he could leave the meta side, the Goddess Mother gestured for him to stay in the throne room. A bit confused, Hermes looked directly at the Goddess Mother to make sure that he understood Her correctly. While looking at Her, he noticed that She was smiling, but the way She was smiling was not typical for Her. Generally, when She smiled, there was this sarcastic sneer associated with it. On this occasion, however, there was no sneer, but a resigned expression, which suggested to Hermes that Alex and I would succeed, together. So, Hermes stood back and observed.

As I refused to move, Alex started pushing me, but I stood my ground, which made me think of what had happened between Esther and her father. I tried to speak some sense into Alex, hoping that he'd come to his senses that way, but he couldn't hear me because the now orange and red, flaming sword was drowning everything else out. At that point, I had become desperate, because I knew that if he actually touched that sword, he would not be able to put it down until it had been satisfied, not with blood, but with the hate, the terror, and the yearning the son feels to replace his father forcibly, which, for Alex, would spiral into an endless escapade of exiled shame, exactly what my grandfather was experiencing even now. And in that state, Alex wouldn't be able to help me prepare myself to take a seat on the Council of the Calf of the White Buffalo, and my mother made it painstakingly clear that he was the only one who could get me there. So, I pushed him back, away from the sword. But that only made him angrier, causing him to hit and kick me multiple times. As I fell to the ethereal ground in the agony of knowing that I had already lost, even before I had tried. I was so angry with myself that I felt like hollering. I thought, at least, that I should holler for being so useless, and it suddenly hit me, why my mother didn't want to save herself. It was because she had foreseen that I would ultimately fail, so by dying, she spared herself that disgrace.

As Alex's hand only had to grab the hilt of the sword and it would be his, Alex stopped, looked at me, then at the sword again, which was green and flaming once again, almost as if his taking it was a foregone conclusion, Alex spoke to me while he kept the sword within his view.

"I am going to bury that man within a much deeper hell than the one he already occupies," Alex said, " one where my mother will never have to be afraid of him again, and I will be able to die in peace, knowing that I have removed him permanently out of our lives."

Sure, I heard what Alex was saying, but all I could see was my failure—my failure to my mother, my failure to Misun, my failure all to my other cousins, my failure to my Kaka, my failure to Esther, my failure to my father, my failure to my Lakota people, my failure to … the world. Although the lion's share of my being was reconciled with my failure, there was this minuscule part of me that only felt this tempestuous rage. I quickly turned to my ancestors, and prayed to them to reveal to me what they have always seen in me. Almost immediately, a slight tickle had formed deep within me. Then, it grew and took hold of my stomach and the rest of my digestive tract. Afterward, it entered my lungs, causing my breathing to become more forceful and quicker. Finally, it had found its way to my mouth, and there was no stopping it now. And as the tickle was on the verge of protruding itself explosively beyond, it came to me.

"I am the Calf of the White Buffalo. That is what I have always been, and that is all that is left for me to be."

On having said those words, the tickle ripped itself past my lips with such violence and force that the sound, the shriek, made me feel both sick to my stomach and disoriented. When I could finally collect myself enough to open my eyes, there was Alex. Not only had he fallen to his knees, but he was bent over with both his hands holding his head and ears. Moreover, his eyes were closed, and he was wreathing from pain. 'So, where did he drop the sword?' I kept asking myself. Canvasing the whole area around revealed no clues. When I looked up, there it was, still in its original spot, but its display of fel color patterns had weakened to what was now a cacophony of lackluster noises and incoherent images., almost as if, for lack of a better word, the sword had been stunned.

Repeating, again, those words to myself, "I have always been the Calf of the White Buffalo, and the only thing for me left to become is the Calf of the White Buffalo," I walked toward Alex and started speaking to him. By that time, the sword was only emitting a very pale shade of yellow.

"Alex it's funny" I started comfortably, "how one of those books you made me read will prove itself most timely, especially since I wasn't going to read any of them. Alex, you think that you are intent on killing the 'dragon,' the evil creature of the hero's journey. But you have been seriously misguided. Your journey has not been that of the hero, but of the heroine. As the heroine's ultimate task has virtually nothing to do with destroying 'dragons,' which never have existed, and everything to do with reuniting with her family. Alex, reuniting with your family has always been your chief motivation, from wanting to help your parents find a lasting reconciliation, to making a deal with a trickster God, who in your mind could be either Yahweh or Satan, depending, of course, on the time of day, so you could get Roya and the kiddos back for good, to doing what you did for me, my Kaka, and my cousins, so we could get Misun back. And now, all you have to do is leave that damned sword alone, take my grandfather and my grandmother, and reestablish the link between the living and the dead. And then, you will have everything that you've ever wanted."

After a few minutes, Alex lifted himself from the ethereal ground, walked over toward me and extended his hand to me.

"Snap daddy!" Alex exclaimed, "From the mouth of babes. You just made me realize that one of my favorite movie trilogies is not about the hero's quest at all, but it's all about the heroine's quest. Wow wee!"

And then, while looking at the Goddess Mother, Hermes noticed that She was smiling and nodding Her head while Her eyes were closed. Hermes then let out a loud "Yeah, boy!"

while raising both of his fists above his head. On remembering where he was, he covered his mouth after saying, "oopsy." The Goddess Mother looked at him gravely, at first. But then She smiled at him very warmly, and with one fel wave of Her hand, the veil separating Her throne room and the underworld was removed. At that very moment, /Caggen appeared in the form of a large, black and green praying mantis. After Hermes struck the ethereal ground with his staff, /Caggen walked up next to Alex and put his Trochanter and Coxa on Alex's shoulder, making sure that his Femur did not prick Alex, which Alex was quite wary of.

"Everyman, after countless symmetrical expansions and contractions of the cosmos," the Goddess mother started as She gestured opening and closing her hands several times, revealing to Alex and me that there wasn't just one Big Bang, but very many, "both the masculine and feminine principles, in concert, have decisively managed to initiate an a-symmetrical synchronicity. In other words, you both, together, have broken through the cycles of expansion and contraction to create something utterly new. To both of you, well done!"

/Caggen took that opportunity to collect Alex and me together for a group hug, and yes, he did prick us.

"Henceforth," the Goddess Mother continued, " let it be known that Everyman, otherwise known as Alexander Herbertus Madden, has successfully concluded these 'Ordeals'. And as a pleasant, though astonishing, consequence, he may help prepare What The Thunder Said Tatanka Youtanka Madden to take her rightful place on the Council of the Calf of the White Buffalo."

After having said that, and with a wave of Her hand, Alex and I found ourselves back in the underworld with my grandfather.

Insisting that I come along, Alex introduced me to my grandfather, and before we left, Alex kissed the tips of his thumb and index finger on his right hand, placing them over my grandfather's eyes, restoring their sight. Because Alex was keen on dancing, I was charged with presenting my grandfather to my grandmother, Afterward, my grandfather introduced me as one of their grandchildren.

"And this little lady is Thunder. She is one of Alex's kids."

After checking in briefly with Pieter and Jussi, Alex returned to Adongpiny, she was going to chew him out for being gone for so long, but she changed her mind.

"If you had taken any longa, we would have to wait until next year to finish, which would leave you with your third ass beating from your biggest sister."

Knowing that he was so close, Alex told Adongpiny to go fetch their newly dead and bring them here, and he would initiate the call and response portion of the dance, which will lead us back here. Adongpiny was silent, but she wouldn't move. And when Alex asked her what the problem was, she remained quiet. Examining her body language, Alex had an idea of what the problem was. She didn't want their parents and sisters to look upon her as a cripple.

"If you want," Alex said, I can place you into a different state of consciousness, one that our oldest ancestors practiced. And after she thanked her baby brother, she closed her eyes, and Alex struck her on her forehead quite forcefully with his open palm, causing her back to first arch upright, followed by her back bending to a ninety degree angle, followed by her elbows extending high over her back. When Alex saw the blood running from her nose, he knew that she would be able to dance without experiencing any pain.

There were more than five hundred people waiting for the dance to begin. As Alex looked into the faces of the children, the women, and the men, he could see that this was a long time coming. Indeed, they will shortly take part in an event that perhaps all of them thought would be impossible. Alex didn't want them to wait any longer than they had to, but he did have to wait for Adongpiny to return with their newly dead, and shortly thereafter, she arrived with everyone. Alex had been so busy that he never had time to consider just how intense it would be to meet people who you already knew, but now, you meet them as your biological parents, not to mention a few girls he had hated who wind up being his sisters. Adongpiny brought them to him immediately. When Alex looked upon his birth mother, there were no traces of her unending sadness.

"Oh, my God! Could that woman smile!" Alex exclaimed when he shared the experience with me later.

When Alex faced his biological father, he instinctively called him, "Bwane," which Alex remembered meant 'Sir.'

"Still, you insist on keeping me at a distance from you, my son," Alex's father said. "I've given this a lot of thought. What about Papa?"

Alex, of course, nodded in agreement, not yet willing to say anything in the event it turned out to be stupid.

"I apologize for never having told you who you were when you were here with us," my other grandfather said. "I truly hope you can forgive an old patriarch as myself."

"There is no need to forgive," Alex replied, "for I always had a functional family. I just didn't know it until very recently."

"And he's gracious about it, too," my biological grandfather said to my biological grandmother.

Then, he turns his attention to Alex.

"Are you ready to dance with the dead?"

"Totally!" Alex exclaimed.

"Good, you should perhaps begin," Adongpiny said.

"Alex, before I forget," Alex's biological father said, "many years ago, my father told me to tell you something today. 'Whatever it is that you need to know, you can find it today because today you will dance with the dead. And Alex, the dead know everything.' I hope that helps you."

After looking a bit perplexed initially, Alex thanked my grandfather for reminding him, which, in turn reminded Alex that he had to fetch a few people. As soon as he reintroduced both halves of his families, including me, he initiated the first steps of the dance, which involved stomping on the ground with the heal of the foot. When Alex came crashing down on the ground, which was the roof, the three women who had originally taught him the dance were there with the gatekeeper, apparently to prevent him from turning their descendants away. And as suddenly as the dance began, it broke off because both the newly dead and the old dead had the strong need to reconnect the severed link between them and the living. Re-establishing that link took precedent. After a while, I found Alex and asked him why they had not yet started dancing.

"Unexpectedly, but not surprisingly, the reunion has taken precedent," Alex replied.

As Alex was saying those words, two men who were holding hands and had both been crying walked up to us. As a joke, but later I realized it wasn't a joke, Alex told me that the taller one had to be the world's most competent gatekeeper. One of the women who taught Alex the dance also joined our circle and put her arms around Alex and me. She gestured to the gatekeeper.

"It seems you are ours," the gatekeeper said with some difficulty. "Here is my older brother. You come directly from his line," the gatekeeper said as he pushed his brother into our arms.

"Alex, do you know who your gatekeeper is?" I asked.

"Oh, my God!" Alex replied while still embracing both our direct ancestor and me, "you're right, Thunder, our gatekeeper here doubled as our 'collateral ancestor'."

18
Cape Town, Here We Come

Later that evening after the consummation of the reunion of the living with the dead, Adongpiny subtly brought it to her baby brother's attention that his ancestral home had been turned into an orphanage, of sorts, for girls. She also brought it to his attention that she had borrowed money from the bank against the house, its outbuildings, and the land. After the miscalculations and the re-miscalculations, everyone concerned agreed on a little more than 90,000,000.00 Ugandan Schillings. You wouldn't believe how relieved Alex was when he realized that it was less than $30,000.00.

Alex invited Adongpiny to come with him to the United States, but she declined, giving the excuse that she had to take care of their family's property. But she did make Alex promise that he would bring his wife and children on her birthday, which was a little more than five months away, on May 23. It was also agreed that Alex would come back next year right before the rites of passage ended to take part in the dance.

And as for my American grandparents, they both agreed to stay with my Ugandan grandparents' people, and Alex was able to cultivate a direct line of communication like I have with my mother's people.

Five days later, Jussi dropped Alex and Pieter off at the airport in Entebbe. Jussi hadn't yet booked his flight to Helsinki. Yes, he was going to study to become an elementary-school teacher. But before Alex would let him leave, he reminded Jussi to reread Wilfred Owen's poem, *Dulce et Decorum est*, replace the detailed substance that is more relevant to Jussi's wartime experiences, and then, Jussi should ask himself, "Is it truly sweet and honorable to die for one's country?" Jussi was laughing at how Alex wouldn't let him go until he promised to do it, which he did.

"Alex, the secret to being a good, competent psychoanalyst is taking on your analysand's issues as if they were your own," Pieter said as they were both looking for a ticketing agent. "You are a natural. You are a natural."

"Merci," Alex replied.

"Alex, I haven't visited the people who raised me in over seven years," Pieter said.

"Piet, I need to get to Maine, so I can bring Roya and the kiddos back home," Alex said. "I know what the problem is now. I just need to go to the house to get some addresses and phone numbers."

"Are you planning on going to Iran?" Pieter asked.

"Well, I will have to plan it out, but yeah," Alex replied.

"And you call me crazy!" Pieter exclaimed.

"Pieter, I know it sounds crazy, but I know she will come back now," Alex said.

"When you are swinging from the highest gallows in downtown Teheran, remember, I told you so," Pieter said. "Alex, I have to go to my home, to the Northern Cape."

Alex did not respond any further. They continued to walk until they reached a ticket office that advertised major American and European airlines. Fortunately, the ticket office did sell tickets for American carriers to New York, and Alex was about to start the process to order two tickets to New York. But when he turned to Pieter to ask him for his passport, Alex couldn't believe what he was looking at. Pieter had become the antithesis of what the trickster was supposed to be, impervious to pain, suffering, the rules, and disappointment.' And what about that built-in subversion?' Alex thought to himself. 'Where the hell did that go?'

Ma'am, do you also fly to Cape Town or Joh'burg?" Alex asked.

Of Course," she replied, "we fly nonstop to Johannesburg and to Cape Town."

"Pieter, are we going to Joh'burg or Cape Town?" Alex asked without looking at Pieter.

There was no response from Pieter, which left an acute pang in Alex's chest.

"Pieter, come on," Alex said as he nudged Pieter's shoulder. "Are we going to Johannesburg or Cape Town?"

"What? What?" Pieter repeated as he came out of his stupor.

"Are we going to Joh'burg or cape Town?" Alex repeated.

"Cape Town, Cape Town," Pieter repeated in very quick succession, as if he were afraid that someone would change his or her mind.

"Would you prefer to fly with SAAS?" the ticket office attendant asked.

"Yes, Ma'am," Alex replied, "and one way."

"Would you like to book a connecting flight from Cape Town to New York?" the ticket office agent asked.

"No, thank you," Alex replied.

Once the ticket was in his hand, Pieter perked up quite remarkably. And as they were walking through customs, Alex thought to himself that 'it is better to give than to receive.' And he was proud of himself for finally understanding why that was the case.

Right before they reached their terminal, a woman who was selling mobile phones asked if they would be interested in a smart phone. Alex declined, but Pieter asked her if she had a SIM card that he could use to call South Africa. Although she didn't have any separate SIM cards, she did offer them her phone to call South Africa. After having made four calls, Pieter had arranged a ride from the Cape Town Airport. On returning her phone to her, Pieter thanked her and asked her how much money she wanted for the four calls to South Africa. Initially, she said $75.00, happy go luckily, as if it were a mere $0.10. Alex laughed at her and thought that if it weren't for the fact that she was trying to rob him blind, he could have liked her. But after the smoke, haggling, and dust had cleared, they all settled on $30.00, which, according to Alex, was still quite exorbitant.

19
The Blessings Come Full Circle

In the Jordan District of Teheran, not everyone in Roya's household was getting a good night's sleep.

BAM-BAM! BAM-BAM!

"*Ma'man*, wake up!" Marjan screamed. "Wake up!"

"*Q' que c'est, ma fille?*" Roya asked as she scrambled to find and put on her robe.

"*Ma'man*, Sana'a is crying in her sleep. I tried waking her up, but it didn't work," Marjan said.

After taking Marjan back to her bed and tucking her in, Roya entered Sana'a's room where Roya found her mother trying to comfort Sana'a. After telling Sana'a that her mother was there, the grandmother rose up from Sana'a's bed and moved away but stayed a while in the room.

"*Ma'man*, Baba is dead, he is dead," Sana'a repeated. "I saw him. He was swinging from a long rope, and we all had to watch."

"*Ma coeur,* if your father were dead, surely Pieter would inform us," Roya replied.

"Pieter wouldn't know because it happened here," Sana'a retorted.

"Here, in Teheran?" Roya asked.

"*Bale!*" Sana'a exclaimed.

"Sana'a, listen to me carefully," Roya said. "Are you saying that your father has already come here, or will he be coming here?"

It took a while for Sana'a to answer the question, but as Roya could see that Sana'a was composing herself as she looked for Alex, Roya waited patiently, kissing her daughter's forehead and cheeks every now and then. As it was evident that Sana'a was calming down, her grandmother took leave of them, but before she left, Roya asked her to check-up on Marjan and the boys. After about twenty minutes, Sana'a fell asleep. Relieved that her daughter could sleep, Roya quietly rose up from the bed, walked to the door, switched off the light, and exited the room. As Roya's mother's bedroom light was on, Roya tapped on the door, opened it, and informed her mother that Sana'a was sleeping. When Roya entered her bedroom, she walked over to her night stand and called the landline number in Bozeman, but there was only the answering machine, on which she left no message. Then, she called Alex's cell phone, and, again, got only his cell phone's answering machine. She never thought she would ever do it, but she even found herself dialing Pieter's number, and yet again all she got was his answering machine.

'If Pieter came with him, he would surely get caught,' Roya thought.

At a little after 5:00 am, Ssana'a entered her mother's bedroom and sat down next to her. They were now in reverse postures. Roya was laying down, and Sana'a was sitting next to her.

"Are you feeling better?" Roya asked Sana'a.

"No," Sana'a replied.

"I tried calling your father and Pieter, but no one picked up," Roya said.

"*Ma'man*, Baba isn't here yet, but he will come," San'a said, "and they will catch him and hang him."

After breakfast, Roya asked her mother to watch the kiddos because she had to go out on a few errands. Roya had her driver take her to the central police station because on her mother's side there are several senior officers. In Shiraz, she had a third cousin who was the top cop, Guardian Major General. But on this occasion, she was going to pay her cousin Omar a visit, who held the rank of Guardian Lieutenant Colonel. As soon as Roya arrived at the police station, she was whisked away to her cousin's office with all the pomp duly deserving of a VIP. After a few minutes, Omar entered his office with a police officer of comparable rank. On seeing Roya seated on one of the chairs, the other officer nodded to Roya and left.

"I do apologize, cousin. But none of these bastards told me I had a guest," Omar said as he walked over to Roya to exchange the customer kisses on the cheek. "How are my auntie and my nieces and nephews?"

"They are all quite well," Roya replied. "And how is Nadine?"

"She is spending all of my money," Omar replied. "That's what she's doing. The only time when she can't spend my money is shortly after America enforces those embargos on us, to prevent us from building atomic bombs that we have absolutely no intention of building. But what can you do?"

Roya reached in her purse and pulled out a carton of cigarettes that were gift wrapped and handed it to Omar.

"Oh, cousin!" Omar exclaimed. "You shouldn't have, *merci*."

After patting his various pockets multiple times each, Omar realized that he was fresh out of cigarettes. While frantically ripping off the wrapping paper, he smiled at Roya. As he opened the carton with a little more care and took out a pack of his favorite American cigarettes, Omar was clearly delighted.

After first offering Roya a cigarette, which she, of course, declined, Omar took one, threw the pack on his desk, lit the one he had between his fingers, and took a voluminous drag.

"Cousin, we are very well met!" Omar exclaimed as he exhaled. "Now that we have dispensed with the niceties, what can I do for you?"

Knowing all too well that her cousin held very little patience behind the façade, she jumped right to it.

"Omar, if I knew that a foreigner was going to try and enter the Islamic Republic illegally…"

"Are you reporting an imminent breach?" Omar interrupted.

"No! No!" Roya stressed. "It's only that I have reason to believe that my husband will try to come here."

"To kidnap the children?" Omar asked.

"No! no!" Roya stressed once again. "I think he will try to convince me to go back to him."

"Roya, I don't even like my own domestic affairs, let alone those of others," Omar admitted still with a hint of patience. "How do you think he will come here?"

"I think he will come via Abu Dhabi or Dubai," Roya said.

"Ah, by way of our white and blue cabbage boats," Omar surmised. "So, he plans on stowing away on one of those boats. Of course, you understand that he will be caught, tried, and hung?"

Visibly alarmed with what her cousin had said, Roya started proposing ideas.

"Wouldn't it be possible to create a net or web, trap him in the net, keep him for a few days at my home, and then return him to the Emirates in one piece?" Roya asked.

"Certainly, certainly, if this were America, where everything and everyone is for sale, even their honor," Omar said. "But as you aptly said, cousin, this here is the Islamic Republic, where corruptibility is rewarded with shame and death, a most macabre death. So, to answer your question, if you were not the daughter of my favorite auntie, I would relish hearing you scream as you are being tortured, and finally, after I fit the noose snug around your fat, bourgeoisie throat, I would push you. Get the hell out of my sight before I change my mind!"

As Roya was escorted out of the police station, she managed to hold back the tears until she was outside of the building and she had walked away from the main entrance. Again, she called Alex as well as Pieter, and again, her efforts bore her no fruit.

***

When Alex and Pieter arrived in Cape Town, they were met by a Bushman couple. Alex was surprised to hear them speak Afrikaans with Pieter. Alex also realized that he had only heard Pieter speak Afrikaans a few times. But the Bushman couple turned out not to be a couple after all. They were siblings. Alex was also surprised to see that when they started speaking with clicks, Pieter replied back to them in their language, clicks and all.
"Pieter, you speak San?" Alex asked.

"Don't say San, Alex, say *Ju*," Pieter corrected Alex, and yes, I do understand a smidgen. Their parents raised me from the age of two till seven, but I am nowhere near proficient."

Pieter did introduce them, to Alex, but because Alex couldn't pronounce their names quite right, the woman told him to call her Sarah, and her brother told Alex to call him Solomon, like the wise king. After three and a half hours of driving due North from the airport in Cape Town, Alex saw a sign that read 'Botha Farm and Game Park.'

"Pieter, is this your family's farm?" Alex asked.

"This was once part of my family's holdings a very long time ago," Pieter replied. "But from what my siblings and I inherited, my brothers and sisters sold most of their shares, but I kept mine, and I even managed to buy a bit of theirs before they sold out."

"How large is it?" Alex asked.

"It's a little more than five hundred hectares," Pieter replied. "Originally, when my first Dutch ancestor came here, he took more than 10,000 hectares from the Bushmen and the other tribes that lived here."

"He took that much land and resources for himself?" Alex asked.

"Alex, you have absolutely no idea what the original Dutch Reformed settlers did here," Pieter replied.

"Then, what happened to the indigenous people who lived here first?" Alex asked.

"If they were sound in body, they could stay and work," Pieter replied, "but if they weren't, they had to go, and where they went was of no concern to the Blanks."

"What if they refused to leave the only home they ever knew?" Alex asked.

"They were killed," Sarah interjected.

"Do Mrs. Sarah and Mr. Solomon work for you?" Alex asked.

They all laughed at his question.

"Alex they are my sister and brother," Pieter replied. "When I was seven, my father got rid of their family because he heard me speak their Bushmen dialect. When I was sixteen, I found them. They were working on another farm. I always kept in contact with them, and when my father died, I brought them back home. And to carve it in stone, so to speak, I sold 250 hectares, 625 acres, to them for one rand. There is also a fund, so they will always be able to pay any property taxes or other fees."

"Why didn't you stay here and live the good life?" Alex asked.

"Our shaman told me at a very early age that I had the gift to heal people," Pieter replied. "She told me that it was imperative that I go out and cure everyone who has the 'White People's' Disease. When I met you, I felt sorry for you because although you were black on the outside, the 'White People's Disease' was corrupting you on the inside. So, I decided to make you my long-term project. And I am pleased to say that you are well on your way to recovery."

Curious as to what disease he had, according to Pieter, Alex asked him.

"Pieter, what is the 'White People's Disease?'"

"Why Alex, it is when you put money and things before people and animals," Pieter replied.

"In other words, you put dead things before life, and in this way, you reduce, diminish, your own humanity to such a degree that you become what you value most, some thing."

"But very important, Solomon started, "we can sometimes live and hunt and gather and be together like in the old days. We can still honor our ancestors."

Listening to Solomon made Alex think of me and my Kaka.

'So, there is actually something that is sacred to Pieter after all!' Alex thought to himself, astonished.

After having ridden in the van for four hours straight, not including the bathroom break, Alex was starting to get numb in the right butt cheek. So, he asked Pieter how much longer it would be before they arrived. Pieter would say that it's not much further, but after about 45 minutes, Alex would ask again. But after having sat in the van for five hours, Alex wouldn't accept Pieter's standard answer, so Pieter was obliged to inform Alex that they had only traveled halfway.

"Are you telling me that it's a thousand fucking kilometers from Cape Town to Kimberly?" Alex asked.

"Alex, you've been so nice lately, so I didn't want to ruffle your feathers by sharing with you such minutiae" Pieter said.

Alex wanted to scream, but he managed to control himself, mostly because of Sarah and Solomon. After another 525 kilometers, which included one stop to get gas, eat and drink, they arrived at the Botha family farm. It was a surprisingly green spot.

"It's so green here," Alex commented.

"Yes, my forefathers made a point of always controlling more than a sufficient amount of water for themselves," Pieter said.

"What kind of wild animals do you have here?" Alex asked.

"We have almost everything," Sarah said smiling. "We have zebras, giraffes, lions, some leopards, some cheetahs…"

"Oh, cheetahs are my favorite!" Alex interjected.

"We have elands!" Solomon asserted. "They are the most important animal for us."

"Do you have any elephants or rhinos?" Alex asked.

"When we were children, there were a few," Pieter said, "but poachers have long since killed them all off."

"What about hippos?" Alex asked.

"We don't have them, but we can take you to see them, if you want," Sarah offered.

When they arrived at the house, Sarah, Solomon and Pieter reverted back to speaking Afrikaans with a Bushman word or two inserted here and there. After a few minutes, two teenage Bushmen girls came to the main house to take Alex to the cabin where he would be staying. It was only about three hundred meters away from the main house, and Alex was impressed by the solar panels that covered the entire roof. When he entered the cabin, he was pleasantly surprised to see that the bed was made. He even inspected the sheets, which were crisp and clean, no bed bugs. Afterward, he walked to the light switch and turned it on. One of the girls told him to save the light for the nighttime because there will only be three hours of light, and it is getting dark. Alex looked around for the bathroom, but there wasn't one. When he asked about that, the girls told him that there was an outhouse, of sorts, in the back of the cabin, but he would have to go to "the big house" to wash. Before they left, they showed Alex the water that was in the refrigerator just for him.

Alex wanted to wander around, but standing face-to-face with a leopard or a pride of lions didn't sit well with him, so he simply sat on the cabin porch and took all the sights and sounds in. About two hours later, shortly before 9:00 pm, Sarah and the two girls brought Alex some food. That's when Alex found out that the two girls were Sarah's daughters. When Alex asked about Pieter, Sarah told him that Pieter was visiting his sisters, but tomorrow he would come and "fetch" Alex to take him near the Namibian border to a big Bushmen celebration. When Alex asked her what the occasion was, Sarah shrugged her shoulders as if she didn't understand the question. But her older daughter said something in Bushmen, and then Sarah laughed and said, "We celebrate that we can be together."

The Goddess Returns

At 6:00 am the next morning, Pieter woke Alex up and brought him to the main house for breakfast. At the big house, Alex met Sarah and Solomon's other three siblings, one man and two women, and most of their children. Although Sarah and Solomon's parents had passed away, they did have two very sweet and ancient looking great-aunts whose faces were full of grooves that gave their features the effect of being full of character and strength. And all of the children, all twelve of them, were absolutely beautiful. They looked as though they had the faces of all the various peoples of the world in their own, Oriental, Latina, Caucasian, Black, everyone.

When breakfast was over, Sarah informed Alex that he had had ostrich egg and eland for breakfast. At that time, Alex didn't know how significant the eland was in Bushman culture, and because he didn't respond to what Sarah had told him about breakfast, she called one of her girls, and asked her how to say something in English. The girl repeated it to her mother under her breath, so Alex would not hear it first from her lips. Then, Sarah turned to Alex, took a deep breath and spoke.

"The eland is the most potency and the most important animal for the Bushmen people. We prepared it for you because Pieter calls you his brother. And that makes you our brother, forever."

She then moved her head towards his, until her nose and forehead touched his. Alex closed his eyes, but the oldest girl told him to open his eyes and look at her mother. Afterward, the two girls repeated the gesture with Alex.

When Alex saw Pieter again, he asked him how far the Namibian border was from his farm.

"Alex, we are not only going to the border, but we will be going beyond it, into Namibia," Pieter said.

"Why do we have to go to Namibia?" Alex asked, wondering if he will ever get to see Roya and the kiddos again.

"You see Alex, some of the Bushmen I am related to live in the Northern Cape, here, in the Upington area, and others live in Namibia," Pieter said. "And now that they all know that I am here with … you, they all want to meet you. And most of them are already gathered in Namibia."

It was amazing that Alex knew what Pieter was saying without ever saying what their relationship meant to him. And Alex felt ashamed that he would have missed this if Sarah hadn't said what she said earlier that morning. But suffice it to say that everything regarding what they thought and felt about each other was tacitly understood and would always be.

After some thought, Alex politely informed Pieter that he would not be riding in the van to Namibia primarily because that trip would last at least five hours longer than the one from Cape Town to Kimberly, which was already too long. However, Pieter did manage to persuade Alex to

fly to Namibia in a single-engine plane. Of
course, there was the added stipulation that Pieter
would not end up being the pilot. Alex assumed
that the pilot would be a Bushman, but it was a
27-year-old German from Magdeburg, Germany,
which was a city in the former German
Democratic Republic. His name was Thomas
Mueller. He told Pieter that he came to Southern
Africa after he saw a documentary about the
Bushmen people. He was first attracted by their
beauty, and when he heard that everyone alive
today comes from them, he decided to come to
Southern Africa to get to know them. He first
went to Botswana. Afterward, he went to
Zimbabwe, but it was in Namibia where he found
his husband, who was an artist. When Alex asked
him if he will eventually move back to Germany
with his husband, he told Alex that he felt Alive
in Africa.

"Ich fuehle mich lebengig hier in Afrika.
Aber nicht in Deutschland."

After a little more than an hour and a half,
Thomas started his descent.

"Are we in Namibia?" alex asked.

"No, this is Upington," Pieter said. "Thomas
has to pick up his husband. He is visiting some
family members here."

After Thomas had turned off the plane, he
disembarked, placed two blocks of wood in front
and two blocks behind the wheels of the landing
gear. And while he refueled the plane, he told
Alex and Pieter that it will take him an hour to

pick up his husband, say hello to his family, and return to the plane. Because it would take so long, Thomas asked them if they preferred to wait or come for the ride. Pieter and Alex decided to go with him. They took a taxi from Upington International Airport to the Dr. Harry Surtie Hospital, which was less than ten minutes away.

"Mein Swager hat sich drei Rippen gebroched," Thomas said as he exited the taxi.

When Pieter asked how Thomas's brother-in-law broke three of his ribs, Thomas simply shrugged his shoulders. At the hospital, the receptionist took them to Thomas's Brother-in-law, and the room was crowded with family and friends. Because the windows were closed, the air was quite stale, and Alex smelled what he thought was vomit. So, shortly thereafter, he left the room telling Pieter that he was going to the bathroom. Alex did not make a point of remembering where the room was in relation to the main entrance, where he went, to get some fresher air.

After a few minutes of relative isolation, not wanting to be left behind in the middle of Upington, Northern Cape, South Africa, which bordered the Kalahari Desert, Alex decided to return to the stifling, crowded room. However, as soon as he entered the hospital, he took the first left turn, when he should have taken the second one. Thus, he ended up on the wrong wing of the hospital. Thinking that he was at the correct door,

Alex opened it and entered the room. When Alex entered the room, five pairs of eyes were looking at him, the patient who was laying in the bed, three young men, and an older white woman. The others, including the patient, were all Bushmen. Alex excused himself and was about to leave the room, but the older white woman begged him not to leave. She spoke English with a British accent, telling Alex that the patient, her sister, and the three younger Bushmen's great-grandmother was in a coma for more than two weeks.

"But two days ago, she suddenly woke up and said, 'He is coming.' So, we waited, and after two days, you opened the door," ethe White woman said.

The patient, who was quite light-skinned, had wrinkles, not only on her forehead but throughout her face, horizontally, diagonally, and vertically. Yet, her skin still glowed, and she was beautiful.

As soon as she saw Alex, she sat up, drew her hands together, and waited for Alex. Again, all the other eyes turned to Alex to see what he would do. Not believing what was happening, Alex walked right up to the bed, and started telling the story of how and why my kaka gave him what was called, "Blessings." The older white woman translated what Alex was saying in Bushmen, and the patient became more and more animated as the story progressed. After Alex finished relating the story, he drew his hands together. And blew slowly into them, and the patient cried out and blew warm, loving air into her small, wrinkled hands as well. Then, Alex placed his hands on the patient's chest, and she did the same to him. And after a minute or so, the patient collapsed. When Alex turned around, he was afraid that the others would be angry, but they all looked relieved, and surprisingly so. Everyone could see that she was still breathing, so Alex could also relax. The older, white woman looked at Alex, smiled, and asked him his name.

"My name is Alex," he said.

"I bet you were lost," she said laughing.

Alex nodded, and she volunteered to get him where he needed to be. While she escorted Alex to the receptionist, he asked her a question.

"Do you happen to know what that was about?" Alex asked.

"From what my mother told me years ago," the woman started.

"Ah, she raised you," Alex interjected.

"No, that woman is my sister," she replied, "but our mother told us about it very often. Tens of thousands of years ago, when the various tribes were migrating throughout Africa, bands would split up and join with others. It was a very fluid time. My mother was told, when the blessings were handed down to her that when their band separated, for example, the one that you are connected to and the one that we are connected to, split up. The blessings were how they said good bye, and it would be the way that they could identify each other if they ever met again. My siblings doubted whether what happened here today could ever happen. They thought it was lost for good, but here you are. Thank you!"

When Alex got back to his crowded, stifling room, Thomas, his husband, and Pieter were ready to go.

"I was afraid that you were lost," Pieter said.

"I was," Alex replied.

"Oh, yes, Roya emailed me and told me to tell you to get in contact with her," Pieter said as he handed Alex his cell phone.

"What time is it in Iran?" Alex asked.

"All I know is that we are seven hours ahead of Bozeman time," Pieter said.

As it was 6:30 pm in South Africa, Alex figured that Iran was two, maybe three hours, ahead, which meant that it couldn't be later than 9:30 pm in Teheran.

When He called, the phone rang only once before Roya's voice was on the other end.

"Alex, is it you?" Roya asked.

"Hello to you, too," Alex said. "And yes, it is me."

"Where are you?" Roya asked.

"I'm in South Africa," Alex replied.

Alex expected her to ask him why he was there, but she didn't.

"Don't do it Alex!" Roya exclaimed.

"Don't do what?" Alex asked.

"Sana'a dreamt that you came here, but they caught you and lynched you," Roya replied. "So, don't do it!"

"But I know what happened," Alex said. "I know why you left me."

"You can't know that, Alex," Roya replied. "No one knows that but me, and I have never told anyone."

"Roya, you went some place and found your brother Shotvah with a man," Alex said. "His name was Kivih, or Kevih."

"Kaveh," Roya interjected. "His name was Kaveh. He was my fiancé."

"Oh," Alex said, realizing that things had just become a bit more complicated.

"Do you know what I saw them doing?" Roya asked.

"Yes, Shotvah was performing fellatio on Kaveh," Alex said. "They both saw you look at them. Kaveh smiled at you, but Shotvah was ashamed. Because you regarded him as cheating on you, you never spoke with him again, but he thought you shunned him because he wasn't a man. As a result, he joined the army and was killed in the war with Iraq."

Roya was silently crying while listening to this.

"Roya, Roya," Alex called her name. "Are you there?"

"*Bale*, yes, I am here," Roya replied.

"You said that if I found out what was wrong, we could be together again," Alex said.

"But Alex, you once told me that there is no forgiveness," Roya said. "I only wanted to tell my brother that I love him unconditionally, Alex. But I can't do that. And if there is no forgiveness, I can't live."

"Roya, Jacques Derrida said what's the point of there being forgiveness, if it can't forgive everything, even the unforgivable?" Alex said. "And I think he's right."

After an extended silence, Roya promised Alex that she would come back home to Bozeman, but, of course, her mother would be coming along. When Alex asked about her mother having her friends around, Roya told him that for her mother, her family is most important.

When they hung up the phone, it suddenly dawned on Alex that /Caggen had kept his part of the deal. So, Alex had to keep his and help me become the best Calf of the White Buffalo that I could be.

Epilogue

It finally happened--after all these years, I have
finally been "definitively" named 'the Calf of the
White Buffalo' by my people, and yet, I still have
less of an idea of what I should say at this 60th
session of the Commission on the Status of
Women here at the UN headquarters in New
York than I did that morning eight years ago
when my Kaka and I had that early morning
discussion over breakfast, day-old cinnamon fry
bread and coffee.

Although I am only required to be here for one
day, for the keynote address, which I will give, I
decided to attend the last five days of the eleven-
day event. My minder, Sharon Reed,
continuously insists that I have to, "circulate, mix
and mingle. That's what the UN is all about,
networking." After I had arrived, a surprising
number of people, mostly journalists, and mostly
women with about half-a-dozen men, asked me
all kinds of questions, many of which were
repeated during the Q & A sessions.

"Following patriarchy's demise, how shall
that new world order look?" a British reporter
asked me. Several other women wanted to
interview me. However, I didn't feel comfortable
with the idea of a formal interview. But I did
agree to a more informal question-and-answer
session in a small, out-of-the-way conference
room. Out of habit and decorum, I guess, the
organizers wanted an impeccably dressed French

woman named Clydia to introduce me with a speech that was so—what I thought—inappropriately erudite that I had to quickly switch gears and really focus on what she was saying to follow her:

"Thank you, Clydia," I said, "for your dissertation on me. Now, I not only know how I have to dress, but I also know that I have to prepare five years in advance if I'm ever asked to introduce a Nobel Laureate in either Stockholm or Oslo." Then the questions came.

"Dr. Madden,"

"Don't call me that!" I insisted.

"Sorry, Thunder, how do you define phallocracy? Do you believe that there are multiple phallocracies or just one, and do you really believe that they, or it, will cease to exist within our life-time?" a middle-aged black woman asked.

"'Primacy of the phallus', 'phallocentrism', 'phallologism', and now 'phallocracy'. And it goes on and on. My sister, we do not lack a penis; we are the ones who have the babies and our bodies can feed them, too. Have any of you ever thought that perhaps that's where it—patriarchy--started, men realized that after contributing their seed that they were no longer necessarily needed? I personally believe this--the trauma that they experience from this realization was so utterly poignant that in their desperation they found it necessary to create patriarchy, to redeem their self-image. So, we are not suffering from penis envy, but men, especially patriarchal men, are suffering, perhaps unconsciously, from womb envy. Think of just how flimsy the argument supporting patriarchy is: Biologically, men are bigger and stronger than women. That's it. And on the basis of that, men assumed that they were better than women. As Gerda Lerner and many other sisters and brothers tell us, our role in the formation of civilization was and still is so stupendously imperative that without women there would not only never have been 'civilization,' but neither would there be any men, which reminds me of conversations I have had with some of my more radical feminist brothers and sisters who sincerely wish that we were like those bees who can reproduce females without the services of sperm from a male bee. But I constantly have to remind them that many of us live and would die for hetero-sexual coitus, even if our husbands and partners, at times, are jerks. The problem has always been that we have not been in a position--much like Blacks, Hispanics, the Indigenous Nations, and anyone else without clout—to have a voice that is heard, valued, respected, and counted. For example, the 13th Amendment abolished slavery. That's a good thing, right? Of course, it is! Indeed, it is so good that we failed to consider the possible ramifications of the inserted clause, 'except as a punishment for crime whereof the party shall have been duly convicted.' And here we are today where it is being used to incarcerate and exploit an exorbitant number of Black, Hispanic, and Indigenous men and women, in many instances to work as slaves, for a mere pittance. They continue to be regarded as property to be exploited for anyone else's benefit, as long as it is not their own..."

"Pardon me Thunder," an elderly ostensibly effeminate man said, "are you suggesting that the 13th Amendment requires some amending of its own?"

"Most indubitably!" I answered. "When you look at the history of private property," I continued, "you learn that the first form of private property was the ownership of human beings, us females and our bodies; it started around the advent of agriculture. And I think that's because men feared—and still fear--that power that is part and parcel of being a woman— it must have been like having your very own genie in a bottle. And they wanted to control that power, the power of our bodies, especially as we moved from the hunter-gather economy to horticulture, and then to full-blown agriculture. And yes, we have been languishing under male domination, 'patriarchy', for millennia—indeed, some authorities believe that it may have started as many as six thousand years ago. I remember reading one authority who believes that it may have even started eight thousand years ago--and, yes, our despair is as palpable today as it has ever been, but we won't get anywhere by obsessing over men's penises, 'the rule of the penis', or the primacy of the male utterance. Actually, I believe that men are obsessing far more over our vaginas, wombs, behinds, and breasts than we could ever be over their penises. Besides, there are many men who are desperately waiting in the wings for that moment to step out from under the shadows of the domineering males in their lives and with us women, all of us sisters, again, everywhere, rise up and say no more to female genital mutilation; no more rapes, sanctioned or otherwise; no more to gender-based violence; no more pitting sister against sister; no more to fathers, brothers, husbands, or anyone else telling a woman what she may and may not do with her own body; no more to child slavery or any other form of bondage; no more to child marriages; no more to women and children being made destitute, especially when it is due to men's bellicose folly; no more to the gender-wage gap and denying women complete equality—not the kind of equality Orwell describes in "Animal Farm"--and the deserved recognition as fully honored members in society; no more to racism or any other form of superiority b-b-bigotry; no more to distributive bargaining when it comes to people's lives; no more mindless destruction of our eco-systems; and no more to anyone using his or her power capriciously or otherwise just because they can. But to realize that future, we will need men's help to turn the tide, so let's not antagonize them more than we have to, okay!" I stressed. "What's the next question?"

"So, you do make a distinction between feminist rights and emancipation?"

"Definitely!"

"Would you please explain?" a man asked.

"Sure,…"

"This future utopia that you envision is as preposterous as it is naive! It will never happen because the action, the sheer momentum required for this 'revolution' of yours would be colossal," a very short-cropped, red-headed man who reminded me of Van Gogh's self-portraits, but with both ears intact interrupted.

"Could we blease maintain a more respectful and less adversair tone for zis question and answer session, si vous plait?" Clydia interjected with her commandingly mesmerizing French accent.

"That's okay, Clydia. I don't take his comment offensively at all. In fact, I think he's making a very valid point," I said. "Indeed, it's utterly terrifying to witness—with my own eyes and ears--just how adept some people have become: They have the almost uncanny knack of making poor, under-educated, and unemployed people believe that they can have the self-same interests as the wealthy, and for millennia, all kinds of men—sons, brothers, husbands, fathers, uncles, etc.--and women--have been convincing girls and women, sometimes coercively, that it was their duty to support anything that was in the best interest of the family, or the community, or even the nation, often at her own economic,

political, emotional, moral, and spiritual
detriment. Women were made to hate and deny
themselves, abandoning everything feminine,
wanting only to endeavor masculine pursuits,
forgetting all sense of solidarity with their sisters,
as if we were all enemies. Today, because of
mass media, we know that our sisters and their
kids in various parts of the world—Syria, Iraq,
Uganda, Guatemala, Lebanon, the United States,
Greece, Palestine, Nigeria, Venezuela, The
Democratic Republic of Congo, etc.—are
undergoing unimaginable suffering. I'm going
off on a bit of a tangent, but the point I want to
make is that emancipation is the general call to
everyone's freedom, all men's freedom, all
women's freedom, regardless of orientation,
color, religion, etc. Feminist rights make all
those freedoms detailed and explicit. To press
my point even further that emancipation includes
men's freedom, when I was in Durban, South
Africa last year, an Afrikaner gentleman came up
to me after the conference and told me the
following: 'Yes, you are right. As a white man, I
am a prisoner of both apartheid and patriarchy. A
little more than seven years ago, my son, our
only child, announced his engagement to a well-
known, black journalist. I told him that I would
disown him immediately if he didn't break-off all
contact with this woman. Of course, he didn't, so
I did. My wife tried to talk to me, telling me that
we are living in a new time and that the old ways
are dead. I smacked her hard on her cheek; I

remember feeling so outrageously incensed that she could actually think of that, let alone say it to me, to me out-loud. Needless to say, she left me. After a while, part of me acknowledged that I missed and needed her as well as my son, who by that time was going to be a father. But the other part of me, the obstinate, patriarchal side, was far too proud to admit my error. After divorcing me, my wife, my ex-wife remarried, surprisingly with a more progressive Afrikaner, who accepted the miscegenation between my son, his wife, and their children, my grandchildren.' I told him to make a point of re-establishing a relationship with his son and his family. But he screamed frantically, 'It's too late! It's too late! It's too late!' At first, I couldn't understand what he was saying, which he eventually saw on my face. And then, he said that they all died in a car accident when they were driving from Bloemfontein, where my ex-wife lived, to my son's second home in Port Alfred. You would not believe how much I would give to have died in that collision with them.' I looked into this gentleman's eyes, and I saw at that moment that white South Africans, especially the men. were also front-row-seat victims of that prison, apartheid, which was of their own making. A few days later, I realized that most men were also prisoners of patriarchy."

"Thunder, from your books, your articles, and the interviews, we know your views; you do not believe in establishing a matriarchy, for you acknowledge that masculine values are necessary," a younger woman in a faded jeans jacket said.

"And, although there are matrilineal cultures, such as the Dine' and various ethnic groups in southern India, where the females inherit the family's property, it seems that there have never been any matriarchies," I added.

"However, they must not have free reign; feminine values are also needed in the world to temper masculine values." The woman in the jeans jacket continued.

"Exactly! The feminine principle as well as the masculine principle must not only work together in the world, but in order for each and every person to be whole, complete, the feminine as well as the masculine principle must be actively present in each and every one of us as well, otherwise known as *Anima* and *Animus*. *Anima, according to Carl Jung,* represents the feminine principle in men, and *Animus* represents the masculine principle in women," I said.

"So, they are like *Yin* and *Yang*," a gray-bearded man said.

"Yes, but don't see them as being two halves of the whole; they also have to intermingle and engage in each other. In other words, there shouldn't be pure feminine value or pure masculine value. The problems seem to arise when we started delineating, prescribing, and pegging the gender roles. Males had to carry out only so-called masculine functions and women could only carry out so-called feminine functions. But as women also have to express themselves in some masculine ways just as men have to express themselves in some feminine ways, why shouldn't women and men be left alone to pursue their own happiness?" I said. "Anyone else?"

"Thunder, my name is Karen Green and I'm with the Ezine 'Women Now'. In a few days, as you are the 'Calf of the White Buffalo', you will address the 60th session of the UN's Commission on the Status of Women here in New York, which is a pretty big deal. Your ascension to fame has been nothing less than meteoric, to say the least. Yet, with regard to your background, we know very little about you," an older woman said while knitting what looked like a sock.

"We know that your mother was a Lakota Sioux and a shaman and that your father is an African-American, a school principal as well as a shaman. We also know that you have a Master's degree in Ethnic and Women's Studies from the University of Arizona, and that several universities have bestowed upon you honorary doctor degrees for your work. And still, we don't really know that much about 'you,' the 'private, personal you.' Many of my readers are dying to find out how you got here," a woman with a flowery green, yellow, and red scarf said.

"I don't know if you really want to hear about that; it would be quite a long, boring story," I said.

The Goddess Returns

"Thunder, my name is Marion. Your voice is impacting die Welt in major ways. Zum beispiel, I read just dis morning zat zere are countries in Africa, Zud America, Europa, und auch a handful of states here in Amerika zat, az ve speak, are debating ob—I mean vheser--to introduce legislation zat vill finally make gender equality the law, with tees!" a bald woman with a heavy German accent said.

"It's amazing how several news agencies have hired teams of investigators for the sole purpose of digging up dirt on you to discredit you," a stern, hard-boiled looking man with black-rimmed glasses said almost disdainfully. But they've come up with zilch, nada. I want to know how that's possible. I want to know your story!" he demanded.

"Thunder, I'm a man as well as a captain of industry, and although I agree that our present political and economic state of affairs leave much to be desired, especially when billions of people in the world are suffering needlessly because of it..."

"Not only people, but entire species! Remember, we are living in the Anthropocene, coined by Paul Crutzer, and Noam Chomsky tells us that, 'we are the asteroid.' In other words, we are the cause of what some scientists call 'the sixth extinction event,' and I personally believe that there won't be much left to witness the seventh. This extinction of countless species—perhaps, notwithstanding our own—should evoke images of how it must have been when that asteroid slammed into the Earth some 65,000,000 years ago, and all the mayhem it caused," I said.

"Uh, what was I going to say?" the captain continued. "Oh, there it is, I'm afraid that if you actually, somehow managed to end patriarchy-- and I am certain you also have capitalism in your crosshairs—in the world, there would only be massive chaos and pandemonium. I need something reassuring, something that will allay my fears, especially since we do not have any models of how a truly egalitarian society, let alone an egalitarian world, should look. I don't know, but maybe something from your story can do that for me."

"Ladies and gentlemen, I don't know if telling you my stories would be a good idea, because this shouldn't be about me. It is about making the best possible world for everyone, even for the men who are in perpetual power. For, in his Lord-Servant or Master-Slave Dialectic, Hegel tells us that the master isn't genuinely free either, but dependent on what the slave produces, and he tells us that the slave is the one who displays real agency."

"Thunder, if you don't, there are those who will construe your silence as a coverup, that you have something to hide," the journalist from the ezine said.

"For the record, I have absolutely nothing to hide, and I do not appreciate these attempts at manipulating me…But I will tell you my stories, if that's really what you want."

"Wait, wait! Can we record it?" a woman said who was elbowing the man sitting next to her who was ostensibly making some form of love with his cell phone.

"Yes, of course," I replied.

"Thank you, thank you! Just give us a minute to set up," the woman added.

"Ladies and gentlemen, some of you—if not most of you--will find much of what I say as rather, how should I put it, implausible, and if you change your mind about being here, feel free to leave, but please do so quietly," I said.

***

On the day before I would give the keynote address, which would also be the last day of the conference, Esther, Jerry, Sana'a, and Marjan all came to support me. Esther, Jerry, and their son, Misun, arrived first.

"There he is. Haung, Misun," I greeted Esther's first born. "Where is your ina?"

My eyes followed Misun's pointed index finger, and I saw my sister.

"Esther, Esther, it's so wonderful to finally get to be with you again!" I exclaimed.

"This is the day when we finally become free," Esther said as we rubbed our noses and faire le bise. "How could I miss it!"

"How far are you?" I asked as I rubbed Esther's belly.

"We're in the beginning of the third trimester," Esther replied. "Still a few months to go."

"Where's Jerry?" I asked.

"He's parking the car," Esther replied. "He'll be here in a few. But what about you? Your nerves must be at least a little frazzled."

"No, not really," I replied. "Our ancestors are with me, and the message we have for the world is powerful."

"Thunder, remember that day when that reporter came to our school to interview you?" Esther asked.

"How could anyone forget Mrs. Simmons!" I replied.

It seems like it was just yesterday," Esther added. "Oops, that's Misun's potty signal."

"I'll be on lookout for Jerry," I said as she and Misun entered the women's bathroom.

While Esther and Misun were in the restroom, a woman from Palau and another woman from Malawi approached me to inform me that a group of people would be "delighted to casually speak" with me, after the keynote tomorrow.

Just as I assented, I saw Jerry walking towards me.

In an excited flutter of energy, the two women congratulated each other and sped off.

"Dere she go wit he' bad self," Jerry said as we hugged each other.

"For how long can you miss your students?" I asked.

"T'day, t'mar', and Friday," Jerry replied. "These charter-school students are pretty mature an' responsible. They can get by a couple of days witout me."

"I'm glad you, Esther, and Misun are here,"

"What about Alex and Roya, are you expecting them?" Jerry asked.

"No, Roya has a recital in Portland on Saturday, so she's busy practicing, and Alex is playing the good househusband," I replied.

"I hear dat!" Jerry exclaimed.

Shortly after Esther and Misun returned from the restroom, Jerry apologized for having to leave so quickly, but he was afraid that something "funky" would happen to their hotel room if they didn't check-in before 4:00 pm.

"Let's eat breakfast together tomorrow morning," I shouted as they were leaving.

"Wha' time?" Jerry shouted back.

"Is 8:00 too early?" I asked.

Jerry looked at Esther who then looked at me and said that they would be in the restaurant next to our hotel—we were staying at the same hotel.

A few minutes after they had left, Sana'a called, asking if she and Marjan should come to the UN, or if we should meet at the hotel. Looking at the clock on my cell phone, I told them to meet me in the lobby of the hotel in thirty minutes. Then, we hung up. I figured that they had to be very tired, after having driven all the way from Maine. Marjan was a freshman at the University of Maine at Farmington, where she was planning on becoming an elementary-school teacher, and Sana'a was a junior at the University of Southern Maine, where she was working toward her B. FA in Creative Writing. She liked writing short stories, but she was passionate about her poetry, some of which was written in French and in Farsi.

When I arrived at the hotel, Sana'a and Marjan were already there. Marjan was speaking on her cell phone when I saw her. She then saw me, waved, and tapped Sana'a on her shoulder and pointed towards me. They both stood up, and I walked toward them.

"Haung," I said as I embraced and kissed them both.

"Che taw ri?" they both asked in unison.

A few years back, we decided to greet each other in our mother tongues.

"Shotvah and Darioush are disappointed in us because, according to them, we didn't do enough to convince *Ma' man* to let them come," Marjan said.

"Are you speaking to them now?" I asked.

"No," Marjan replied, "they left a voicemail message. I tried calling them, but neither one of them is picking up. I think that they are too angry to speak with us."

After going up to our room, they quickly unpacked, and afterward we called Alex and Roya to let them know that the girls had arrived safely. Sana'a wanted to go to Chinatown for dinner, but I wanted to stay in our room, so I could stay warm with my speech. But Sana'a was still able to get her Chinese food, which was delivered to our hotel.

The next morning when we met for breakfast, Jerry was the one who asked me if I had a chance to catch any news last night.

When I told him that I hadn't, He showed me his cell phone , and the title of the article read, "Thunder Tatanka Youtanka Madden becomes member of the Council of the Calf of the White Buffalo."

"These are no random coincidences," Esther exclaimed. "Thunder, I can smell it."

"Smell what! Marjan asked.

"Freedom," Esther replied, "for all of us, including the wasicu."

When Esther said that, it reminded me of the pain she felt as her father was abusing her, her mother, and her sister. I only wanted to protect them, but I couldn't, which Is why I have always felt inadequate. And as I thought about my speech, I had to admit that it, too, was so woefully inadequate.

"What is it?" Esther asked, sensing that something was very wrong.

"I'm just going over my speech in my head," I lied.

When we arrived at the UN, I was hard-pressed to latch-on to something to say for my keynote address. Clydia was the first person to greet us when we arrived. After she and I had faire le bise, she escorted us to our seats. She was impeccably dressed to the nines, as always. Curiously, though, Marjan told us that she thought she had seen Alex, but when she waved at him, he ignored her. Jerry, Esther, Marjan, and Sana'a were all on the lookout for him. I had to put Alex aside in order to piece-out a keynote address.

Fortunately, by the time my name was announced, I knew roughly what I was going to talk about.

"All human progress, up till this point, has been *ad hoc*," I said following my greeting to the assembly. "And we've managed to muddle our way throughout the millennia with innumerable starts and stops. To be honest with you, considering the sheer volume along with the complexities of today's mounting issues, dealing with those issues individually will not do. For, if we take the time to look, we will find that we are at a plethora of precipices. I don't have to innumerate them because you all know what they are, and you know what the core issue is —for many of us it is the lack of compassion in our hearts, in our communities, and in the world in general. And this is how we know that we live in a male-dominated space. Yes, we all live within a patriarchal context that is strangling us all, men, women, children, animals, insects, plants, microbes, minerals, everything. In the bigger scheme of things, it wouldn't matter if we, as a species, if we were to go extinct. We know this because the dinosaurs were here for hundreds of millions of years, and then, they weren't here anymore." But the thing that gets me is something Noam Chomsky said, 'we are the asteroid.' We are our own patriarchal asteroid."

Then, I shared my concern about Europe, about how deluded so many Europeans were that a substantial war couldn't happen Europe, which reminded me of "Nie wieder." And that was said after WWI.

Despite the fact that this new European war was seven time zone away from us, ahead of us, in New York City, it disturbed me something terrible, and I made that known to my audience. And because many of them nodded, I had to ask the question.

"Does it bother you, too?"

It seemed as though everyone there nodded her and his head, and many of them actually said, "Yes."

"You know, between climate change and this new European war, which could easily escalate into WWIII, I wonder if we have already passed the Rubicon."

"Going back to the piecemeal, *ad hoc* solutions that I mentioned just a little while ago, I recently listened in on a conversation between several automotive union leaders and a reporter.

Among other things, the reporter asked the union leaders if they believed that climate change was real. Although they said they did, one of them said that the most important thing was that their members had good-paying jobs, and right now EVs are not union jobs, nor are they good-paying jobs. For her, having good-paying jobs for her union members trumped climate change. Managing climate change should be tantamount to waging a war, and just as in the case of war, which is a real existential threat, we will all have to make sacrifices, heavy sacrifices, if we hope to make it to the other side. However, when I look around, I don't hear sacrifice. I don't see sacrifice, which means we will fail, miserably and completely."

After a few seconds, I continued.

"My sisters, there are susurrations of revolt, violent revolt in the air. Please, pay them no heed."

"I don't even have control over my own body anymore!" a woman with a southern accent cried out.

"They rape us, and they are still getting away with it," another woman said.

"I know," I said, "but we will not change the world by trying to do it their way."

"*Was tun wir gegen die Entfrempdung?*" a woman shouted in German.

"We will have to do it our way, with a huge, continuous dose of compassion and love, one that doesn't stop until the world is saturated with them, because our lives, the lives of our children, and all children are our children, and the lives of all those we love, including all those assholes, are at stake. My sisters, it is up to us to save this world, and us alone, unfortunately."

"*Qu'est-ce que vous nous demandez de faire exactement?*" I heard Clydia ask from the side of the stage.

"What do we have to do?" I repeated the question in English. "If we are serious about saving the planet, my sisters, and brothers, we will have to organize ourselves and mobilize. Let me explain. Many of you are in your respective countries' foreign service. Haven't you seen and heard of memos and policies that disadvantaged the poor, the invalid, the elderly, women, and children? What did you do? Others of you are doctors, nurses, teachers, school-board members, social workers, journalists, nannies, lawyers, judges, economists, CEOs of major corporations, scientists, investors, and a few of you are even heads of state. When that unsavory memo or policy change made its way to your desk, what did you do? What will you do? My sisters and brothers, it is not enough to be a just, compassionate, and understanding individual if we want to impact the world, so we can save it. We will have to create compassionate, loving, inclusive, and understanding contexts in our hearts, in our communities, and throughout the world. When someone says or does something sexist, racist, xenophobic, anti-nature, homophobic, or anything that dismisses the weak, challenge it, confront it, without letup, until it is quashed. The old, and not so old, white men are desperate. They are actively seeking international support to revert back to the good, old days. I don't know when that was, but hey. They are reactionaries. They are in retreat. We must make a point of making multi-cultural democracy the norm where we can all live our lives to the fullest and thrive, including those old, white men."

When I ended my address, there was an applause, but I wasn't sure of hitting the mark that I had hoped. Yet, there was a nice applause, but all I could think of was that they were all just being polite. A few minutes later, while the conference was coming to a close, an elderly, white woman with metal-framed glasses and gray hair that was in a bun rose up and started walking to the podium. She did seem vaguely familiar, but I couldn't place her. Then, after she had come about ten yards closer, I was pleasantly surprised.

"Mrs. Simmons," I said, interrupting the speaker who was wrapping the conference up.

When the conference had adjourned, I rose up, jumped off of the podium, and ran to Mrs. Simmons. As we hugged each other very warmly, she repeated, "You did it, What the Thunder Said, you did it, you did it."

After she cupped both of my hands and gestured to a black man who was behind her, he placed his hand in what looked like a white buckskin satchel and pulled up the chanupa, the sacred pipe, and carefully handed it to her. Once she placed the chanupa in my hands, she said a blessing. Then, she backed away from me, always smiling, and she took off her glasses. By now, Esther, Jerry, and Misun came to us. Mrs. Simmons turned around and hugged Esther and rubbed her belly, saying something under her breath as if she were blessing Esther's unborn child. Afterward, Sana'a and Marjan had reached us. What followed was too spooky for both Esther and me—Mrs. Simmons, how do I say this? Mrs. Simmons transformed into an actual buffalo, a black buffalo, and then into a brown buffalo, and into a red buffalo, and finally into a white buffalo calf. That's right! Mrs. Simmons was Pte San Win, White Buffalo Calf Woman. She had returned and She was captured on video and T.V.

"My daughters, and my sons, the era of harmony and love is now upon us," Pte San Win said after She returned to her human form, not as Mrs. Simmons, though, but as Pte San Win, an Indigenous woman in full, splendid, Native, buffalo skins, white, of course. "In other words, it is time for the feminine principle to rise and temper the masculine principle. You all have been forewarned! Aquarius is racing toward you, and were she to find you ill-disposed toward her, well, let Us just say that it shall not be pretty."

As she was leaving, the people in the assembly hall moved out of her way. Just before She had left the hall, Sana'a shouted, "Baba!"

Then, someone ran past me toward Her.

"Why doesn't Baba see us?" Marjan asked.

"Don't worry," I said, "that's not Alex."

"He sure looks and moves like Baba," Sana'a said.

"If he's not Baba, then who is it?" Marjan asked.

"He's a very ancient trickster god with a crazy name, who just may have finally pulled off his comeback," I said wryly.

When /Caggen reached Pte San Win, he grabbed Her wrist. Not looking at who it was, She glared at the offending hand, which caught fire instantaneously and burned most of /Caggen's blue suit and white shirt. Once Pte San Win realized who it was, She smiled at him. They rubbed their noses joyously and very affectionately, as if they hadn't done that in a very long time, and then slowly, they faded out of our view.

The Goddess Returns

www.ingramcontent.com/pod-product-compliance
Lightning Source LLC
Chambersburg PA
CBHW030549260626
47157CB00006B/2243